Financial Initiation

Chester Vittorio Franklin

chestervittoriofranklin@yahoo.com

FIRST EDITION

ISBN 978-1-7376014-4-9

With thanks to Juliet, Joseph, Anne, and Jack

Other Books by Chester Vittorio Franklin

Financial Execution

Financial Retribution

Prologue

Professor Krakaris welcomed the students as they arrived for the initial session of his Philosophy 101 class. He asked each their name, shook their hand, and invited them to take a seat. Once there were no further arrivals, he walked to the front of the classroom, slid down the dual-layer chalkboard, and revealed the following quote:

> *True wisdom comes to each of us when we realize how little we understand about life, ourselves, and the world around us.*
>
> *Socrates*

As was his practice, the professor then commenced a dialogue with and among the students regarding the meaning of the quote. He also asked probing questions, including whether the perceptions of a man who lived so many centuries ago could possibly still be valid in the Internet age. By the end of the hour, the Professor identified those students most likely to benefit from his class in multiple ways, and those individuals apparently destined for education by a life of painful experiences.

Chapter 1

Friday June 29, 2001
Paso Robles, California

The northern half of San Luis Obispo County was shrouded in an intense rainstorm, fueled by strong winds blowing from the southwest. The storm and the lack of a moon produced almost complete darkness by 7:30 PM.

Fifty-five-year-old Dale Huffington drove carefully to avoid hydroplaning on the 101 freeway, leaning over the steering wheel to maximize his vision of the road surface. After about an hour of driving, Dale slowed further and took the first exit for the City of Paso Robles. The Paso Robles Inn, founded in 1889, the same year as the city, was less than two miles from the freeway. Upon arriving at the Inn, Dale pulled his raincoat tight, opened his umbrella, and sprinted for the door to the bar.

Once inside, Dale put his raincoat and umbrella on the stand by the door and peered into the room. He quickly identified Joel Johnson, seated at a booth at the rear of the bar. He walked over and sat down across from Joel.

"What a night for an out-of-town meeting," said Joel.

"We can't take any risk of being identified or overheard," replied Dale.

"I understand."

"Have you finished the calculations that I requested?"

"Yes. Here's my best estimate, with contingency points highlighted on the right side. The plan you developed is excellent. I never could have produced anything like that on my own," advised Joel.

As Dale reviewed the document, the bar waitress approached the booth.

"What can I get you to drink?"

Dale responded, "We'll take two cosmopolitans. Thank you."

Once the waitress was out of earshot, Dale, his face tense and presenting a stern look, turned back to Joel and continued, "Tonight is the point of no return. If we're going to proceed with the plan, we need to start immediately."

"You're right. I would need to go into the office tomorrow morning and use both days of the weekend to commence the implementation."

Joel paused, and then said, "I know this is a really difficult situation for you given your family history."

Dale responded, "Do you realize that my great grandfather and bank founder, Kenneth Huffington, may have had a drink in this very location? This hotel opened about a decade before the bank was formed, and was one of the few stopping places on the road north to Monterey and the San Francisco Bay Area."

"All the more reason for us to proceed. Doing nothing would present severe consequences for both of us."

"On the other hand, if our planned actions fail, our lives would likely be completely ruined, both professionally and personally," sighed Dale.

"True, but at a certain point, does being any worse really matter?" asked Joel.

Dale took deep breath and stared at the ceiling, contemplating how his life would be forever changed if they did not take action and achieve success.

Joel again looked over the document he had prepared.

"I think we have a decent chance at succeeding. We need to put this problem behind us as quickly as possible."

The waitress arrived with their cosmopolitans. Both Dale and Joel took long sips of their drinks. Several minutes of silence followed.

Dale shuddered, and then spoke, "The master plan looks good. I can't think of any way to improve it further. We initiate the steps starting tomorrow morning. We both need to be careful to not allow any evidence to be left at the bank. We speak about this only in person and away from the office. No written, email, text, or fax communication on the subject. No phone calls either if we can avoid it. We will need absolute secrecy to succeed."

Joel nodded his understanding and concurrence.

The two men clinked their glasses and downed the remainder of their cosmopolitans. Dale placed cash on the table for the drinks. The bank officers donned their raincoats, picked up their umbrellas, and walked out into the darkness.

Chapter 2

Friday February 1, 1901
Santa Maria, California

The Santa Maria Valley, located about 150 miles north of Los Angeles, extends from the Santa Lucia Mountains toward the Pacific Ocean. This part of the central coast of California had become a significant source of agricultural production during the final decades of the 19th century, blessed by fertile soil and moderate year-round temperatures that permitted a long growing season. The City of Santa Maria also enjoyed increasing prosperity over the past twelve years because of the discovery of oil in the vicinity of the town. The city had grown up substantially since its formal founding in 1874, just twenty-four years after California became a state.

It was a cloudless mid-morning in the valley. By 9:30 AM, the temperature had risen to seventy degrees Fahrenheit, where it would remain for most of the day. Forty-five-year-old George Anderson, attorney at law, was finishing breakfast before making the short walk from his home to his law office located near the primary intersection of the city, Broadway and Main Street. Despite being born into a family of limited means, through hard work, George was a member of the first graduating class at the Hastings School of Law (established in 1878) at the University of California at Berkeley. He and his family moved to Santa Maria in 1897 after recognizing its potential while traveling through the area on an extended vacation down the California coast a year earlier.

"Marjorie, thank you for breakfast this morning. The omelet with the ham, cheese, and onions was prepared perfectly."

"We're blessed with having access to fresh eggs, milk, cheese, and butter each day. Cooking here is so much easier than where I grew up in Oklahoma."

"Thank you again for your patience over the past month. With all of the recent activity, I've neglected both you and George Junior."

"It's all right, dear. George Junior and I understand that the work you're performing now is very important. You've shared with me how these opportunities will establish a strong financial foundation for our family for years to come."

George then kissed his wife, hugged his ten-year-old son, and departed their modest house.

Upon entering his law office, demarcated by a hanging sign under the portico of the wooden building, George called out to his legal assistant in the next room, "Betty, do you have the conference room set up for the 10:30 meeting?"

"Yes, Mr. Anderson. Five sets of the documents for the new partnership have been typed and spaced around the table. A pitcher of water and glasses, along with fresh baked buttermilk biscuits from Molly's, are on the sideboard. Your stamps and seals have been placed next to your seat at one end of the table."

"Thank you, Betty. This is going to be a momentous day for us. Are the sets of documents also prepared for our 2:00 PM meeting this afternoon?"

"I have four sets of the associated documents, including the articles of incorporation and the bylaws, ready to be placed around the conference table as soon as the morning meeting concludes. The stock certificates for the new bank are also ready for processing. I'll swing by Molly's between the meetings to replenish our supply of biscuits."

"Excellent. Is the new bottle of Armagnac brandy and the snifters stored in the side bar, as we discussed?"

"Yes, Mr. Anderson. I do say that you'll need to measure your consumption after the first meeting in order to be ready for the second. That ornery and lecherous Kenneth Huffington can be a challenge even on his most pleasant of days. I can't help but observe his undressing me with his eyes every time we meet."

"Unfortunately, I'm all too aware of Kenneth's proclivities. However, he has been a great resource into organizing the new bank."

"I see Mr. Cook coming down the street. I'll greet him and then show him into the conference room. That will give you time to position yourself," said Betty.

"You're always thinking ahead, Betty. No wonder you're one of the few women working in the legal field in California these days."

The front door to the attorney's office swung open. John Cook entered. John was a mountain of a man, standing six feet, four inches tall, with broad shoulders, a barrel chest, and huge biceps developed over a lifetime of farming. John was the current manager for the Cook family agricultural operation, following in the footsteps of his uncle Rudolph, one of the settlers and founders of the Santa Maria valley and city. The Cook family maintained over 1,500 acres of row crops, varying the mix of vegetables each year to support the long-term health of the land and in order to respond to market prices for different types of produce. The mild weather allowed three crop cycles per year on a given parcel, thereby enhancing profitability vis-à-vis farms located farther north.

"Good morning, Mr. Cook," said George, following with a firm handshake.

"It's always a pleasure to come into town for business other than selling vegetables and buying seed and fertilizer. The farmer's life is not an easy one."

"I appreciate that. Please, have a seat at the table. Betty will serve you a glass of water and one of Molly's famous buttermilk biscuits."

The front door to the office again swung open. Entering together were Mr. Matthew Thornburg and Mr. Daniel Fesler. Like Mr. Cook, these two men were also the current generation of manager for their families which had helped settle the valley and found the city.

"Gentlemen, please take a seat at the table and allow Betty to serve you some refreshment. I know you are well acquainted."

Mr. Cook, Mr. Thornburg, and Mr. Fesler had known each other for years. Their fathers or uncles had been in the valley since soon after statehood. They all attended the Episcopal church in town. The Thornburg family interests included one of the larger cattle grazing operations along the central coast. The Fesler family business interests included ownership in several railroads back east, plus a large swath of farmland on the north side of town which included extensive frontage on the Santa Maria River.

"We're waiting for Mr. Miller, as usual," stated Mr. Fesler.

"I'm not surprised given his diversity of business interests. I often wonder how that man gets any rest," said Mr. Thornburg.

"Not to mention the energy he devotes to his young and attractive wife," interjected Mr. Cook.

All of the men shared a hearty laugh, sampled Molly's biscuits, and drank some water.

George then spoke up, "This business opportunity would

not have been possible without Mr. Miller's relationships with various interests throughout the state, both business and political."

Mr. Thornburg replied, "George, of course we recognize James' special talents for generating wealth. His long history of success speaks for itself. We're just a bit jealous that such an ordinary looking fellow could attract such a lovely and personable wife as Mildred."

The front door to the office again opened, followed by a small breeze off the Pacific Ocean to the west. A short man, balding, and wearing thick eyeglasses joined the group.

"Good morning, Mr. Miller," said George.

"Great to see you all. I apologize for delaying the start of our meeting this morning. Shall we get right down to business?"

The other four men in the room nodded in concurrence. Mr. Miller and Mr. Thornburg sat on one side of the conference table, with Mr. Cook and Mr. Fesler seated at the other side. George sat at the far end. He was the first to speak.

"Please allow me to recap where we are and what we aim to accomplish this morning. Through each of your contacts, and in particular Mr. Miller's, we have become aware of the possibility of a substantial amount of oil being located underground at reasonable depth in an area comprising about 1,200 acres south of town. Even if oil is not found on this real estate, about seventy-five percent of the land is suitable for agricultural production, with the remaining twenty-five percent viable for animal grazing. Based upon what we know of the local hydrology, there should be ample groundwater supply below certain segments of the acreage. The current owner of the land is the grandson of one of the original land grant recipients from early in the past century. The land has been left fallow and unused for decades. The grandson is a physician living and working in San Francisco, with a wife and five children."

"Mr. Anderson, how recently have you been in contact with this grandson?" asked Mr. Cook.

"I received a letter just last week. That letter confirmed his interest in selling the real estate at the price we tentatively offered."

"No effort to bid us up at all?" asked Mr. Thornburg.

"None whatsoever. From my one in-person meeting in San Francisco and the follow-up letters we've exchanged, the owner has not been on the property for at least fifteen years. He has no interest in developing or operating the land. His wife and children revel in the San Francisco social and cultural scene. In fact, his wife is from a wealthy family widely known for the lavish parties thrown at their estate in the Pacific Heights section of the city by the bay."

George then paused to drink some water.

"Please continue, Mr. Anderson," said Mr. Fesler.

"The documents before you are those necessary to form a new partnership named Blue Pacific Ventures. Each of the four of you will own 22.5% of the partnership, but contribute 25.0% of the initial capitalization. I will own 10.0% of the partnership, but not contribute any capital. In return, my legal services to the formation and ongoing operation of the partnership shall be provided for no charge. In addition, I shall function as the General Partner for the partnership for no remuneration. Each of you are defined as Limited Partners. This will provide you and your families with certain legal and financial protections should our plan not progress as envisioned. The initial capitalization of the partnership will be sufficient to purchase the subject 1,200 acres and also provide adequate liquidity for our projected undertakings."

Mr. Miller then stood up, although such was only moderately observable given that the table height came to almost mid-chest.

"Please allow me to recap our planned operations. The first step will be for me to coordinate drilling exploratory wells on that part of the acreage we believe to have the most potential for significant amounts of oil. The acreage not identified for drilling and not suitable for agricultural production will be managed by Mr. Thornburg for cattle and sheep grazing. We will leverage the results from our oil well drilling to identify additional sources of groundwater. Mr. Cook will establish one or more additional groundwater wells for use in agricultural crop irrigation on that portion of the land not being used for either oil production or cattle grazing."

Mr. Miller then paused to ensure all of the meeting participants were of like mind with his presentation thus far. All were. Mr. Miller continued.

"As we all know, the Southern Pacific Railroad extended a spur to Betteravia Junction in 1899. That location is less than ten miles from the 1,200 acres we are discussing this morning. Mr. Fesler, your role will be to either negotiate further spurs and extensions with the Southern Pacific to serve our aggregate business interests, or to form a short line railroad in the valley for connection to Betteravia Junction. With improved railroad service, all of our varied commercial interests will benefit, plus there will be the option of using railroad tank cars to transport our oil to the Southern California refineries."

Mr. Miller sat down and nodded toward George.

George followed. "Thank you, Mr. Miller. That was an excellent summary. If there are no questions, might I suggest that we each execute the various documents before us. After that, the four of you should provide me with your capital contribution for deposit into a new bank account under the name of our partnership. I will advise each of you as soon as I return from San Francisco with the executed deed and other documents necessary to complete our purchase of the real estate. Each of you may then commence your portion of our plans for land development and operation."

The men signed the various documents and handed George their capital contributions in cash. This part of California was far more rural than the well-developed cities of Los Angeles and San Francisco. Most business in the county was still conducted in currency. George verified the amount of each man's capital contribution and issued each a receipt.

George handed the documents and the cash to Betty for packaging up for the long trip north.

George then turned to the other four men and said, "Gentlemen, might I suggest a toast on this most momentous of days?"

"Most appropriate and appreciated," said Mr. Thornburg.

George opened the sideboard and removed the bottle of Armagnac brandy and the glass snifters.

"Well, this is a pleasant surprise," bellowed Mr. Cook.

"I see great prosperity in our future endeavors," said George with a broad smile. "Such a future is deserving of special recognition and celebration."

The men each shared a serving of the French brandy, with George being careful to pour his serving last and in a smaller amount than the others. Toasts were made to each other and the prospect of great success for Blue Pacific Ventures in the new 20th century.

By noon, George and Betty were again alone in the law office.

"Betty, let's both go down Main Street. You buy some additional biscuits from Molly and I will purchase us some lunch. We'll meet back at the office by 12:30 to eat and to recap our plans for this afternoon's meeting."

The attendees at the 2:00 PM meeting were representatives from the other financially dominant families in the area other than those with the surnames of Cook, Fesler, Miller, and Thornburg. The Huffington family owned many of the commercial properties along both Main Street and Broadway. Some of the real estate was leased to tenants, while other buildings were utilized for various family-owned businesses. The Huffington family also owned a minority interest in a commercial bank in Los Angeles. The Phillips family maintained substantial acreage along the coast, some used for farming, and some devoted to shipping and warehousing services in conjunction with the long pier they maintained into the Pacific Ocean. The Kehoe family owned and operated the largest and most upscale hotel in the city, along with several diners and restaurants. The Kehoe's also owned several of the earliest drilled and still producing oil wells in the valley.

By 2:10 PM, Mr. Huffington, Mr. Phillips, and Mr. Kehoe were seated at the conference table along with George, each having been served a glass of water and a fresh biscuit. George then stood up from his usual seat the far end of the table.

"Gentlemen, please allow me to summarize the documents in front of you and recap our plan. We're forming a new commercial bank. Each of you is contributing one-third of the initial capitalization. In return, each of you will receive stock certificates representing a thirty percent ownership in the new company. I will not contribute any capital, but will own ten percent of the bank. This is in recognition of my providing my legal services for free and also serving as the initial Secretary of the company for no remuneration. Once I return from

San Francisco with the required State approvals, we will open Green Valley Community Bank in the building owned by the Huffington family at the corner of Broadway and Main Street. This location will provide us with maximum visibility. Mr. Huffington's son, Frederick, will serve as the first President of the bank, leveraging his experience in Los Angeles in that industry."

"That's exactly as we've discussed," said Mr. Huffington. "If we each bring all of our family's business to Green Valley Community Bank, plus encourage our closest friends to do so, the bank should enjoy great success. Our valley has certainly grown since adopting the name of Santa Maria fifteen years ago. I believe this growth is poised to continue. There is substantial fertile land that has yet to be placed into crop production. At the same time, the rapidly expanding populations in both Los Angeles and San Francisco will drive demand for food. There will simply be too much business occurring in the area to require repeated, long trips to the nearest existing bank offices in either Santa Barbara or Monterey."

Mr. Phillips stood, rubbing his full beard in thought. He was well known in town for his thoroughness, honesty, and work ethic.

After a brief pause, he said, "I concur. With the new railroad spur to Betteravia Junction and my family's planned expansion of our pier and warehouse facilities on the coast, Santa Maria is destined to become a major hub of business for at least fifty miles in each direction. Our new bank will be well positioned to both foster that business and earn profits from providing various financial services."

Mr. Kehoe spoke, "The longevity of my family's oil wells indicates that the reservoir of oil in our valley is quite deep and probably also expansive in area. Over the past year, we've achieved an eighty percent viability ratio for new wells dug, which is far above the typical result for the industry, even in locations such as Pennsylvania. Our new bank will be well positioned to finance purchases of capital goods necessary for expanded oil exploration and production, not to mention furnishing a local facility for ongoing receipts and disbursements."

George stood to gain the floor and advance the business to be conducted.

"Gentlemen, such concurrence regarding the excellent prospects for our new bank is quite encouraging. Shall we now execute the documents?"

Once the documents were all signed, George collected them and stated, "If you'll each provide me with your initial capital contribution, I will hold such in an escrow status pending final governmental approvals. As soon as we receive the last required authorization, I will issue stock certificates to each of you. Your capital will of course provide the initial liquidity for Green Valley Community Bank."

The three men each handed George a large envelope filled with currency. George counted the money and issued a receipt to each of the investors. George then handed the documents to Betty for packaging up for the long trip north. The cash would be safekept in the large safe bolted into the floor of George's office until his departure.

George then turned to the other men and, mirroring the events of this morning, said, "Gentlemen, might I suggest a toast on this most momentous of days?"

"A fine way to conclude our business today," said Mr. Kehoe.

Just as hours earlier, George again opened the sideboard and removed the bottle of Armagnac brandy and the glass snifters.

Seeing the Armagnac brandy, Mr. Kehoe exclaimed, "One of

my favorite beverages, and difficult to obtain in this part of the world."

"Yes, a true indulgence," echoed Mr. Phillips.

After George poured and distributed the servings, including a normal sized one for himself, he raised his snifter and said, "Let me share my favorite quote about banking, by no less than our nation's most profound early capitalist:

> *It is not by augmenting the capital of the country, but by rendering a greater part of that capital active and productive than would otherwise be so, that the most judicious operations of banking can increase the industry of the country.*
>
> *Adam Smith*

Here, here!"

The four men clinked their glasses, inhaled the intense aroma of the Armagnac, and savored the brandy. Mr. Kehoe drained his snifter quickly. He then politely inquired if a second serving might be available. George obliged him.

Mr. Kehoe raised his snifter and said, "Gentlemen, a toast to our future prosperity in this new 20th century!"

The men again clinked their glasses, all smiling in anticipation of their future success. Once they emptied their snifters (Mr. Kehoe, his second), Mr. Huffington, Phillips, and Kehoe bid goodbye to both George and Betty and departed the office.

George turned to Betty and said, "Betty, thank you for also packaging up this second set of documents. I'll start the journey to San Francisco first thing tomorrow morning."

Betty replied, "Of course, Mr. Anderson. We're so fortunate that with the extension of the railroad to San Luis Obispo in 1895, we can travel from Santa Maria to San Francisco in just three days. That journey used to take a week or more."

"Betty, I believe this new century will present wonders beyond our imagination. Best for me to get home for dinner soon and a good night's sleep. I'll leave for San Luis Obispo on horseback at dawn tomorrow. I should return in eight or nine days, depending upon how quickly I can complete both sets of business in San Francisco."

"Mr. Anderson, you'll be carrying quite a bit of currency. Make sure you bring your pistol."

"We're now a long way from the wild 1850's in this state. That said, your advice is prudent. My Colt 45 will be on my hip."

"I'll manage the office as usual while you're gone. Documents for any pressing matters will be drafted and awaiting your review upon your return."

"Thank you, Betty. I don't know what I would do without you."

George departed his law office and commenced the short walk home. Yes, he thought, February 1, 1901 would be a day to remember. Without cash investment and by leveraging his skills, he would maintain a meaningful ownership position in two new enterprises with excellent prospects for the future. He would be able to provide a lifestyle for his wife and son far more accommodating than his experience growing up in the San Francisco Bay Area right after California became part of the United States.

Chapter 3

Saturday May 3, 1980
Goleta, California

It was the final year of Jimmy Carter's single term presidency. The Iran hostage crisis was among the front-page news stories, along with inflation exceeding fourteen percent in the United States. The 1980's were off to a challenging start.

Goleta is located on the central California coast, just north of the city of Santa Barbara. The area is home to the University of California at Santa Barbara. In addition, most of the socio-economic lower classes who work in upscale Santa Barbara and even more affluent Montecito live in Goleta because of the lower cost of housing.

At 4:00 PM, seventeen-year-old Joel Johnson was in his bedroom, putting on his rented tuxedo. The cummerbund and jacket partially hid his excess weight, the result of limited exercise and a diet centered on inexpensive, processed food. Joel's mother, Cheryl, knocked on the door.

"Joel, honey, can I see how you look?"

"Sure, mom. I'm having trouble with the tie."

Cheryl Johnson entered the bedroom and frowned at the clearly incorrectly tied tie.

"Let me redo the tie for you. Do the shoes fit?"

"Yes, mom. We ordered the right size."

As Cheryl fixed Joel's tie, she thought back to herself at his age. At seventeen, she had already been raising Joel for almost a year. She never had an opportunity to finish high school, much less attend her senior prom. Her promiscuity with older boys starting at age fifteen soon caught up with her. She never did ascertain who Joel's father was.

"There you are. Now everything looks good. I've asked our neighbor, Mrs. Lucas, to take some photos of us together before you depart. She should be here any minute."

Joel and his mother lived in an 800 square foot house constructed early in the 20th century, with two small bedrooms, a kitchen, bathroom, and one sitting room. Electricity had been added to the house in the mid-1930's. Mrs. Lucas lived in a similar house next door. She was the elderly widow of a construction worker whose career had centered on the building of the 101 freeway which now ran up and down much of California.

There was a knock on the front door.

"Mrs. Lucas, thank you again for helping us this afternoon. It's a very special day for Joel and me."

"My pleasure, Cheryl. Do you have the camera ready, loaded with film?"

"Yes. I splurged and purchased the high-end Kodak film. Let me just slip on my best dress for the photos, while you and Joel test the lighting and decide where to take the photos."

"Hello, Mrs. Lucas, good to see you," said Joel.

"How handsome you look! Where's Dos Pueblos High School holding the prom this evening?"

"We were fortunate to receive a donation from one of the original alumni, so our class was able to book the Biltmore on the beach in Santa Barbara. No Dos Pueblos senior class has ever held the prom there. I heard that almost one hundred percent of my class is attending."

Cheryl joined Joel and Mrs. Lucas in the sitting room. She was wearing her most elaborate outfit, a sparkly indigo blue dress that fell off the shoulder, along with matching heels.

"Shall we take several photos inside and then several in the garden out back?" asked Mrs. Lucas.

"That sounds like a good plan," replied Cheryl.

"You two stand together next to the fireplace and we'll start."

Joel and his mother stood side by side in front of the fireplace, each with an arm extended around the back of the other, squeezing together tightly. Mrs. Lucas clicked away with the camera. They then repeated the pose and took more photos outside.

"I think that will have to do. I've taken the whole roll," said Mrs. Lucas, handing the camera to Cheryl.

"Thank you again Mrs. Lucas."

As Mrs. Lucas walked out the front door over to her house, she thought to herself. Those two certainly have a close relationship, perhaps so close as to be a bit strange… Well, at least they're good neighbors.

Back inside, Cheryl turned to Joel.

"I never had a chance to attend either my junior or senior prom."

"I remember your telling me that before, mom. It was my fault."

"Oh, Joel, honey, having you was the best thing I've ever done. Never talk like that. Now, tell me who your date is."

"Susan McNichols. I don't think you've ever met her. She was in my lab group this semester. Susan also hasn't dated much, but, like me, didn't want to miss an evening at the Biltmore, standing on the beach watching the sun set over the Pacific. In fact, as the prom date approached, it was Susan who asked me."

"Is she pretty?"

"Well...not nearly as pretty as you are, mom."

Cheryl gave her son a long kiss on the cheek. Joel gave his mother a final hug, walked out the front door, and climbed into the family car. While Joel had washed and waxed the 1971 Ford Pinto, the car showed its age and mileage. Cheryl sighed as she watched her son drive away. Raising a child as a very young, uneducated, and single mother had not been easy. However, they enjoyed a very close relationship, fostered by, in a way, their growing up together.

Chapter 4

Friday August 2, 1909
Santa Maria, California

It was a warm summer day in Santa Maria. The town had incorporated in 1905, about four years ago. The town and the surrounding valley had recently enjoyed several years of impressive growth. Economic development and its related investment were strong, fueled by the volume increase in agricultural harvests and significantly greater oil production.

California's population maintained a steady expansion throughout the early part of the 20th century due to both births and domestic and international immigration. This population growth provided ready markets for the vegetables, fruit, beef, and oil produced in the valley. Blue Pacific Ventures enjoyed particular success since its founding. Oil was soon discovered on the 1,200 initial acres purchased by the partnership. Additional drilling over the past eight years demarcated a wide and apparently deep oil reservoir, leading to a doubling of oil production every twelve to fifteen months. The diversification of the partnership allowed for strong profitability, even when the price for one or more of the commodities sagged.

Green Valley Community Bank opened for business in 1902. As was typical for a new bank, a loss was recorded for each of the first two years, followed by another two years of break-even performance while the bank's balance sheet was established. Profitability was first achieved in 1906, with earnings increasing each year for 1907 and 1908. 1909 results to date indicated a likely further improvement in annual income.

George Anderson departed his law office at 4:30 PM, just

after he and Betty finished drafting and executing a will and last testament for one of the local businessmen. The walk home took more time now, as the Anderson's had sold their nearby small house for an estate in the best part of town, about a twenty-minute walk from the office. Upon arriving home, George greeted his wife and son.

"Good evening, Marjorie and Junior."

His wife and now 18-year-old son both gave George a hug.

"Do you need my help in packing for Junior's travels tomorrow?"

"No, Dad, Mom and I have the Model T stuffed with everything I'll need at Stanford University."

The Anderson's were one of the first families in the county to purchase a Tin Lizzie, as the Ford Model T cars were often referred to. The black cars hadn't yet been in production for a year when George had taken the train down to Los Angeles to purchase one just a few months ago.

"Junior, we're really going to miss having you around. However, we're also so proud of your being accepted into the Stanford University class of 1913."

"I couldn't have done it without the support of you and mom. I'm planning on taking the classes designated as prelaw. That way, if I get accepted into law school as planned, I'll be well prepared. My goal is to return and help you and Betty with the practice."

"The way the valley is growing, we're going to need another good attorney in town."

"You two, always talking law and business!" exclaimed Marjorie. "Now, wash up and let's sit down to enjoy our favorite family dinner. While Stanford is a prestigious school of learning, I doubt they can match my specially seasoned Santa Maria tri-tip steak!"

Chapter 5

Wednesday February 10, 1982
Santa Barbara, California

Santa Barbara City College was founded in 1909, almost sixty years after the incorporation of the city itself. The public community college offered a wide range of associate degree and certificate programs. The college was also the gateway into the University of California system for students of modest means and / or average academic achievement in high school. Joel Johnson was in the second semester of his sophomore year. His appointment this morning was with Mr. Sampson, one of the community college's guidance counselors.

Joel knocked on the door to Mr. Sampson's small office.

"Yes, please come in."

"Good morning, Mr. Sampson."

"Hello Joel. Please have a seat. How can I help you today?"

"I've completed drafting my application to enter the University of California system next year, with an indicated preference for UC / Santa Barbara. That way I can live at home to keep costs down."

"That makes sense. Remember that the federal student loan program is available to help with education costs. I'd be happy to assist you in that regard should you be interested."

"I was wondering if you might be able to look over my UC application package prior to submission."

"I'd be happy to. That's an important part of my job each

year at this time. Let me also pull up your transcript."

Joel sat quietly while Mr. Sampson reviewed the documents and the information from the computer terminal. After a while, Mr. Sampson turned to Joel and began asking questions.

"Joel, what do you plan to major in at university?"

"I'm thinking of music theory. My mother has taken piano lessons with me since I was eight years old. That was one of the few indulgences we could enjoy given her modest income from the department store plus my part-time work at the fast-food restaurant."

"UC / Santa Barbara has an excellent music program. Are you thinking of being a composer, teacher, or performer?"

"I'm not really sure yet. I need to learn and experience more before I could make that decision."

"It's not unusual for a sophomore to be less than certain regarding his career path, so don't worry about that right now."

Mr. Sampson then again turned his attention to the computer terminal.

"Joel, its looks like you'll meet the requirements for our AA degree based upon the classes you have completed, plus the ones which you're currently taking. However, examining your grades, they appear to be just barely adequate for acceptance into UC / Santa Barbara. You'll need to maintain your current GPA through this final semester of classes here. Do you think you can do that?"

"I think so. The only class I'm having particular difficulty with is Philosophy 101. I needed a class in the social sciences to complete the Associate of Arts requirements here, and that class fit perfectly into my schedule."

"I know Professor Krakaris quite well. If you continue to

have difficulty, don't be afraid to make an appointment during his office hours. Professor Krakaris is one of our most popular professors, despite conducting his classes with academic rigor."

"Thank you for the advice."

"Your application looks complete. As you know, we here at City College take great pride in the ratio of our graduates who continue on into either the UC system or the Cal State system and earn four-year college degrees. Best of luck, and please contact me if I might be of any other assistance."

"Thank you, Mr. Sampson."

Joel rose to his feet and walked over to the library. He had two hours before his next class, which would give him time to complete some of the required reading for Professor Krakaris' course.

Chapter 6

Tuesday October 20, 1959
Santa Maria, California

Eisenhower was in the seventh year of his presidency. The Baby Boom was still in full force, rapidly increasing the number of Americans. Rock and roll music was rapidly evolving, setting the stage for its explosion in the next decade.

The directors and senior officers of Green Valley Community Bank were assembled in the board room of the bank's new headquarters building. The bank had grown at a steady, strong pace over the decades, with the exception of the 1930's, fueled by the population and economic growth of the state. The California population growth rate increased markedly following the conclusion of World War Two. Significant numbers of jobs were being created in various industries, such as aerospace and entertainment in the Los Angeles basin. The bank's original branch office in downtown Santa Maria was now complemented by a headquarters building on Main Street and a branch office in the city of San Luis Obispo, about thirty-five miles to the north.

George Anderson III, esquire, the bank's new Chairman of the Board, walked over to the podium, signaled the assemblage for quiet, and then commenced speaking.

"It is with great pride and anticipation that I welcome all of you here this afternoon. We are blessed to live in a time of burgeoning opportunity. Just two years ago, the space age was commenced with the launching of Sputnik 1 into earth's orbit. Two months ago, we became the fifty states of America with the entry of Hawaii into statehood. Tomorrow morning, we will release the bank's financial results for the first three quarters of the year. Not only are we on pace to achieve a record level of annual profitability this year, but, as of September 30, Green Valley Community Bank's balance sheet exceeded $100 million in totals assets for the first time. This is an impressive milestone for our community bank."

The attendees erupted in applause. In addition to Mr. Anderson, three other descendants of the original founders were on the nine-member Board of Directors: the two Huffington brothers and Steven Kehoe. Another five descendants of the original founders were bank employees, including a woman with the maiden name of Kehoe and four Phillips', each of whom was immediately recognizable by their full beards. Family and community roots ran deep in the Santa Maria Valley.

Perhaps most proud among those in attendance was George Anderson II. Now 68 years old, but in failing health, Junior smiled broadly watching his son perform so effectively as Chairman of the Board. George III had followed in his father's footsteps, also obtaining a degree from the Stanford School of Law. George II had been one of the earlier graduates of that esteemed institution, attending just twenty years after its establishment in 1893.

Once the applause quieted down, George III continued.

"To mark this special occasion, each bank Director and employee will receive this commemorative plaque."

George III held up one of the plaques, rotating his positioning so that everyone in the room could get a good look.

"As you can see, the base of the plaque is redwood, known for its strength, long life, and California heritage. The small brass plate at the bottom contains the words:

Green Valley Community Bank

$100 Million In Total Assets
September 30, 1959

The large brass plate is in the shape of the bank's logo and bears the following inscription:

Far and away the best prize that life offers
is the chance to work hard at
work worth doing.

Theodore Roosevelt

Catherine and Madeline will distribute the plaques as you depart. Now, please join me in celebrating with some tri-tip kebabs and chardonnay wine from one of our clients."

The crowd again broke into applause.

Steven Kehoe loudly called out, "Let's drink to that!"

George III stepped away from the podium and began shaking hands and thanking the Directors and employees for all of their contributions to the bank's success.

Chapter 7

Monday March 15, 1982
Santa Barbara, California

Joel ran across the Santa Barbara City College campus. He did not want to be late for his 3:00 PM appointment with Professor Krakaris. Being overweight and out of shape, he arrived on time, but clearly winded.

"Good afternoon, Joel."

"Good afternoon professor."

"You look flushed. Can I offer you some water?"

"Yes, thank you."

Professor Krakaris removed a chilled bottle of water from his small, in-office refrigerator and handed it to Joel. Joel took a deep gulp. Once it appeared that Joel was breathing normally, the Professor continued.

"How can I help you this afternoon?"

"I know I'm not doing well in your class, despite my desire to do so. If you'll remember, my mid-term paper received a 'D' grade."

"Let me pull up my records... I see that you've achieved 'C' and 'C +' grades on the multiple-choice testing in the course, but your two papers thus far have both received 'D' grades."

"Yes, despite my devoting many hours to the writing of the papers."

"Did you bring the two papers with you?"

"Yes, here they are."

Joel reached into his backpack and handed the two documents to the professor. Mr. Krakaris leafed through both papers to refresh his memory.

"Joel, what do you think my objectives are in teaching Philosophy 101?"

"Well... the 101 courses are usually broad introductions to a given subject. They are typically designed to provide students with a foundational education and also furnish them with sufficient background on the subject to decide whether to pursue additional education or even major in that field."

"That's true. Anything else?"

Joel pondered for a moment and then replied, "Nothing that I can think of."

"Let me share a quote with you and see if that helps:

It is one thing to show a man
that he is in error,
and another to put him in possession
of the truth.

John Locke

Does that bring anything to mind?"

Joel thought for a while and then replied, "I'm sorry, professor, not really."

"Let me share one more quote:

If you would be a real seeker of the truth, it
is necessary that at least once in your life
you doubt, as far as possible, all things.

Rene' Descartes

"Did that help you answer my question?"

Joel was embarrassed, but answered honestly, "I'm sorry, professor. I'm just not getting what you're driving at."

"Okay, then let me be more direct. Joel, my second objective in teaching Philosophy 101 is to help my students learn to think, to analyze, to ponder. Many 101 series courses are simply a memorize and repeat process on the given subject. In contrast, my approach as a professor of philosophy is to also teach you *how* to think productively."

"Now I see what you are saying. Thank you for your patience."

"Did that lead you into identifying my third and final objective for teaching Philosophy 101?"

Joel began to sweat. He felt embarrassed enough already by the conversation. However, think as he might, he could not develop an answer to the professor's question.

"I'm embarrassed to say I'm still drawing a blank."

"Let's take a moment and consider what a couple of our philosophers have said. These quotes are from your reading thus far this semester.

There are no extra pieces in the universe.
Everyone is here because he or
she has a place to fill,
and every piece must fit itself
into the big jigsaw puzzle.

Deepak Chopra

True wisdom comes to each of us when we
realize how little we understand about
life, ourselves, and the world around us.

Socrates

Do you remember reading that material?"

"Yes, professor. I've made a particular effort to memorize the key philosophical quotes and identify their originator."

"Joel, what you just said tells me that you're not on track to identify my third objective. So, I'll again be direct. I aim to teach my students to utilize their enhanced thinking skills to consider and examine what is occurring around them. In other words, to learn how to evaluate what they are seeing and hearing in light of the environment. I want my students to be able to integrate the smaller, tactical aspects of their lives with the bigger picture."

"Ah, now I see what you're saying. Thank you for your patience with me this afternoon."

"I'll look forward to your next two papers. Now that you know what I'm looking for, you should perform much better."

"I assure you, professor, that I'll make every effort to work even harder in your class."

"I see that my next appointment is here."

Joel stood up, retrieved the two papers from the professor, placed them in his backpack, and departed the office. On his walk back to his car, he committed to twice reading the upcoming material for the class. He needed at least an overall 'C' grade to meet the criteria for acceptance into UC / Santa Barbara.

Later that afternoon, as Professor Krakaris was closing up his office, he thought back on his meetings today. The Johnson student was clearly earnest in his commitment to do well in the class. On the other hand, he doubted that Joel would ever develop the synthesis and perspective he was trying to teach. Some people were just wired that way, focused on what was immediately in front of them, without the ability to think through to the bigger picture. The professor made a mental note to give Joel a 'C' in the course regardless of how poor his forthcoming papers were. It made no sense, in the grand scheme of things, to deny the student the opportunity to complete his AA degree and move forward in life simply due to how his brain operated.

Chapter 8

Thursday February 8, 1996
Santa Maria, California

50-year-old Dale Huffington was energized this morning, even before having his usual cappuccino. He had been promoted from Senior Business Development Officer to President of the bank a month ago. The promotion boosted Dale's already larger than average ego. He enjoyed being known as a mover and a shaker throughout the valley. Dale's investment in his education had paid off. He earned an undergraduate degree in business from the University of Santa Clara and an MBA from UC / Berkeley. Dale was blessed by good genes and above-average intelligence.

Yesterday was Dale's first Board of Directors meeting as President. All had proceeded smoothly. Green Valley Community Bank was in acceptable financial condition, with average earnings versus its peer group and a low level of delinquent loans. The national and regional economies were both experiencing an accelerated rate of growth, fueled in part by the burgeoning Internet businesses. While the front side of the Treasury yield curve was relatively flat (versus the steeper yield curve generally preferred by banks), the nominal level of interest rates was high enough to facilitate the bank's earning a favorable net interest margin.

Dale's wife, Anne, was waiting for him in the kitchen, having prepared his usual breakfast of one poached egg and some local, seasonal fruit. Several of the valley's farmers had constructed greenhouses in recent years, thereby extending the growing season to virtually year-round.

"Good morning, darling. How are you today?" asked Anne.

"Feeling excellent. The Board meeting proceeded well yesterday, Linda has transferred over from the Business Development Division and is settled in, and we have a great pipeline of potential new business."

"Your ancestors would be proud. Was it your great-grandfather who helped form the Bank?"

"Yes, Kenneth Huffington was my father's grandfather. The Huffington family was one of the pioneer settlers of the valley."

"Well, I'm off to San Francisco this morning. We have a three-day showing at a new gallery just south of Market Street."

Dale smiled at this, hiding his grin behind his cup of cappuccino. Anne was both an artist and an art exhibitionist, coordinating showings throughout the state. Anne's trips provided Dale with ample opportunity to utilize his condominium on the other side of town for an array of trysts. While Anne's personality exhibited a zest for life that was immensely attractive to Dale, her physical appearance was a bit mousy and her sexual performance was at best mundane. Dale had secretly purchased the condominium about five years ago, with all of the associated bills sent to his office at the bank and paid for via a separate checking account that was unknown to Anne. Linda Morris, Dale's assistant for the past ten years, was utterly loyal to Dale and facilitated his lifestyle. Dale had offered Linda a job years ago when she was desperate for income following a bout with prostate cancer by her husband, Carl. Dale had also provided Linda and Carl with a no-interest loan from his personal funds to cover the deductibles and copayments arising from Carl's cancer treatments.

"What's the nature of this showing?"

"All oil-based paintings by a new and upcoming artist. His combination of color and perspective is unique. He has the opportunity to become famous with more visibility and continued progression in his art."

"He's fortunate to have found you. I can't imagine anyone better suited to advance his career."

"Thank you, dear. Will I need to defrost something for you for dinner tonight?"

"No need. I've got a business development dinner with one of the larger agricultural packing companies in the valley. They would make an excellent account for the bank."

This was another lifestyle aspect loved by Dale. He was a master of small talk and a great salesman. He arranged for most of his lunches and dinners to be for attracting and retaining clients, all paid for by the bank. This allowed Dale to keep his personal expenses low, thus freeing up cash flow to support the condominium. This also facilitated Dale's regularly eating chef-prepared meals. Upscale food and wine, plus sexually adventurous women, were Dale's primary weaknesses.

"The bank is lucky to have you. I hope the Chairman of the Board recognizes that."

"Yes, George Anderson IV supported my ascension to President, and was helpful during yesterday's Board meeting."

"Good to hear. Well, I've got to hit the road. I'll see you Sunday night."

Dale and Anne kissed, and then she departed. As Dale watched her pull out of their driveway, his pulse quickened. While he intellectually knew that his sexual compulsions were both risky and obsessive, he was simply unable to control himself. That was an inherent part of his personality, similar to an addict being hooked on a drug.

As Dale drove to the office, his thoughts wandered to Heather Perkins. He had been flirting with Heather for months now. She was a 40-year-old former Miss San Luis Obispo County, with a curvaceous figure, long flowing blonde hair, and a vibrant personality. Her husband frequently traveled to Los Angeles on business. Perhaps this would be the weekend when his lust for Heather might be fulfilled.

Chapter 9

Saturday May 21, 1984
Santa Barbara, California

It was a cloudless, but already hot, morning as Cheryl Johnson took her seat for the graduation ceremony at UC / Santa Barbara. She was so proud of her son, Joel. He had received his AA degree in two years from Santa Barbara City College and then transferred to UC / Santa Barbara as a junior. Two years after that, he was now graduating with a Bachelor of Arts degree. Joel majored in music theory. Cheryl smiled to herself. All those years of piano lessons together had paid off. Joel's accomplishments were all the more impressive given that he had continued working in the fast-food restaurant throughout his college years in order to supplement his mother's modest income.

The loudspeakers began playing a traditional march, followed by a stream of robed students taking their seats at the front of the amphitheater-like setting. The ceremony was almost perfectly designed and executed. Speeches by two graduating seniors and three members of the faculty were well written and effectively delivered. The university choir provided musical interludes, plus a closing song to send the graduates on their way.

Cheryl arranged to meet Joel at the university's fine arts building, where he would collect his physical diploma.

"Joel, I'm over here," called out Cheryl.

Joel instantly responded to the sound of his mother's voice and ran over to her. They embraced in a swirling hug.

"Honey, I'm so proud of you. You're the first member of our family to earn a college degree."

"Mom, you're always so kind. I did just barely graduate, with a 'C minus' grade point average. At least I got some 'B minus' grades in some of my core music theory classes."

"Don't sell yourself short, Joel. You were raised by a single mom in a household of quite limited income, yet still managed to graduate from a quality university."

"Thanks mom. I never could have done it without your support and encouragement."

They hugged again.

Cheryl said, "I promised you a nice graduation dinner. Did you decide where you would like to eat and if you wanted to bring one of your classmates?"

"A steak at The Swiss Restaurant on North Broadway in Santa Maria would be great. Most of my classmates have been together since they were freshmen, so, arriving as a junior, I never really developed any deep friendships. Being a day student didn't help, either."

"That's okay, honey. I'm happy for just the two of us to celebrate this big day."

That evening, as Joel and Cheryl were waiting for their entrees to be served at the restaurant, the topic of conversation turned to Joel's future.

"Joel, did you have any luck landing a job through the UC / Santa Barbara career center?"

"I visited them five times during the past semester. I mailed more than a dozen cover letters with my resume to various organizations in the fine arts field, as they suggested. Those did not result in any follow-up communications. I also signed up for four on-campus interviews with various non-profit entities somehow related to music or artistic or cultural endeavors. I didn't get called back for a second interview with any of them."

"It's okay, honey. It's a competitive world out there. It took me six years and three tries to finally get appointed Department Manager at the department store."

"I'm just not sure what to do next. I feel that I've exhausted all leads through UC / Santa Barbara, especially now that the summer is here and many of the career placement staff will be taking vacations. I'm also thinking that perhaps I need to be more realistic, mom. I'm no better than an average student with a degree in music theory. That's quite a bit different profile than the really smart students who graduated today with degrees in mechanical engineering or computer science. Maybe I need to pursue some other line of work, outside of the fine arts."

Their steaks arrived. This meal was a real treat for Cheryl and Joel. They rarely ate out given Cheryl's limited income. When they did, it was typically at one of the chain restaurants where Cheryl could use a coupon for a free entrée. After they both consumed about half their dishes, Cheryl's eyes lit up with an idea.

"Joel, didn't you have a good experience with a counselor at City College. What was his name?"

"Oh yes, Mr. Sampson."

"Why don't you give him a call and make an appointment. After all, you're an alumnus. Maybe he'll have some good ideas regarding employment opportunities."

"That certainly can't hurt. I'll give him a call first thing on Monday morning."

Chapter 10

Friday July 11, 1997
Santa Maria, California

George Anderson IV, esquire, was at his law office, located in one of the most upscale commercial buildings in Santa Maria. The office was paneled in mahogany, complemented by marble floors. The practice was small, comprised of George, one paralegal, and one legal assistant. This was by design. George earned enough income from his fractional ownership interest in Blue Pacific Ventures to live an extravagant lifestyle, if he so chose. George I was truly prescient in establishing that entity, with his ten percent interest passed down to the eldest male from generation to generation. By George IV's generation, most of the descendants of the original founders had grown up with wealth, and had little motivation to actually work the land. As a consequence, the partnership now functioned primarily as a collection of leases. The oil production occurred under a lease to one of the large energy companies, with the partnership receiving a royalty payment for each barrel produced. Similar arrangements were made for the farmland and the grazing land, generally with some profit participation on top of the base lease payments. George was the current General Partner, following in the footsteps of his great-grandfather. The work of the General Partner was now simplified to administering and renewing the leases, collecting monthly royalty and similar payments, and making periodic disbursements to the owners of interests in the partnership. On top of the significant Blue Pacific Ventures income, George also received a handsome stipend for serving as Chairman of the Board for Green Valley Community Bank. Therefore, George did just enough work through his law firm to fill up his days and help his friends throughout the community. Any legal matters of great depth or complexity were referred out to larger law firms.

George looked at his calendar and saw that he was having lunch today with Al Cook, the bank's Chief Financial Officer. The Anderson and Cook families were well acquainted, with their relationship dating back to the late 1800's and the initial settlement of the Santa Maria Valley. George checked his watch, grabbed his coat, and started the short walk to the restaurant. Upon entering, he had no difficulty finding Al, seated at a booth towards the back of the dining room.

"Hello Al. How are you today?"

Al stood up to shake George's hand, which disappeared into Al's palm. Good nutrition and access to quality health care had facilitated the Cook family genetics over the generations. Al was a full six feet, eight inches tall, and must have weighed close to 300 pounds.

"Just fine. Thank you for agreeing to meet with me today, outside of the bank's offices."

"My pleasure."

A waitress approached the two men, inquiring what they would like for lunch. George ordered the tri-tip sandwich, a Santa Maria specialty. Al ordered the ribeye steak accompanied by a baked potato with all of the fixings. Both men also requested a draft beer.

"Al, how's your wife doing?"

"Very well, thank you. Lately, she's been studying Italian at City College."

"That's a bit unusual. What prompted that endeavor?"

"If you'll remember, Peggy has a master's degree in art history. She loved studying the Renaissance period, analyzing the progression in style, technique, and sophistication, starting as early as Giotto, and all the way to Botticelli towards the end of the era."

"Yes, that's right. I've discussed that topic briefly with Peggy at various bank events over the years. But, how did that lead to wanting to learn to speak Italian?"

"The answer to that question dovetails with my reason for inviting you to lunch today."

"Okay. You've piqued my interest."

The waitress arrived with their beers. Both men took a gulp, and then continued the conversation.

"George, we're both descendants of the founders of Blue Pacific Ventures, and current owners of a portion of that partnership."

"Yes..."

"As General Partner, you know how much income I received from the partnership each year."

"Of course. And I'm happy to say that this year might be the most profitable one yet. Strawberry production is up at the same time prices are due to some farming issues in Mexico, so our agricultural operations are well positioned to throw off a record amount of cash flow."

"That's the point, in a way. George, Peggy and I have decided that I should retire from the bank and spend the rest of our lives pursuing our dreams. Our income from Blue Pacific Ventures alone is more than enough to allow us to indulge in any passion. Peggy wants to start this next stage of our lives by living in Florence, Italy for a year. That would provide easy access to many of the great Renaissance art works, starting with the Uffizi Gallery, Palazzo Vecchio, and Santa Croce."

"But you're only, what, 53 years old?"

"I just turned 54, and I know that's young to retire. Peggy and I have discussed this at length. We want to be able to travel and have experiences now, when we're both healthy. You remember that my father died at 58 from a heart attack."

"Yes. He was a great man. I still remember the hundreds of attendees at his funeral, and the eulogies delivered by family and friends. He was also a dear friend to my father. But, Al, are you sure you want to do this? You've got an undergraduate degree in business administration, a graduate degree in accounting, and are a licensed CPA. That's a lot of personal and professional investment to walk away from."

"I recognize that. I will miss the business world in general and the many colleagues at the bank in particular. However, Peggy and I have our minds made up."

"I see... I'm disappointed for the bank, its shareholders, and its customers, but happy for you and Peggy if this is what you both really want to do."

"George, tell you what. Peggy has another semester of Italian scheduled at City College. I'd be happy to stay on the job until you and Dale decide on a replacement. I'd never leave the bank hanging."

"I appreciate that. Not unexpected coming from you, Al. Have you discussed this yet with Dale?"

"Not yet. I wanted to speak with you first, given your intricate knowledge of Blue Pacific Ventures. I was hoping you'd help me break this news to Dale, while of course keeping my ownership interest and related income associated with Blue Pacific Ventures confidential."

"I see where you're coming from. I'd be happy to do that. I'll check my calendar back at the office and give you and Dale a call to schedule."

"Thank you, George. That's much appreciated."

The waitress arrived with their lunches. The tri-tip sandwich was delicious, perfectly seasoned and cooked. Al tore into his ribeye steak and baked potato. It took a lot of calories to fuel someone the size of Al.

Chapter 11

Friday May 27, 1984
Santa Barbara, California

Joel parked in the large lot in front of City College. He was a bit early for his appointment with Mr. Sampson, and so took a leisurely walk across campus, thinking back to his experiences there several years ago. His one regret was not having dated much. The odds for such were stacked against him. He was not athletic, and almost twenty pounds overweight, all of which was carried on his stomach. As a day student commuting in from Santa Maria, he did not spend much time on campus outside of classes and labs. And, as Joel admitted to himself, he was an introvert with a less than fascinating personality. Small talk was never his forte. The women on campus seemed much more drawn to the athletes and the business majors. Good looks and money were always attractive.

At the 11:00 AM appointment time, Joel knocked on the door to Mr. Sampson's small office. Mr. Sampson opened the door and welcomed Joel to take a seat.

"Hello Joel. Good to see one of our alumnae. How have you been?"

"I graduated from UC / Santa Barbara last week with a major in music theory."

"Congratulations. I'm very happy for you. What prompted you to make this appointment?"

"Despite about four months of effort, and extensive use of the UC / Santa Barbara career center, I haven't been able to land a job. I can't keep asking my mother to support me, plus I want to begin a career."

Joel handed Mr. Sampson a copy of his resume. Mr. Sampson ran his finger down the page as he reviewed the document.

"What types of jobs have you been applying for?"

"Almost anything tangentially related to music or the fine arts, and from San Francisco to San Diego."

"Your experience is not unusual. There simply aren't that many jobs in the fields you've mentioned. In addition, the competition for the limited number of positions that exist can be quite intense. If I remember correctly, you play the piano, but are far from a virtuoso."

"That's true."

"Did you develop an expertise in music composition at UC / Santa Barbara?"

"While I did classwork in that regard, none of my work was particularly notable. My grades confirmed that perspective."

"I see... Let me think for a bit..."

Mr. Sampson leaned back in his chair and stared at the ceiling for a few minutes. He turned back to Joel and asked several questions.

"Joel, would you say that music is somewhat mathematical by nature?"

"Yes. The notes, chords, harmonies, etc. can be viewed as a form of mathematics."

"Would you also say that playing or composing music requires a certain amount of discipline?"

"Yes, I would also say that."

"Joel, this may sound out of left field to you, but might you possibly consider working in the accounting field?"

"Accounting? I never even thought of that."

"I mention accounting for two reasons. First of all, there is a high demand for people with accounting skills right now. City College placed 100% of our accounting certificate holders in jobs this year. Second, your background in music theory might indicate a potential facility for accounting work. The starting pay for even low-level accountants is attractive, plus generous benefits packages are often available."

"Wow! This *is* an unexpected conversation... What would I have to do to pursue an accounting job?"

"City College offers an accounting certificate to individuals with at least an AA degree who successfully complete four accounting classes. There are two classes in basic accounting, one class in cost accounting, and one class in managerial accounting. They are designed to be taken sequentially, and we offer them as part of our summer program. Thus, you could have the certificate by the end of next summer. Also, taking one class at a time would give you a chance to work a perhaps more professional part-time job than the fast-food position I saw on your resume. That would build your work experience and profile, plus of course provide enhanced income."

"And there would be an almost 100% chance of landing a job?"

"While I of course cannot guaranty that, the probability is good."

"Do you have the forms necessary to enroll in the accounting certificate program?"

"Let me find them... Here they are. The tuition cost is very low, consistent with our mission as a community college."

"Thank you, Mr. Sampson. I'll discuss this with my mother

tonight. I can't thank you enough for taking the time to meet with me today."

"That's what guidance counselors do."

Joel shook Mr. Sampson's hand, took the application documents, and walked back to his car. He thought at length about this potential new direction in his life as he drove back to his house in Goleta.

Chapter 12

Saturday August 24, 1985
Goleta, California

It was 4:00 in the afternoon when Joel drove up to his mother's house, where he continued living after graduation from UC / Santa Barbara. He was hungry after working five hours straight at his part-time teller position without more than a bathroom break. This had been a busy week for Joel. The final examination for his managerial accounting class at City College had been on Wednesday. The Bank of America Branch Manager (Santa Barbara) scheduled him for three straight shifts Thursday through Saturday to cover for vacations by other employees. He would finally be able to rest this evening, and then have a leisurely Sunday after attending church with his mother. The house was empty upon Joel's arrival. His mother was working the late shift at the department store in Santa Barbara this evening.

As Joel entered the small kitchen to get something to eat, he noticed an envelope addressed to him on the table. The return address was for Green Valley Community Bank in Santa Maria. His heartrate increased to 60 beats per minute. He interviewed there for an Accountant position three weeks ago, following being advised of the open position by Mr. Sampson. He thought that the bankers were impressed with his being willing to go back to City College for the accounting certificate. The woman from Human Resources smiled when they discussed his having worked part-time as a teller while completing the accounting curriculum. Joel tore open the envelope and began reading the enclosed letter.

Dear Mr. Johnson:

We are pleased to offer you the position of Accountant. This position reports to the Controller and is located in Santa Maria. In addition to your starting salary, the Bank will provide medical, dental, and vision benefits. You will also be eligible to participate in our 401(k) Plan. Your requested start date is September 16, 1985. This offer is contingent upon your receiving the accounting certificate from City College of Santa Barbara. We are pleased to offer you a starting salary of $28,000 per year. Please indicate your acceptance of this offer by signing below and returning this letter to our Human Resources Department. If you have any questions, please contact ...

At this point in the reading, Joel dropped the letter onto the table and leaped into the air. Finally! He would be fully employed and have a career. He could not wait to share this great news with his mother. With the addition of his salary, they would finally be able to replace the leaking roof on their house and, after that, purchase a dishwasher to make his mother's life easier. The one hour commute each way was an easy drive and quite manageable.

Joel then calmed a bit and remembered the contingency in the offer letter. He had passed the first three accounting classes with grades from 'C plus' to 'B minus', and he felt confident that he had performed reasonably well on the final examination for the managerial accounting class. Grades would be posted early next week. He made a mental note to stop by the City College campus each evening to check the bulletin board where the grades were posted, and to call Mr. Sampson once he knew he had passed the fourth course.

Chapter 13

Saturday January 3, 1998
New York City, New York

At 8:00 AM, it was a bitterly cold winter morning in New York City. A polar front was moving south from the Canadian arctic, resulting in a forecast high temperature of just 12 degrees Fahrenheit this afternoon. Twenty-four-year-old Jennifer Eastman was sitting at the small kitchen table in the similarly small apartment she shared with her roommate, trying to warm herself with a cup of hot tea. The radiator for the 600 square foot apartment was again on the blink. Thank goodness their apartment was on the seventh floor, partially warmed by the heat rising from the floors below. Jennifer's roommate, Mandy Barnaby, jumped down from the upper bunk bed in the bedroom they shared and joined Jennifer in the kitchen.

"Good morning, Jen. Did you sleep well?"

"Thank goodness I bought that extra wool blanket on clearance in Woolworth's basement. Another icy night for us in this tenement."

"I wish we could afford a better place. The rents in the Theater District are just so high."

"I made a decision this morning while sipping my tea."

"What was that?"

"I'm not going to continue living like this. I studied hard for all four years at NYU in graduating cum laude with a fine arts degree. In the three and a half years since then, I've worked forty or more hours per week waiting tables in order to have enough money for food, rent, and acting lessons. The only parts I've gotten have been understudy roles to supporting characters in off-Broadway productions. Those types of roles don't pay squat."

"As we've discussed, my experience is quite similar to yours. I've asked myself many times whether to abandon my acting dreams and pursue a more predictable, normal life. Is that what you decided, to give up?"

"Just the opposite. I've observed that the better female roles have generally gone to the best-looking women. Customers don't want to pay Broadway prices to watch average-looking people. Beauty also drives opportunities in television, even in commercials for mundane products like cat litter."

"I agree that talent alone is not enough for women to succeed in the entertainment business. That's a deplorable situation that's just not right. However, I can't see a way to change that. The culture is just so damn embedded in the industry. It goes way back. I'll never forget reading the quote:

The casting couch? There's only one of us who ever made it to stardom without it, and that was Bette Davis.

Claudette Colbert

Decades later, and Colbert is still correct."

"That's why I've decided to spend every dollar I've saved, plus borrow money from my parents, to have the plastic surgery performed."

"What are you talking about?"

"I know that my nose is large enough to shield a small child from the sun."

"Jen, you're exaggerating again. It's hardly that big."

"Big and with a hump in the middle. Not exactly the nose of a starlet."

"I've heard that nose jobs can be quite painful."

"It can't be more painful than continuing to live in a roach-infested building with no heat."

"You have a point there. By the way, we've been quite successful with the roach traps. We could advertise as big game hunters."

Jennifer laughed. She didn't know what she would have done these past several years without a best friend like Mandy. The two of them experimented with a physical relationship a couple of years ago, but reached the conclusion that they were both fundamentally heterosexual.

"But that's not all."

"What else are you thinking about?"

"The entertainment industry has a breast fixation. How many leading actresses have small B-cups?"

"We've discussed many times that sex sells. We've also chatted about trading sexual favors for career opportunities. Neither of us has sunk to prostituting ourselves."

"The plastic surgeon says I have the frame to support large C-cups to small D-cups, with good projection."

"But what about all of the issues with breast implants? Women have reported a wide range of related maladies, some severe. Why would you want to take that risk?"

"Look, Mandy. I'm twenty-four years old. If an actress does not land at least a couple of major roles by twenty-eight, it's all over for her career. I only have a small window of opportunity, and I'm going to take it."

"You certainly sound determined."

"I am, and there's a favor I need to ask you."

"I'll be glad to arrange my shifts to be able to help you recover."

"That's kind of you, but too much to ask. Instead, would it be okay if my mother stays with us for the first week after the surgery? She can sleep on the couch. I'll have a post-surgery follow-up appointment and will be limited in mobility and function for the first week."

"Of course, but I insist that your mom sleeps in my bed. Someone over fifty years old should not be couch-surfing. I'm fine for a week, and will, despite what you said, adjust my shifts to be able to help you during the second week."

"Oh, Mandy, I couldn't ask for a better friend and roommate."

The young women hugged each other tightly. Their deep friendship was fostered by their shared experiences and frustrations with breaking into the entertainment business.

Chapter 14

Monday January 5, 1998
New York City, New York

The offices of Huffman Brothers were elegant. They were located on the 60th floor of one of the marquis skyscrapers in the Financial District at the base of Manhattan Island. Huffman Brothers was a mid-sized investment bank, operating in the equity, bond, and derivative markets, while also conducting initial public offerings, mergers and acquisitions, and fixed income securitizations. The booming economy in the late 1990's had accelerated the firm's pace of growth, as did the expanding size of markets for comparably new financial instruments, which in turn were enabled by the advances in technology over the past several years.

As soon as the closing bell for the markets sounded, Ben Cohen, one of the Managing Directors, called for everyone's attention on the trading floor.

"Good afternoon, everyone."

"Good afternoon, Mr. Cohen."

"We had a great trading day this afternoon. Our new private label collateralized mortgage obligation sold out across all of the tranches, on the initial day of offering, at our asking prices or better."

The assembled employees all clapped loudly, with a couple of whistles thrown in.

"But that's not the only reason I'm speaking to you this afternoon. I would like to introduce our two newest teammates."

Ben gestured for two men, apparently in ther late twenties to early thirties, to step forward. Both were impeccably dressed in the latest Wall Street style.

"Duane Scott is our newest bond trader, with a focus on the Agency and private-label CMO market."

One of the men stepped forward and waved to the group.

"Troy Helmsley is our newest fixed income salesman. While Troy will sell our entire suite of bonds, from Treasuries to Junk Bonds, he will also have a focus on the collateralized mortgage obligation market."

The other man stepped forward and similarly waved to his fellow employees. Ben then continued.

"We see an excellent opportunity to significantly grow our volume and earnings in the CMO market. For those of you on the equity side, I'll explain a bit. The initial securitization of residential mortgages was in what we now call the pass-through mortgage-backed security market. In other words, firms originated and / or purchased thousands of, for example, thirty-year, fixed-rate, residential mortgages. These loans, typically with certain common characteristics such as interest rate, balance, and maturity, were then pooled into securitizations. For Agency MBS, a portion of the interest income from the mortgages was paid to FNMA, FHLMC, or GNMA as guaranty fees and portion was paid to the servicer for the mortgages. The remainder of the cash flows from the residential mortgages were passed-through to purchasers of the MBS on a scheduled / actual basis. In other words, investors could buy a fixed income security with a thirty-year final maturity, receiving monthly principal and interest payments, with the amount of scheduled interest guaranteed to be paid each month. Complete principal recovery was also guaranteed by the Agencies, although the timing of that principal recovery depended upon the payments on the underlying mortgages."

The employees in attendance who focused on equities (common and preferred stock, stock options, and restricted stock) nodded their heads in understanding. The employees who specialized in the fixed income markets yawned. Ben then continued.

"With the advances in computer technology, the CMO market was born later. Similar to MBS, a pool of mortgages is assembled. Rather than passing through a common interest rate and all security holders having the same final maturity, in a CMO the incoming cash flows from the mortgages are sliced and diced into a wide array of what we call *tranches*. For example, a given tranche may receive all of the initial principal payments until it is paid off, resulting in a short average life. To balance this, a tranche with a long average life is also created. This second tranche would not receive any principal payments until the first tranche is paid off. As another example, one tranche may pay out all of the interest available from the underlying mortgages, while its offset tranche would pay out all of the principal available from the underlying mortgages. We call these 'interest-only' and 'principal-only' tranches, often abbreviated to IO and PO. As a final example, one tranche may be designed as floating interest rate above an index such as LIBOR. Its offset tranche would be an inverse floater, which pays a lower interest rate as the index rises."

Ben paused at this point, seeing a hand raised in the back of the room.

"Yes, do you have a question?"

Harold Creighton, one of the younger employees in the room, stood up.

"Yes, thank you. Can you explain why the CMO market is

growing at such a faster pace than the MBS market?"

"That's an excellent question, Harold. The reason is twofold. First, firms such as ourselves are financially encouraged to create CMOs, as we can often sell the totality of the tranches at an aggregate price that is higher than would be received for a pass-through MBS based upon the same underlying mortgages. Second, the special cash flow characteristics of the various CMO tranches help many types of our customers with their business. For example, a life insurance company with very long-term obligations, in other words, waiting until the deaths of the policy holders, often desires an investment with a fixed interest rate over a similarly long average life. Because such a CMO tranche helps the client mitigate his risk, he is willing to pay a premium for the particular profile of cash flows."

Ben then paused and surveyed the room. It was the end of a workday, and the faces communicated their fatigue and desire to leave.

"Enough about the fixed income markets. Let's conclude by giving a round of applause and welcome to our two newest employees, Duane and Troy."

The room erupted in applause. Duane and Troy smiled broadly. Ben then departed the floor, signaling the other employees that they were welcome to also leave. Quite a few employees paused to shake hands and share a few words with Duane and Troy.

Chapter 15

Monday January 5, 1998
Santa Maria, California

Dale walked into the bank at his usual time of 8:45 AM. He typically used the gym down the street from the bank for an hour early in the morning, part of his effort to stay in shape and be attractive to younger women. He was lost in thought thinking about possibilities for future trysts when he almost walked over Norman Miller.

"Ouch!"

"Oh, Norman, excuse me. I apologize. I didn't see you."

"That's not an unusual circumstance for me."

Dale cringed at both his behavior and his wording. Norman was a good employee and a descendant of one of the valley's founders. He was also very short.

"Are you okay? I'm very sorry. I should watch where I'm walking."

"No problem, Dale. Have a good day."

Dale then continued walking to his office, now focused squarely on what was in front of him.

"Good morning, Dale. Can I get you a cup of coffee?" asked Linda, his executive assistant.

"That would be great."

After Linda returned to Dale's office with the coffee, he asked, "Is the cleaning service for the condo working on Wednesday this week, as usual?

“I haven’t heard differently. They’ve been quite consistent for the past couple of months.”

Dale wanted to avoid bumping into the cleaning service while he was entertaining at his condominium in town.

“Good to hear. Did you make the monthly mortgage payment on the condo, using the red checkbook?”

“Yes, plus I used the red checkbook to pay the utilities last week. All the condo invoices are up to date.”

“Thank you. Same situation with the house invoices from the blue checkbook?”

“Yes, everything paid on schedule.”

“Linda, I don’t know what I would do without you.”

Linda beamed. She had one of those personalities that thrived on regular, positive feedback. Dale recognized this, and so made a particular effort to praise Linda whenever the opportunity arose.

“What’s on the calendar for today?”

“You have a meeting at 9:30 this morning with George Anderson.”

“Oh, yes, he’ll want to discuss our search for a new Chief Financial Officer.”

“Then you have a lunch with the Gonzales brothers. You’ve been courting them for bringing their business to the bank.”

“Yes, they would make an excellent account. Their vineyards are highly productive, with excellent quality grapes as well. Those two really know how to operate a vineyard and sell their grapes for top prices. Anything else scheduled for today?”

“Not until the evening. You and Anne have a dinner reservation at the event for the combined Rotary Clubs of the valley. It’s a big fundraiser for the proposed new wing for the hospital.”

“Having advanced cardiac care right here in the valley would help save lives. Too much heart damage can occur by the time an ambulance travels to San Luis Obispo or Santa Barbara.”

“I’ll leave you to catch up on your email. I didn’t see anything that appeared important in your Outlook account this morning, but you’ll want to check if any of the emails require an immediate reply.”

Dale had granted Linda complete access to his email account to help manage the flow of communications he received as President of the bank. Linda similarly monitored his voice mail and all incoming faxes.

As Dale scrolled through his email, he noticed one from Veronica Sharp. Veronica operated a good-sized retail store on Main Street, and was a most attractive woman. Dale had made sure that the bank’s prospecting for the retail store’s financial business was assigned to himself. Dale typed in a reply message, suggesting their getting together for lunch sometime in the next week. Just as with his business duties, Dale’s personal activities also focused on maintaining a strong pipeline of prospects. In Dale’s case, this meant prospective sexual partners.

Promptly at 9:30 AM, George Anderson IV, Chairman of the Board, approached Dale’s office. Linda greeted him and showed him to the round table that Dale used for in-office meetings. Linda gently closed the door behind her.

Dale walked over from his desk and joined George at the round table.

"Good morning, George. You're looking fine this morning."

"Thank you, Dale, and good morning to you as well. How are we doing with the CFO search? Al Cook has been most gracious in agreeing to stay on until we hire his replacement. However, it's been quite a few months now, and I don't want to abuse Al's good graces. Plus, I know that his wife Peggy has their entire year in Italy thoroughly planned, starting April 1. My wife and I had dinner with the Cook's the other night. Peggy has developed quite the Italian accent and vocabulary. Most impressive. And we both know that Al loves Italian food!"

"Al loves *all* food! That said, I do know that he has a special yearning for fresh *tagliarini* with meat sauce, and also *arancini* cooked the traditional way."

Both men shared a laugh. Dale then returned to the subject at hand.

"George, as you know, the bank hired an executive search firm about five months ago. We sorted through a list of potential candidates, eventually interviewing five. Of those finalists, we first made a job offer to our preferred candidate. The fellow was an MBA and CPA with fifteen years of financial management experience. It turned out that he received three job offers besides ours, eventually selecting a Silicon Valley technology firm that offered a stock option package with which we could not compete."

"I remember your reporting that to the Board a while back."

"We then extended an offer to our second preferred candidate, with a similar result. With the Internet economy exploding and NASDAQ racing to a record high, the technology companies are swallowing up substantially all of the experienced CFO candidates in California."

"What has the executive search firm said about this situation?"

"They have never seen a market for CFOs like the current one. Between the rapidly expanding technology companies and all of the start-ups, there is far more demand for CFOs than the current supply."

"Did the executive search firm have any suggestions?"

"They said that we could double our compensation package and try to buy our way in."

"Hmmm... That would disrupt the salary structure among all of the senior officers. We'd have to similarly increase the pay of every Executive Vice President to avoid hard feelings, which would not be financially reasonable for the Bank. We're solidly profitable, but hardly in the realm of the large technology companies."

"I concur."

"Any other ideas?"

"The executive search firm did ask if there was any way we could cover the CFO position with an internal promotion. They communicated this despite the fact that such would not result in a commission for them."

"Wow! That clearly shows what the current market for finance professionals must be like. I've never heard of a search firm willingly walking away from a commission."

"Agreed."

"What do you think?"

"Well, our Controller, Joel Johnson, has been with the bank for thirteen years now, having worked his way up the ladder. For the past three years, he's been working closely with Al. Al has routinized most of the bank's accounting, finance, and tax work with excellent procedures."

"I hear a 'however' in your tone of voice."

"You're perceptive as usual, George. With Al, we've had a CFO with an undergraduate degree in business administration from the College of William and Mary, a graduate degree in accounting from the University of Southern California, and a California CPA license. In contrast, Joel has an undergraduate degree in music theory from UC / Santa Barbara and an accounting certificate from City College. While we've invested in Joel over the years by sending him to various finance and accounting training classes, that profile just doesn't match up with Al's."

"I see your point. On the other hand, we're at a recruiting disadvantage being located here in the valley, so far from both San Francisco and Los Angeles. In addition, no community bank can compete for talent with the Internet companies in today's economy. What if we convince Al to stay on until after the 1997 Annual Report is completed and the 1997 federal and state tax returns are filed? If I know Al, he could have that wrapped up by the end of March, allowing him to meet Peggy's schedule. We could also ask Al to make a special effort to tutor Joel during that timeframe in the areas where Joel has not had as much exposure or education."

"The more I think of it, the more I feel that we don't have any other choice."

"I'm thinking the same way you are."

"George, let me ask a related question. Isn't Melvin Needham related to you in some way?"

"Yes, he is, but not by blood. He is the son of my wife's sister."

"Would you be okay with promoting Melvin from Assistant Controller to Controller in conjunction with Joel's promotion?"

"I'm very sensitive to any appearance of nepotism, especially in our closely knit valley. Do you think Melvin is ready for the Controller position?"

"Well, I haven't spent much time with him. In fact, I have to admit that I barely know him. We haven't spoken much over the years, especially when I worked in the Business Development Division. However, I hear that he is highly focused on having his debits equal credits and balancing the accounts regularly. Those are great attributes for a Controller."

"As long as you and the other senior officers believe that Melvin is the best candidate for the job, I'm okay with his promotion to Controller."

"That way, we can recruit an Assistant Controller or a Senior Accountant from one of the regional colleges. That should be much easier to accomplish than the CFO search. In addition, paying, say, twenty-five percent more for an Assistant Controller is infinitely more affordable than paying up across our entire pool of Executive Vice Presidents."

"We're agreed. Dale, this has been a productive meeting as usual. I'll leave the implementation and announcement details up to you."

George rose, shook Dale's hand, and exited the building. As he walked back to his law office, George had no idea about what he had just helped set in motion.

Chapter 16

Monday January 19, 1998
Santa Maria, California

All of the bank's employees received the same email this morning. The key content of the email included the following:

> *Please join me in congratulating Joel Johnson on his promotion to the bank's newest Executive Vice President and Chief Financial Officer. Joel will officially assume those duties on April 1, following the retirement of Al Cook on March 31. In addition, we are pleased to announce the promotion of Melvin Needham to Controller. It gives me great pleasure to announce internal promotions for our fellow employees. Such highlights our commitment to career development for all Green Valley Community Bank team members. Both Joel and Melvin are locals, having grown up and obtained their education here on the Central Coast of California. I'd also like to highlight the twenty-five years of excellent service furnished by Al. The bank's total assets have doubled during Al's tenure, and every one of those twenty-five years was a profitable one for our bank despite several being in recessionary periods. Al's long and successful tenure validates our approach to hiring superior professionals and then providing them with the resources and support to be successful...*

Joel had shared the good news with his mother over the prior weekend. He still lived at home with her, but had used his income over the years to upgrade the house, its contents, and their cars. Cheryl was overjoyed at her son's promotion. The extra income would advance both of their retirement savings, something Cheryl was thinking about more often now that she was over fifty years old.

At the headquarters building that morning, at least half the employees stopped by Joel's office to offer him congratulations. That was the right thing to do in the valley, where the closeness of the various families fostered a form of decorum. Outside of the bank, however, quite a few of the employees questioned the promotion. Their general conclusion was that Joel was at best an average banker, not particularly intellectually nor socially intelligent, but blessed by good fortune to be in the right place at the right time.

Towards the end of the day, Linda stopped by Joel's office.

"Congratulations, Joel."

"Thank you, Linda."

"You're in luck. I needed some 'retail therapy' today, and you're the beneficiary."

Linda handed Joel a beautifully wrapped box. Whenever Linda had too much work to do or became stressed for any reason, she pursued retail therapy, or shopping to buy something. The shopping experience helped her feel more in control. Because Linda wasn't particularly bright and was by nature an emotional individual, she became stressed quite often, as reflected in her monthly credit card statement.

"Joel, aren't you going to open it?"

"I was going to take it home, but if you'd like, I'd be happy to open it now."

"Please do!"

Joel slowly and carefully unwrapped the package. This was a habit from his childhood, when he and his mother would save money by re-using wrapping paper.

A round, brass object emerged from the box. Joel looked puzzled. Linda noticed this.

"It's a compass! It's in recognition of your new responsibilities to help chart the course for our bank," explained Linda.

"Oh, I see… Thank you very much, Linda. I'll do my best."

Linda threw Joel slightly off balance by giving him a hug, and left his office. She was surprised that Joel didn't recognize the significance of the compass. She thought she had done a great job selecting that gift.

Joel performed his final tasks for the day and then prepared to drive home. During the trip, he thought to himself and noted that he must send Mr. Sampson an email, sharing his good news.

Chapter 17

Monday February 2, 1998
New York City, New York

The trading floor at Huffman Brothers was even louder than usual this morning. Equity, fixed income, and derivative salesmen were working the phones and email to drive buy or sell orders. The corresponding traders were monitoring their inventories and the effectiveness of their hedges as the capital markets fluctuated.

Troy Helmsley was on the phone with one of his new accounts, a mid-sized pension fund.

"I agree. That CUSIP is an excellent fit for your fund, filling a gap in your liability matching. Do you want to make an offer to buy?"

"The dollar size is over my authorization limit. I'll need to get approval upstairs."

"Okay, but the bond could trade away from you."

Duane happened to be walking by Troy's station at the time with his second cup of coffee this morning. He overheard the conversation and signaled Troy to place the client on hold.

"Can you please hold for a minute?"

"Okay."

"Troy, if you enter this code onto your terminal, the security will be circled, or held in stasis for you, for fifteen minutes. Huffman Brothers added this feature just for situations like this, to avoid losing a trade while waiting for a higher-level authorization from the client."

Troy took the client off hold.

"I just got approval to circle the bond and hold it for you for fifteen minutes. Can you get in contact with upstairs and call me back?"

"Thank you, Troy. Will do."

The client hung up.

Troy turned to Duane and said, "Thank you. I didn't know we had that feature here. You just helped me save a $20 million trade."

"My pleasure. All of the investment bank systems are slightly different, although substantially all of the companies use the Bloomberg terminals, like us."

"I owe you one. Thanks again, Duane."

Chapter 18

Saturday February 21, 1998
Santa Barbara, California

Dale Huffington didn't wake up until 9:30 this morning. He had been out late the night before, serving as Master of Ceremony for a dinner / dance fundraiser for the local chapter of United Way. The event had been a huge success, with the tickets sold out a month in advance and donations far exceeding the target. Dale had worked the crowd, smiling, complimenting, inquiring --- all leading up to his soft sell of making a donation to the cause. The local chapter would now have the funds necessary to operate one of its primary missions, a food bank that was a lifeline to the valley's poor.

After an hour ride on his mountain bike through the valley's agricultural heartland, Dale took a shower and packed his car. He left Santa Maria around noon for the drive down toward Santa Barbara. It was an unusually warm day for this time of year, with the Santa Ana winds blowing outward toward the Pacific Ocean.

Dale's wife, Anne, was in Sacramento, the state capital, all weekend, directing an art show. Dale had met Debbie Donegal at a fundraiser for ecological causes about a month ago. She was passionate about shutting down the remaining California offshore drilling platforms. So much so that she had recently penned an article for the local paper encouraging residents to never forget about the devastation caused by the massive Santa Barbara oil spill almost 30 years ago. As Dale drove south, he smiled to himself at this. That was before Debbie was even born. As a Porsche flew by his Cadillac, Dale also contemplated that Debbie was far younger than his usual trysts, and that he was about twice her age. However, he sensed that Debbie returned his physical attraction. Dale pulled off the 101 freeway at a little used exit north of town. He followed the directions Debbie had given him over the phone, arriving at a little dirt parking lot just inland from a small cove.

As Dale stepped out of his car and looked toward the ocean, he saw an umbrella, easy-up, and blanket positioned on the sand. Debbie saw him at about the same time and came running over. She was wearing a minimalist bikini, displaying a body that exceeded Dale's high expectations.

"We picked a perfect day for the beach!"

"I'm a county native, but I never knew about this cove."

"It's a well-kept secret. Secluded, with clean sand, protection from the wind, and a great view out into the ocean."

"Thank you for sharing this with me."

"That's not all I'm looking forward to sharing today."

Debbie gave Dale a deep kiss on the lips. Once he came up for air, he smiled at Debbie's aggressiveness. This was a nice change of pace from his wife's sexual passiveness.

"Did you bring another blanket, the food we discussed, and the wine?"

"Exactly as instructed."

Dale and Debbie emptied his car of the provisions and added such to what Debbie had already brought down to the beach. Once they had everything laid out under the umbrella and easy-up, Debbie took a slice of the soft camembert cheese, rubbed it on her breasts, and coyly said "Your appetizer is ready."

That began what evolved into an overnight stay on the

beach, with Debbie orchestrating a symphony of sexual experiences. She creatively integrated all of the food and wine into their pleasures, with a pause to watch the sun slowly set on the water. Dale had never experienced a woman with such a robust and varied sexual appetite.

As daylight entered onto the cove the next morning, they slowly awoke.

Once they were both sitting up, Dale said, "Debbie, this has been a wonderful time. I feel so fortunate that we met."

"It was more than just good luck."

"Okay..."

"Spending a night on a beach like this only reinforces my feelings about the environment. Why would society allow this to be placed at risk simply to line the pockets of huge oil companies? I hope you can appreciate where I'm coming from."

"You make a good point."

"I'm glad you agree with me. As Treasurer of the Central Coast Ecological Society, I'll look forward to you and / or your bank's $10,000 contribution."

"I'm happy to be supportive, but isn't that a bit steep?"

"Oh, I think that's a quite modest price to avoid having your wife receive the naked photos I took of us after you passed out last night."

Dale initially panicked. After taking several deep breaths, the reality of the weekend became clear. He was a person of influence in the county, and President of the local bank. He was also a member of one of the valley's founding families. Debbie had applied her best assets as part of her effort to evoke change. Her youth and beauty had blinded him to her ardency in pursuing her cause.

"My assistant, Linda, will have a check waiting for you, in exchange for the negatives and all copies of the photos."

Dale began quickly packing up his items, anger evident on his face. He was also frustrated with himself, for allowing his carnal desires to override his better judgment.

Debbie added, "Dale, I really did have a good time. Your enthusiasm was energizing. I hope I showed you the importance of protecting the environment."

"I sure learned about the importance of protecting my environment."

With that, Dale walked briskly over to his car and drove away. The sand in his boxers wasn't the only thing that chafed on him on the drive north back to Santa Maria.

Chapter 19

Friday February 27, 1998
New York City, New York

Nearing the end of the trading day, Troy Helmsley walked to the other side of the bank of Bloomberg terminals and caught the eye of Duane Scott. Duane saw this, and rose from his chair, following Troy. As Troy grabbed a chilled bottle of water from the employee break room, he turned to Duane and initiated a conversation.

"Duane, we've both been working at Huffman Brothers for almost two months, but we've hardly had a chance to become acquainted."

"It's been so hectic. You've been almost frantic, cold-calling potential accounts to build your book, while I've traded more bonds in one month here than I traded in six months at my prior job," said Duane.

"The economy is booming. This Internet revolution is driving an incredible surge in business activity, leading to an increased demand for credit. At the same time, the Federal Reserve is fostering a faster growth rate in M2 Money Supply, injecting liquidity into the economy. That liquidity is searching for a home, resulting in good demand for investments."

"We certainly picked a great time to come to work at Huffman Brothers."

"Do you have time to get a drink together after work?" asked Troy.

"I do. Nothing on my calendar for this evening."

"Great. I know a place nearby which stocks top quality beverages and provides a great view of Battery Park and the harbor."

"Sounds good."

The two investment bankers then returned to their seats to complete their workday.

At 4:45 PM, Troy concluded his final sales call for the day and looked over to Duane. Duane gave him a thumbs up. They exited the Huffman Brothers office, took the elevator down, and walked about four blocks to a bar and grill named Gino's Place. Upon entering, Troy navigated them to a booth towards the back, but with a line of sight out a window to the park and harbor. The two men sat facing each other in the booth.

"What's your favorite beverage?" asked Troy.

"While investment bankers are famous for their consumption of top end hard liquors, I must admit that I prefer wine."

"That's fine with me. Red or white?"

"Are you open to getting some appetizers? I didn't have much of a lunch today."

"Sure. Gino's has some family specialties."

"Then red."

A very attractive waitress approached the booth. She was of slightly above average height, had long blonde hair, a delicate face, and an apparently terrific figure.

"What can I get for you two?"

Troy responded, "We'd like to order two of Gino's specialty appetizers. Do you have the *frico* and the *suppli* available tonight?"

"Yes, both, still made according to the recipes from Gino's Italian grandmother."

"Great. We'll take a dish of each. What red wine would you suggest to pair with those?"

"Do you have a price range in mind?"

"Price doesn't matter," replied Troy.

"Well then, I'd recommend a bottle of *Brunello di Montalcino*. It's Gino's favorite wine, from the area his ancestors farmed in Tuscany."

"We'll take your recommendation."

The attractive waitress then departed to input their food orders and retrieve a bottle of the wine from Gino's cellar. Troy restarted their conversation.

"Duane, we don't know much about each other. What's your background?"

"I'm from Greenwich, Connecticut, just over the state line from New York. My father was also an investment banker, working most of his career for Merrill Lynch, primarily on the merger and acquisition side. My mother is a country club wife, socially well connected. I attended Cornell University and obtained an undergraduate degree in economics. I then worked for two years in operations support at Merrill Lynch in a job facilitated by my father, before obtaining an MBA with a specialization in Finance from the University of Chicago."

"Chicago is quite a quant program. I've heard that it's academically rigorous."

"True. However, that prepared me for being an effective bond trader, particularly in the more complex and esoteric corners of the fixed income universe," advised Duane.

"Where did you work after receiving your MBA?" asked Troy.

"I then took a trading position at one of the smaller investment banks. I wanted to chart my own path, distinct from my father's connections. After several years in that job, I was ready to move upstream and landed the position at Huffman Brothers."

"Interesting. Are you married?"

"No, not even a steady girlfriend. However, that's been partially by design. I must admit I've enjoyed dating a wide range of women in New York City. Working at a prestigious firm and having a healthy income hasn't hurt in opening doors in that regard."

The waitress returned with their wine, plus two glasses of iced water with lemon slices. She showed the bottle's label to Troy.

"I don't recognize that winery, but I'll trust your recommendation."

The waitress replied, "You won't be disappointed."

Both men stared while the waitress opened the bottle of wine. She had a face that looked lifted from a perfume ad in Cosmopolitan. Her arms were firm, indicating some time spent at the gym. She poured a small taste of the wine into a glass for Troy's approval. The aroma was superb, the taste akin to liquid velvet.

Troy responded, "That's wonderful. Thank you for the recommendation."

The waitress poured full glasses for both men and departed. Duane spoke next.

"So, please tell me a bit about your background."

"Fairly similar to yours, except that I grew up in an upscale Boston neighborhood. My father is still working, in an executive level position at the largest regional bank. My mother initially had a career in marketing, but gave that up to raise me and my three siblings, plus support my father's career ambitions. I obtained a business management degree from Boston College, worked three years in commercial business development for Citibank, and then went to Harvard for my MBA. My graduate studies were also concentrated in finance. After Harvard, I returned to Citibank for a few years, this time working in fixed income sales. I eventually decided that I wanted a career working for an investment bank, and so made the jump over to Huffman Brothers."

"That's quite a similar background. I would not have guessed Boston, based upon your lack of accent."

"My parents were both from New York, so our family never really adopted the Boston way of speaking."

The waitress returned to the booth, this time carrying a steaming dish of *frico*.

"Be careful, this is quite hot. I'd recommend cutting it open to cool a bit before eating."

"Duane responded, "Thank you for the advice. What exactly is *frico*?"

"Gino's recipe is a well-guarded secret. However, in general, *frico* is a soft cheese combined with potatoes, onions, and herbs, and then fried in extra-virgin olive oil."

"Sounds delicious. Thank you for the education," said Duane.

After the waitress left them, they toasted with the *Brunello di Montalcino* and sampled the *frico*. Both the food and the wine were excellent. Troy then returned the conversation to business.

"Duane, tell me, what are you thinking about career-wise?"

"Working for an investment bank is demanding. By that, I first mean intellectually, managing the various bond positions, deciding when and how to hedge, bidding to buy and sell securities, etc. I also mean physically demanding given the long hours. I saw what this career did to my father. An energetic, fit man was converted into an overweight, constantly tired individual with high blood pressure by age fifty. I'm twenty-nine now. I'm aiming to start a second career, of whatever type, by age forty."

"I agree with everything you said. I'm thirty now, and need to be doing something else no later than a decade from now. As a salesperson, I've got to travel and entertain in building a book of clients, in addition to all of the time at the office trying to source buy and sell orders from my customers. I'm already having trouble hitting the gym as regularly as I would like, and I'm probably only serving about forty percent as large a client book as the firm would ideally like."

Duane added, "My experience is that a good trader working with a good fixed income salesman can achieve synergies, the concept of one plus one equals three. Might you be interested in directing much of our activities to each other?"

"Absolutely. And I agree with your comment about synergy."

The men each downed some more of the red wine, and finished the dish of *frico* in the process.

Duane then asked Troy, "I don't think I asked about your marital status?"

"Very close to yours. There are a couple of women with whom I regularly spend time, but nothing as serious as an engagement. I've also enjoyed being seen as a quite eligible bachelor in my business and social circles. That profile has led to some memorable experiences."

Duane imagined what Troy might be talking about and smiled. The waitress then arrived carrying a plate of *suppli*.

Duane looked at the small, brown, egg-shaped items on the plate.

"Miss, I will admit my ignorance. What are *suppli*?"

"There is a range of recipes, based upon the various regions of Italy. On top of that, Gino has his unique family recipe. However, in general, *suppli* are somewhat like the *arancini* of southern Italy, although smaller. The outside portion is *risotto*, or Italian style rice. The inside is stuffed with a range of sauces, vegetables, and / or meats. The entire *suppli* is deep fried in extra-virgin olive oil. The plate I just served you contains two each of three different types of *suppli* we serve, sort of a sampler dish."

"Thank you for the explanation. That sounds delicious," said Duane.

"I see that you've finished your bottle of wine. Would you like another?"

"What would you recommend with the *suppli*?" asked Troy.

"It appears that you both enjoyed the *Brunello di Montalcino*. I'd recommend a wine from a bit further to the east in Italy, *Vino Nobile di Montepulciano*. It has certain commonalities with the *Brunello*, but also some distinct differences in flavor and finish."

"You're quite the salesperson," said Troy. "We'll again defer to your recommendation."

The men sampled the variety of *suppli*. While they each had their favorite, they both agreed that the dish was quite tasty. The waitress' advice regarding the *Vino Nobile* was again excellent. The luscious red wine paired perfectly with the *suppli*. Now both quite relaxed following one and a half bottles of wine, Troy broached a new topic to Duane.

"Duane, do you think if we both work diligently for a decade, that we will be able to retire by about age forty? By retire, I don't mean moving into a Sun City community. Rather, I mean having a sufficient net worth to do whatever we wanted for the remainder of our lives?"

"While the Huffman Brothers compensation and benefits packages are good, I don't see achieving that level of financial independence in just a decade. There is the high cost of living in Manhattan, plus the high rates of federal, state, and local income taxes. There are also the payroll taxes. I'm also not willing to live like a hermit for ten years. I enjoy Broadway shows, superb restaurant meals, and beautiful women, all of which are expensive."

"I share your perspective and desires," said Troy with a smile.

Both men enjoyed another gulp of wine. Troy then continued.

"You mentioned that your father worked in the investment banking business. Growing up, did you hear about ways various co-workers achieved a higher level of financial success?"

"Oh, yes, quite a few approaches, some legal and some not, most less than completely ethical."

"Might you be receptive to thinking about teaming together to pursue one or more of the legal, but perhaps less than sinless, behaviors?"

Duane paused at this question. From listening to his father

over the years, he was aware of a range of activities that investment bankers could pursue to augment their income. He finished the last of his wine, and then replied.

"I would not be receptive to anything clearly classified as criminal activity. On the other hand, I would consider concepts consistent with the saying that *a fool and his money are soon parted*."

"I share your perspective. Let's continue this conversation at our next meeting. I'm afraid that I've reached my limit for alcohol consumption, even it has been very fine alcohol," responded Troy.

Troy caught the eye of the waitress.

Upon arriving at the table, she asked, "Can I get you anything else?"

Troy answered, "Just the check and your first name. You've provided excellent service and recommendations tonight. I'd like to put in a good word for you with the ownership."

"That's kind of you. My name is Jennifer."

The waitress left the check on the table. Troy removed three $100 bills from his wallet and left them on the table, representing a generous tip. The two men exited the restaurant and called a cab.

Once in the taxi, Duane said, "Troy, the next round is on me. And by the way, I wouldn't mind eating some more of Gino's food and again laying my eyes on Jennifer."

"I knew we'd get along well the first time we met!"

Chapter 20

Friday February 27, 1998
New York City, New York

It was almost 9:00 PM by the time Jennifer returned to her apartment. She had worked the noon to 8:00 PM shift at Gino's and then taken the subway north to the tiny apartment in the Theatre District that she shared with Mandy. Her mail was on the kitchen table, as usual. She was fortunate to have such a reliable roommate. Among the letters was one from a production company with which she had auditioned on Monday. Jennifer eagerly opened the envelope and read:

Dear Miss Eastman:

We are pleased to offer you the role of Jacqueline in our upcoming production. Rehearsals will occur daily from 7:00 AM to 11:00 AM. If you would like to accept this part, please...

A primary role, not an understudy! The part was a supporting character, and the theatre was one of the less elegant on Broadway, but this was real progress! Jennifer smiled from ear to ear. She then heard Mandy cough in the bedroom, and entered.

"Are you okay? Can I get you some water?"

"I just finished my glass of white wine, which went down the wrong tube. I'm okay, but thank you."

"Mandy, I have great news! I was offered a primary role in the production I interviewed for on Monday."

"That's wonderful! I'm so happy for you."

"The money's not rich, but it's more than I've been receiving for the understudy roles."

"We could use the extra income around here. The landlord noticed us for a rent increase today. I spoke to him about it. It seems that the economy is booming and there's a shortage of housing in the city, so he's taking advantage of the situation."

"More for this hovel? Damn! However, I'm not going to let that ruin what has been a great day. In addition to the new role, I received a $75 tip from one of my tables tonight."

"Let me guess. A male lawyer or banker dressed in an expensive suit, stopping in to Gino's after working in one of the Financial District towers?"

"You're close. Actually, two reasonably good-looking guys who were both finely dressed. I didn't get their profession, but their manner suggested that they were well educated and highly compensated. They could have been lawyers or bankers."

"You didn't ask?"

"I had a full load of tables, and they asked me so many questions about the food and wine that I didn't have time."

"I trust you won't make that mistake again if you have a second opportunity? Remember, you have a roommate who is single."

"I promise."

Mandy and Jennifer both smiled. They had developed a close friendship working together to survive in New York City. Later that night, as they were about to turn off the light and go to sleep, Mandy spoke.

"You know, Jen, your good fortune today might not have been luck."

"What do you mean?"

"I mean that maybe your recent investment is beginning to pay off. The world is always nicer to beautiful people."

"I'm not sure about that... I guess we'll see what tomorrow brings, and if good fortune continues to come my way."

Chapter 21

Friday March 20, 1998
New York City, New York

About half way through the afternoon, Troy got Duane's attention down the trading desk and mouthed 'Gino's?' Duane nodded affirmatively.

The two investment bankers departed the office just before 5:00 PM after completing the paperwork for the fixed income transactions they conducted today. Once they were outside and more than a block away from the office, they began speaking.

"I've given quite a bit of thought to the topic we discussed the last time we ate at Gino's. I think I have a good solution," said Troy.

"I've also thought more about things. I look forward to our conversation tonight," replied Duane.

"Shall we aim for the same booth?"

"I'd prefer to aim for the same waitress."

"Good line! That's of course what I meant. The food at Gino's is delicious, but Jennifer is an awesome dessert."

Both men laughed as they entered the bar and grill. They looked over towards the booth where they sat before, observing that it was occupied by four women, all of whom were dressed in expensive business attire. Pausing for a moment, they then saw Jennifer bring beverages to the booth. Troy and Duane then walked quickly and sat down at the adjacent, empty booth.

"So, tell me about your solution," said Duane.

"In a nutshell, I propose that we 'Pump and Dump'."

"Are you talking trade allocation? That's almost impossible to do these days with all of the computerization."

"Not trade allocation in the historical sense. Years ago, in an analog, paper-based world, it was possible to manually allocate the most profitable trades, with the benefit of hindsight, to certain accounts to pump up their performance. Of course, that also resulted in other accounts being allocated the least profitable trades. I agree that we could not conduct that type of operation today."

Jennifer approached the booth. Both men smiled a bit more broadly than was normal.

"Good evening, and welcome to Gino's. Say, you two are familiar... I've served you before, haven't I?"

Troy answered, "Yes, about a month ago. Your food and wine recommendations were excellent. We've returned for another superb meal."

"Yes, now I remember. You enjoyed the Tuscan red wines from Montalcino and Montepulciano."

"You have an excellent memory."

"An actress needs to have a good memory."

Duane interjected, "You're an actress?"

"Yes, I'll be starting a run on Broadway in about a week. It's a supporting part. The show should receive favorable reviews. It's well written, with both humor and drama."

"Are there still tickets available?"

"Let me take your order. When I return, I'll give you a flyer for the show. I have one in my jacket downstairs."

"What would you recommend for dinner?"

"Gino received an overseas shipment of saffron yesterday. The very best. I'd recommend the *risotto Milanese*."

Duane spoke up, "Forgive my ignorance, but what type of dish is that?"

"It's the special Italian rice, cooked with saffron, cheese, olive oil, and Gino's secret list of spices. Trust me, it's delicious. The dish comes with a side antipasto salad."

"You've convinced us. We'll each have that. What wine would you suggest with the risotto?" asked Troy.

"If I again remember correctly, price is not a consideration for you two?"

"Correct."

"Then I would recommend a bottle of white wine from the top DOCG winery in Friuli-Venezia. Northeast Italy is well regarded for high quality white wines."

"Let's give that a try. Thank you."

Jennifer left the booth to submit their orders. The men then resumed their conversation.

"So, tell me about the modern version of trade allocation and exactly what comprises your Pump and Dump strategy," said Duane.

"Let me start with the latter topic. We both know that when we sell a U.S. Treasury Note, the gross commission, to be split between the sales desk and the trading desk is 1/128 of one percent. On a $5.0 million trade, the gross commission is just $391. Of that, I earn about $100 and you receive about $50. That's a difficult way to earn a living."

"Agreed."

"The gross commissions and the allocations to the salesmen and traders are progressively higher across the MBS, PAC-CMO, Municipal Bond, and Junk Bond products. However, for the lower priority and / or more esoteric CMO tranches like the Z-Support and some of the SEQ, the commissions can be quite generous, even surpassing those of Junk Bonds."

"In addition, the Bid / Ask spreads on some of those products are far wider than the U.S. Treasury market, giving us more room to work with," replied Duane.

"Yes, plus the wider Bid / Ask spreads typically result in more money being allocated to the year-end bonus pool for a given size trade."

The men paused to facilitate their digesting the recent conversation. Duane then continued.

"I'm thinking this through... So, what if we identified, say, ten or twelve potential new clients to the firm, who fit a certain profile, where we could pump up the decision-maker, setting him or her up for a future dump of a highly profitable transaction."

"The new clients would need to be accredited investors, with a sufficiently large balance sheet and enough liquidity to buy into a big enough Z-CMO support tranche or an Inverse Floater CMO tranche, for example, to make our efforts worthwhile," said Troy.

"And the decision-maker would need to be coachable, while also having a personality susceptible to being pumped."

"Exactly."

"Doing the math in my head, we could earn over 100 times the commission on trades like that compared to U.S. Treasury

Notes," presented Duane.

"You're spot on with the math, as usual," replied Troy.

Jennifer arrived at the booth with a chilled bottle of the Italian white wine, along with an iced ceramic wine sleeve. She opened the bottle and poured Troy a sample to smell and taste.

"The aroma is deep and complex," said Troy upon smelling the wine. After tasting it, he said, "Wow, that wine has a distinct entrance, a rich middle, and a smooth, lasting finish. I've never tasted anything like it."

"I thought you'd like it," said Jennifer, as she filled their glasses. "Your dishes should be ready soon. Oh, here's the flyer I mentioned. I hope you can see the show."

Once Jennifer returned to the kitchen, the men continued their conversation.

"Okay, I understand the Pump and Dump," said Duane. "But, how does the trade allocation aspect fit in?"

"It's all part of the Pump. Let me provide some examples. Whenever we buy in a bond at a particularly low price versus market, we give our target first look at buying such. Similarly, when we get a purchase order at a good price from another client for a particular security owned by the target, we again give the target first look."

"That's likely not enough to really pump up a target," noted Duane.

"Agreed. To further pump up our targets, we use the wider Bid / Ask spread on the less frequently traded securities to our advantage. My boss allows us salesmen to buy at the Ask and sell at the Bid in order to attract new customers. He views such as a type of marketing or advertising expense. That way, we can provide really good prices to our targets, regardless of whether they are buying or selling securities."

"I can see that. However, even adding up everything you have said, I don't think there's enough juice to Pump a target enough that we can then sell him or her on a Dump."

"Depends on the particular profile of the target, but I see your point. I've already thought of how we address that," responded Troy.

The men quickly fell silent as Jennifer approached with their dinners.

"Here you are. The *risotto* is hot, so let it cool a bit."

"The aroma is intense," said Troy.

"It's the imported saffron, plus the particular cheese and spices," advised Jennifer.

Duane took a small amount of the *risotto* on his fork, blew on it, and gave it a taste.

"Incredible! That's simply delicious."

Jennifer smiled and refilled their wine glasses.

"Please let me know when I can bring you anything else."

She then turned to serve a nearby table.

"This dish is amazing. How did I get to be my age and never eat this before?" said Troy.

"And served by such a lovely woman. Life doesn't get much better than this," added Duane.

After consuming about half of the risotto and sampling the antipasto salad, Troy returned the conversation to their primary topic.

"Look Duane, for Pump and Dump to really work there is one more aspect that needs to occur."

"I won't guess, but am eager to listen."

"We need to identify decision-makers at the client firms whom we can gently manipulate from a psychological perspective. Nothing blatant, just the icing on the cake to complete our plan."

"Such as?"

"Certain individuals can be nudged in various directions through the manipulation of their weaknesses. For example, some people are very egotistical. The way to influence them is therefore first to appeal to their ego in building their comfort with and confidence in us. Other people are hedonistic. Once we identify that characteristic, we facilitate their fundamental personal desires. This also builds comfort and confidence."

"Are you a bond salesman or a psychologist?"

"By definition, both. Any decent salesman utilizes psychology in performing his trade. Haven't you ever bought a car?"

Duane laughed. "Okay, loud and clear, I see what you mean."

Jennifer stopped by the booth.

"Is everything okay?"

"We can't thank you enough for your culinary guidance. As a small expression of our appreciation, we'll order tickets to your show first thing tomorrow. If you know acting even half as well as you know Italian cuisine, we're in for a superb performance."

Jennifer blushed a bit. "I'll let you finish your entrees."

"Troy, how would we identify targets with excellent potential for our plan? We could expend a lot of time and energy and not achieve our objective."

"Fortunately, our firm maintains multiple extensive databases to help us salesmen identify possible new clients. I can tap those, supplementing by reviewing the websites, press releases, and other materials from the potential targets. We'd have to devote some research time, but I need to do some of that anyway in building my book of business."

"That sounds a bit too far removed to lead to a high probability of success."

"That's why we supplement that aspect with a quick psychological reading of our potential clients, along with running various tests. In other words, we aim to quickly validate if a given client is truly suitable for Pump and Dump."

The men then finished eating their dinners, at which point Jennifer again dropped by their table.

"Would you be interested in something sweet or a cordial?"

Troy and Duane each smiled, each thinking that Jennifer would be the perfect dessert for the evening. However, both men maintained their professional composure.

"We're pleasantly stuffed. The risotto was quite filling. Just the check when convenient for you," said Duane.

When Jennifer returned with the check, she asked, "Might you have business cards? I'd like to be able to call you after you attend the performance and hear your impressions."

Both Troy and Duane provided their business cards, attempting to do so nonchalantly despite the quickening of their pulse rates.

Jennifer quickly glanced at both business cards.

"Oh, Huffman Brothers. I've heard of the company. And located not very far away from Gino's. Since you enjoyed your two meals here so much, perhaps you might recommend Gino's to your associates. Gino could use some more business.

He's got quite an extended family to support."

Jennifer departed the booth to pick up another table's meals from the kitchen. On her way, she thought Mandy would be pleased with her. She now had the contact information for the two investment bankers, and had collected such in a calm, non-committal way.

Duane paid the check in cash, including a significant tip.

Once they existed the restaurant, Troy turned to Duane.

"What do you say we do a test run. In other words, identify a handful of potential targets and conduct our plan. We can learn from the experience, improve upon our techniques, and / or cease at any time. Best of all, there is nothing illegal about selling publicly traded securities. It's up to the client to decide what price he's willing to pay and what bonds to purchase. We only provide opportunities."

"Agreed. Let's start next week. And, Troy, you *are* going to buy those two theater tickets tomorrow."

"First thing. I don't want to miss another opportunity to see Jennifer."

Duane slapped Troy on the back and smiled.

Chapter 22

Wednesday April 1, 1998
Santa Maria, California

Joel was full of pride, and more than a bit nervous at 7:30 AM, as he moved his personal belongings and key files into the CFO's office before most of the other employees arrived at the bank. Scott Miller, one of the deposit operations employees, happened to be in the office early that morning, observed what Joel was doing, and offered to help. Scott grabbed a banker's box that was stuffed with documents, plus a large plant, and carried both to the CFO's office. Joel didn't say anything, but thought to himself that Scott must work out regularly. That was a quite a load for someone barely five feet tall.

The bank had sponsored a retirement party for Al Cook the previous evening. The event was held at the most upscale hotel in town, owned by members of the Kehoe family. Almost all of the employees and Directors attended. Al was well thought of, both personally and professionally. The party included a four-course dinner, speeches (including several references to the big shoes to be filled following Al's retirement), and the presentation of several gifts to Al, including the traditional gold watch and, as a gag gift, a laminated map of Italy and a large English-Italian dictionary. Al's and Peggy's retirement plans had become well-known over the past couple of months. As a consequence of the extended event, and the ample wine and beer served by the hotel, quite a few of the employees arrived for work late and / or hung over. Joel recognized this, and decided to keep a low profile throughout the day.

At 8:30 AM, Joel rang Melvin's extension.

"Hello. This is Melvin."

"Hi, it's Joel."

"Good morning. First day of the new quarter, time to work on closing the books for the prior month and quarter."

"Thank you, Melvin. I know I can always count on you. I've completed moving out of the Controller's office, if you would like to begin moving in."

"No thank you. I'll stay where I am. I like it better down here."

The growth of the bank had led to space being tight in the headquarters building. An addition was under construction, but was not yet completed. In the interim, employees were squeezed in to all available space. Melvin had been working out of a small office in the basement for over a year.

"Are you sure?" asked Joel.

"Positive," replied Melvin. "I'll get the standard backdated general ledger entries available for your review by this afternoon. You should go over the investment security reports today. Good-bye."

Joel knew that there was something unusual about Melvin. He was a devoted worker, but maintained a number of atypical personal behaviors. If Joel had more background, he would have realized that Melvin placed on the autism spectrum.

Joel next called his mother at home. She would be leaving soon for her shift at the department store.

"Hello."

"Hello, mom."

"Hi, Joel. Is everything all right?"

"Yes, no problems. I just wanted my first call outside the bank as Chief Financial Officer to be to the individual who supported me for so many years and made this possible."

"Oh, honey, that's sweet of you to say. You worked really hard, too. I'm so proud of you. I need to leave for work now. I'll see you tonight?"

"I should be home for dinner about the usual time."

"See you then."

Joel walked into the Accounting Department and asked for the quarter-end security reports. Joel was familiar with some of the reports through his work as the Controller. Over the past several weeks, Al had devoted quite a few hours to educating Joel about the other reports and the capital markets in general. Joel had never actually conducted any investment security transactions. That had been Al's area of expertise.

The bank purchased a variety of short-term investments and bonds in order to earn extra interest income on its excess liquidity, and in order to have collateral for certain deposits and counterparty transactions. This was common for a community bank. Deposits were typically greater than loans, leaving excess cash available for investment.

Joel approached Rebecca, one of the accountants.

"Good morning, Rebecca."

"Good morning, Joel."

"Do we have the quarter-end accrual report off the security accounting system?"

"I just finished running that. Here you are."

"Thank you. We'll also need the safekeeping report from

our correspondent bank. That report includes the market values for our quarter-end disclosure. When does that usually arrive?"

"That report is addressed to the CFO. Al usually received it in the mail by about the fourth day of the month."

"I'll keep a lookout for it. Have a good day."

The correspondent bank electronically held the bank's securities, processed trades at the direction of the bank, and received payments from the issuers of the securities, primarily the government agencies FNMA, FHLMC, and GNMA.

Joel returned to his desk and dug in to his work. Al had developed checklists and calendars to ensure that all of the required accounting entries were timely made. Joel worked down Al's list throughout the day. Just after 5:00 PM, he departed for the drive south for dinner with his mother.

Chapter 23

Friday April 3, 1998
New York City, New York

Troy and Duane finished their work for the day at Huffman Brothers at about 5:00 PM. It had been another busy week. Huffman Brothers' trading volume was running thirty percent higher than last year, fueled by the high rate of GDP growth, recent hires, and the relatively new products now available in the fixed income markets.

"Shall we get a quick sandwich downstairs at Francesco's and then grab a cab up to the Theatre District?" asked Duane.

"Sounds good. It's closing night for the show. The reviews have been good, so the theatre will be packed. We should arrive early," replied Troy.

As the men ate their *panini*, the conversation flowed onto their plans for Pump and Dump.

"The pace at the office has just continued to build," said Duane. "I now understand even better why people only work in this business for ten years and then either have a heart attack or move onto a second career in self-defense. The hours are getting longer each week, and the intensity of the workday has spiked up. Richard, the leading trader for interest rate swaps, melted down at this desk this afternoon."

"All the more reason for us to make as much money as we can while we can. We've been handed this golden opportunity. We may never be as well positioned again. I'm not going to have a stroke at forty-five and spend the rest of my life drooling," said Troy.

After they finished their dinner, they called a cab and arrived at the theater. Jennifer was not listed on the marquee, nor on the promotional poster. They handed their tickets to the usher and took their seats.

The play was an intense murder mystery, injected with bouts of humor to break the tension. The wife of a wealthy couple was found murdered in their mansion. Jennifer played the small role of the next-door neighbor, being both a motive (for the now widower) and a suspect with regard to the murder, given her ongoing affair with the husband. While the overall performance was both impressive and enjoyable, Jennifer's soft, melodic voice did not carry well. This also limited her ability to communicate to the audience her character's emotions and a couple of the sophisticated nuances in the script.

At the conclusion of the show, the actors and director took the stage for a grand bow. The audience continued its clapping, with most standing to share their appreciation for a quality performance.

As the investment bankers were walking to the exit, Troy commented, "A good show. Well written and executed. The timing of the actors was excellent."

"I hear a 'however' in your voice," said Duane.

"You're getting to know me quite well! My 'however' is that Jennifer came across as among the weaker performers. In fact, I could not clearly hear a couple of her lines despite our having orchestra seats."

"I had the same experience. She is a beautiful woman, but does not appear to have the vocal strength for live performances. Perhaps film or television would be better for her, where they can use electronics to amplify her voice."

Once outside the theater, the two men each grabbed a cab back to their apartments. Meanwhile, backstage at the theater, the director and the producer of the show were sharing a bottle of champagne to celebrate an artistically and financially successful run.

"Great overall results for the show. We need to team again with the writers and have a follow-on performance," said the producer.

"Agreed," responded the director, "With perhaps a couple of minor adjustments."

"The next-door neighbor?"

"That would be one of the changes. Attractive young woman, but without the diction and projection to succeed on the stage."

"You're right, as usual. Based upon my recollection of her audition, she also does not dance or sing particularly well. I'll put a notation in our files. We'll put her on the list of 'attractive wallpaper' for the future."

The director and producer again toasted to their success, eagerly downing the champagne.

About an hour later, after saying good-bye to her fellow cast-mates, Jennifer rounded the block to her apartment building. She was confronted with swirling lights and blaring sirens. Looking further up the street, she saw flames erupting from at least three stories of her building. Two fire trucks were already on site, with a third now arriving. She ran towards the taped off area surrounding the building, and saw Mandy sitting on the edge of the sidewalk.

"Mandy, are you okay?"

Mandy coughed and hacked, eventually able to start breathing normally.

"Some smoke inhalation, but I'm all right. One of the residents who lives downstairs saw the fire just after it started. He ran around the floor, and then up and down the stairs, banging on doors, screaming for everyone to get out. Thank goodness he did that."

The women both looked back toward the building. The old tenement did not have sprinklers, nor was it built with firewalls. The construction included plaster over old wooden slats, which functioned as fuel for the fire. The flames were now more ferocious than before, despite the efforts of the firefighters.

Mandy started crying. She was giving life her all, only to experience one setback or rejection after the other. Jennifer held her tightly.

A woman wearing a Red Cross jacket approached Jennifer and Mandy.

"Are you two residents of the building on fire?"

"Yes," replied Mandy.

"Do either of you need medical attention?"

Both women answered, "No."

"I'll help you get a place to sleep tonight in one of our nearby shelters. The facility is stocked with donated clothing, personal supplies, and food. One of our staff there will give you everything you need."

"That's kind of you," said Jennifer.

"After you get some rest tonight, we'll also help you resettle. Here's my card. Please feel welcome to call me anytime as you go through this process. The Red Cross is here for you. Let me check on a couple of other residents and then I'll be back."

As the Red Cross volunteer started to walk away, she paused and turned back to Jennifer and Mandy.

"Also, if you have renter's insurance, you'll want to drop a text, email, or voice mail into your insurance agent as soon as possible."

Mandy and Jennifer looked at each other, shaking their heads, with an incredulous look on their faces. Poor, aspiring actresses working extra shifts as waitresses didn't have money for renter's insurance; nor did their possessions amount to much in value in the first place.

"Were you able to save anything?" asked Jennifer.

"Just my purse, phone, and our laptop," answered Mandy. "The smoke was already getting thick when I heard our neighbor screaming to exit."

"We'll pull through this together," said Jennifer.

"Maybe the fire was our fault," joked Mandy. "After all, we did ask the landlord to exterminate the roaches."

Mandy and Jennifer hugged each other tightly, watching their apartment building collapse into a pile of rubble.

Chapter 24

Monday April 13, 1998
Santa Maria, California

Dale Huffington called the meeting of the Green Valley Community Bank executive team to order promptly at 9:00 AM. Dale conducted this meeting with his direct reports twice per month, as a means of keeping everyone coordinated and also of building teamwork.

"Before we address the various business matters, I'd like to thank several of you for coordinating our bank's support of the Court Appointed Special Advocates, or CASA, program. We now have a record number of employees volunteering time for that organization. The positive impact that CASA provides to abused or neglected children is heartwarming. CASA has always held a special place in my heart. My father, Henry Huffington, was also a huge supporter of that program."

"It's been a rewarding experience for all the employees involved, plus a great way for our bank to give back to our local community," added Gene Phillips, the bank's Chief Operating Officer.

The attendees nodded in agreement. Dale then picked up his copy of the meeting agenda.

"Joel, can you provide us with a financial update?"

"We completed our closing entries for the first quarter last Friday evening. I am pleased to report that our bank has exceeded $500 million in total assets for the first time in our almost 100-year history."

The attendees broke into applause.

Dale added, "I was hoping that we achieved that milestone. Our bank welcomed quite a few new clients during March, including several large deposit accounts."

Kelli Tang, the bank's Regulatory Compliance Officer, added, "Crossing that threshold is fantastic. However, it does bring with it the likelihood of higher expectations from our various regulatory agencies. It's sort of an unwritten rule that banks larger than $500 million in total assets are expected to operate in a more sophisticated manner and possess expanded policies and procedures."

Traci Horst, the bank's Director of Human Resources, commented, "I used to work for a $1 billion bank in the San Francisco Bay Area. The experience at that bank paralleled what Kelli just said. The regulatory examinations were taken up a notch when we grew past $500 million in assets. More advanced analyses were expected and the regulators wanted to see evidence that the Board of Directors was receiving and evaluating quality information, as distinguished from simply data. In addition, we were assigned more experienced examination teams."

"Thank you for bringing that angle to our attention," said Dale. "I'd like each of you to review our current reporting, analyses, policies, and procedures, all to identify areas where we might consider enhancing what we do. I'd also like you to evaluate whether any additional resources, such as personnel or software, are needed. This bank has been well-run for nearly a century. That is a source of great pride for all of us. However, I acknowledge that we can't simply keep doing the same as in the past. The world around us is evolving at an increasingly fast pace. We need to similarly evolve to stay competitive and meet the expectations of our regulators."

The meeting then continued down the agenda, concluding at 10:30 AM.

Chapter 25

Wednesday April 22, 1998
New York City, New York

The Huffman Brothers sales and trading teams were eating their lunch at their desks, as usual, since the capital markets were all open and actively trading.

Troy swung by Duane's station and asked, "Can you stay after work tonight?"

"Sure."

By 5:30 PM, the office was empty except for Troy and Duane. They met in the lunch room to talk.

"I've done a pile of research over the past several weeks. I've identified twelve potential victims, I mean new clients, for our Pump and Dump strategy. Here's the list."

Duane intensely reviewed the list. He knew a couple of the names, as they were domiciled in New York State.

"How did you decide on these companies?"

"First of all, I noted that there has been a general trend in deregulation in the financial services industry over the past decade. Banks, thrifts, and credit unions now have more latitude than ever before, including being able to invest in a wider range of financial instruments."

"I've read about aspects of that. Please continue."

"I then sorted through the firm's various databases to identify financial institutions with total assets of between $500 million and $1 billion, plus that were located outside of major metropolitan areas."

"I understand the size sort. Companies larger than that are more likely to have experienced staff and more robust internal controls. Why the geographic sort?"

"My concept was that financial institutions in more rural areas would have a tendency to be less sophisticated and perhaps hire less well-educated officers than similarly sized institutions operating in major cities."

"That makes sense. However, you have just twelve names here, so there must have been more criteria."

"Ever the analytical trader! You're of course correct. I then read through the press releases, proxy statements, regulatory reports, and websites of the client candidates. I looked for CFOs or Treasurers who were relatively young, inexperienced, and / or not that well educated."

"That must have been tedious."

"It was. Most firms are quite particular to whom they give their checkbook. However, there were about two dozen candidates that fit all of the criteria we've discussed thus far."

"So, what was the last cut?"

"Actually two. I had to ensure that the candidates were not current or former clients of Huffman Brothers, so that we could be sure to be assigned the accounts. I also eliminated any firms that did not own any securitized mortgage product. I considered that it would be too much work to move a customer from zero mortgage related paper to our Dump scenario."

"Troy, in another life, you must have been a detective or a private eye. Excellent sleuthing."

"My recommendation is that we do not mention these dozen firms by name in the office. Rather, let's just casually refer to them by the city of their headquarters. It's not unusual for investment bankers to have nicknames for their clients. That practice should buy us some extra anonymity inside Huffman Brothers."

"After another brutal day today, I'm ready to give it a shot. Let's make all of the money we can, while we can."

"I'll start the cold calls tomorrow. You'll know that we need to employ one of our Pump strategies when I refer to the client by the city name."

"Let's do it. By the way, I've heard of El Paso, Colorado Springs, and Gainesville, but where in the hell is Santa Maria?"

"A town on the Central California coast holding many tens of thousands of dollars, or more, of our future income."

The two men fist-bumped and left the office.

Chapter 26

Thursday April 30, 1998
New York City, New York

"Tom, I wanted to ensure that you are aware of our attractive position in FNMA PAC-1 CMOs this morning. We bought them in below market on the trade, and the market has only continued rallying since then," explained Troy on the phone.

"I looked at the Bloomberg screen shots you emailed me. Does seem like a good buy. Would you split the piece? I've only got a limited amount to invest right now."

"I'll work with our trader. What type of offer are you thinking?"

"I'll take $2.0 million original face at 100-4/32."

"That would be about $1.5 million current face, plus accrued interest."

"Agreed."

"That's a really low offer. Let me put you on hold and see what I can do with the trader."

Troy placed Tom on hold and buzzed Duane on the inside line.

"Duane here."

"Colorado Springs offers to buy $2.0 million original face of our new PAC-1 FNMA CMO position at 100-4/32."

"Wow, that's low. Our basis is 100-5, which is well below market. I can eat a plus. That would be a screaming deal for

Colorado Springs, especially on that conservative a bond."

"Thanks, Duane, I'll see if I can get the trade done."

"Tom, Troy here. I mentioned that was a really aggressive offer. I arm-wrestled our trader. He'll sell to you at 100-9/64, up a plus. That's still notably below current market."

"Fair enough. Done. Send me the usual trade ticket and settlement instructions."

"Thanks for the business, Tom. I look forward to continuing to work with you."

As Troy hung up the phone, he gave a thumbs up signal to Duane. Colorado Springs was the first candidate off the special prospect list to begin doing business with Huffman Brothers. Later that day, after the close of trading, Troy signaled to Duane to follow him into the hallway.

"Thanks for the support today, Duane. We've opened the door to a rich and rewarding future."

"That proceeded just as we planned. How are the other candidates looking?"

"El Paso wants to meet us face to face next week. The CFO, a man named Billy, likes to talk and talk, but I haven't been able to get him to commit to doing business with us. He sounds like a cowboy in his expressions. In fact, a horny cowboy who has spent too much of his time alone on the range."

"That gives me an idea. Gino's for dinner tomorrow night?" asked Duane.

"By all means."

Chapter 27

Friday May 1, 1998
New York City, New York

Jennifer arrived at Gino's for the 4:00 PM to midnight shift. She was already exhausted before the shift even began. Over the past three weeks, she had auditioned for five new shows, each time only being offered an understudy role or a background part. The theater world in New York City was a tight ecosystem. Word had traveled quickly regarding her performance in the prior production. Jennifer and Mandy had also spent many hours over the last week moving into a new apartment. Like their prior one, it was in an old building located in the Theater District, small, and was imbued with the scents of decades of residents. Worst of all, the rent was higher. The economy continued to boom, creating demand for housing even at the bottom end of the market.

At 5:00 PM, Troy and Duane entered the restaurant, saw Jennifer working her usual section, and selected one of the booths.

"Good evening, welcome to Gino's. Oh, my favorite investment bankers."

"We enjoyed your performance last month. Excellent show," said Troy.

"I seem to remember that you were going to call us to hear our reaction to the production," added Duane.

"Your business cards were lost in the fire that burned down my apartment building. I was hoping you would crave some more Italian food and return to Gino's."

"I'm sorry to hear about the fire," said Troy. "You weren't hurt, were you?"

"No. I was just walking home from the show when the fire broke out, so I wasn't in the building. My roommate was in the building, but got out in time. Oh, enough about my woes. What are you two in the mood to eat tonight?"

"What would you recommend? You've never steered us wrong," said Troy.

"The special tonight is *osso buco*. It's another favorite dish of Gino's family. He only puts it on the menu when he can purchase top quality veal shank."

"Might you explain it a bit more?" asked Duane.

"Sure. *Osso buco* is cross-cut veal shank braised with vegetables, white wine, broth, and of course a secret mix of seasonings. We serve it over *polenta*, which is an Italian version of corn meal. I promise you that the dish is delicious."

Duane and Troy looked at each other, shrugged their shoulders, and agreed to follow Jennifer's recommendation.

"What wine would you recommend with the *osso buco?*" asked Troy.

"Is cost still not a consideration for you two?"

"True," answered Duane.

"Then I would direct you to our DOCG *Barolo* from the Piemonte region of Italy. It is a deep, complex, and rich red wine that will stand up to the intense flavors of the *osso buco*."

"Sounds perfect. Thank you."

Jennifer departed to place their orders.

Troy turned to Duane.

"Do you think she would be receptive to helping us out with Billy?"

"Sounds like she needs the money. We don't know anyone who is better qualified. You're the salesman. I'll let you break the ice on that topic."

About half way through the *osso buco*, which was delicious, Jennifer returned to their table.

"I see by the expressions on your faces that you're enjoying the *osso buco*!"

"Absolutely. And it pairs perfectly with the *Barolo* wine," replied Duane.

"Jennifer, if you have a break tonight, we're aware of a business opportunity that might be a good fit for you," proffered Troy.

"I get a fifteen-minute break at 6:30 PM. I can meet you at the end of the bar."

"Sounds good."

The men then continued eating their dinner, discussing angles of approach for Tacoma, Gainesville, and Flagstaff. A substantial tip was again left for Jennifer. Troy and Duane then occupied two stools at the end of the bar and each ordered a glass of *passito* Italian dessert wine at the recommendation of the bartender. Jennifer joined them just after 6:30 PM.

"Thank you both for the generous tip. I can use the money, trying to replace virtually all of my possessions after the fire. Please tell me about the business opportunity you mentioned."

"Duane and I are working to bring some new clients to the firm. These are individuals, most often men, who have many options for their investment banking relationships. We often succeed because of our financial expertise, our reputation, the depth of our product inventory, and how diligently we work for our customers. However, certain potential clients sometimes need a nudge to give doing business with us a try."

"Just what are you talking about?" asked Jennifer, with a bit of scorn in her voice.

"Nothing inappropriate or illegal, I assure you."

"Okay, so tell me more about this so-called nudge."

"We've found that simply having an attractive woman join us for dinner with the prospective client often softens their resistance to starting to do business with us."

"That's so sexist! It's almost the 21st century."

"Admittedly sexist, yes, but it works more often than not. The pay is very good."

"Oh... Tell me more."

"We'd give you $1,000 in cash up front to purchase a high-end, professional outfit, that also is a bit alluring. After the dinner, you would receive an additional $2,500 in cash."

"Isn't the prospective client going to be suspicious that there is this mystery woman sharing dinner?"

"That's where your skill as an actress comes in. We'll give you a bio for your role, plus a profile of the prospective client. For example, you would be an intern just completing your time at the firm, so your future absence would be logical. You would also utilize an assumed name. We would not want the prospective client, who would be from out of state, to be able to track you down. After dinner, you would go your separate way, while we hopefully take the customer to a suitable bar for a nightcap and a handshake to do business. We have one such potential client coming into town next Thursday night. Here's the role description and a profile of the fellow."

Troy handed Jennifer a piece of paper with her role printed on one side and the profile of a man from El Paso, Texas printed on the other side.

"Let me think about it. Can I have your business cards again? I'll get back to you."

Troy and Duane provided their cards, after which Jennifer said, "I'm back on station. Have a good evening, and thank you again for the nice tip."

Chapter 28

Saturday May 2, 1998
New York City, New York

It was almost 10:00 AM before Jennifer and Mandy awoke in their new apartment. They were again forced to share one bedroom with bunk beds. The kitchen was a bit larger than the prior apartment, which unfortunately provided more room for the local family of roaches. At least they were one floor higher this time, which somewhat lessened the round the clock noise from the streets below.

The women shared a pot of coffee at the kitchen table. While Mandy was catching up on her emails, Jennifer carefully re-read the two-sided document from the investment bankers. The role seemed like a natural fit, something easy for Jennifer to play. The fellow from El Paso appeared normal enough. He was forty years old, married with two children, and had an accounting degree from Texas State University. He was the Treasurer for a four-branch community bank headquartered in El Paso, Texas.

As Jennifer sipped her coffee, she glanced over at the half-filled clothes closet that she shared with Mandy. Even with the donations from the Red Cross, they had not yet been able to rebuild their wardrobes. They had shopped at two thrift stores to meagerly furnish their sitting room and outfit their kitchen.

Mandy then looked up from the laptop they shared and asked, "How did the auditions go last week?"

"No luck. Still only understudy and background parts that don't pay much. I was so hoping to leverage my last role into larger parts, but it's not looking like that's in the cards."

"I'm so sorry, Jennifer. No one has been rooting for you more than I have."

"I know, Mandy."

"You want to shower first or second? We both have shifts starting at noon today."

"You go first. I want to finish reading something."

Jennifer again looked around her apartment. The reality of her life sunk in deeply. What the hell! She picked up her phone and called Troy. Ms. Jessica Jones, Huffman Brothers intern, would be attending dinner Thursday night.

Chapter 29

Monday May 4, 1998
Santa Maria, California

The mood in the Accounting Department at Green Valley Community Bank was positive this morning. The bank generated strong earnings the prior quarter, riding the wave of the economic boom to increase the volume of loans outstanding. The Department had relocated into the new expansion space last week. Everyone now had new furniture and more room in which to work, including two new conference rooms and a larger lunch / break room. Day to day operations were proceeding smoothly, as Joel followed the checklists and calendars provided by Al Cook. Melvin Needham simply continued to be himself.

At 9:00 AM, Traci Horst, the bank's Director of Human Resources, entered the Department and called out for everyone's attention.

"Good morning, Accounting Department! I'm here this morning to introduce you to our latest addition, our new Financial Analyst, Angela Falcone."

A good-looking woman, apparently in her mid-twenties, with long black hair and a radiant smile stepped forward, waved, and said, "Hello."

Joel stepped forward and added to the announcement.

"With the growth of our bank, we've arrived at the point where we need to augment our various financial analyses, including regarding capital allocation, interest rate risk, and pricing. Angela is a great fit for this new position. She grew up in San Luis Obispo, attended high school there, obtained an undergraduate degree in business administration from Santa Clara University, worked two years in consulting for one the national accounting firms, and then pursued an MBA from UC / Berkeley with a concentration in finance. Angela will report directly to me. Please join me in welcoming Angela to Green Valley."

The Department broke into applause. Joel, Traci, and Angela all smiled. The crowd called for Angela to say a few words.

"I'm very happy to be joining an organization with such a long and storied history. As Joel mentioned, my family lived just up the 101 freeway throughout my childhood. My father is still working as a detective for the County Sheriff's Department, while my mother is the primary caregiver for my grandmother. I have one sibling. My brother is a priest, assigned to a parish in Northern California. I look forward to getting to know all of you and contributing to Green Valley's continuing success."

The next morning, Angela spurred her welcome into the Accounting Department by bringing in a large plate of freshly made *sfogliatelle*, a scrumptious Italian pastry composed of layer upon layer of thin, buttery dough interspersed with a spiced custard filling. Angela's charming and friendly personality complemented her cooking skills. After just two weeks at the bank, she was already well integrated as part of the team.

Chapter 30

Thursday May 7, 1998
New York City, New York

Troy and Duane arranged to meet Jennifer at Delmonico's Restaurant in the Financial District at 6:15 PM. Delmonico's, founded in 1837, was widely regarded as one of the premier steak houses in the entire country. Several of the specialty dishes were famous, including the Delmonico potatoes.

Once the three of them met at the entrance to the restaurant, Troy gave the maître d' his name. Duane and Jennifer were led to a private booth at the back of the restaurant, complete with walls on three sides and a draw string curtain on the side for access. Troy waited up front for the arrival of Billy Landon from El Paso.

Duane was impressed with Jennifer's selection of attire. She was wearing a gray, high waisted skirt that contained a soft pattern in the material. The skirt fell to ankle length, with slits up both sides to the knee. The skirt was complemented by a short jacket that was just enough of a difference in color from the skirt to provide some visual interest. Jennifer's white blouse appeared to be silk, adorned by delicate embroidery down the center. Matching high heeled shoes and handbag completed the ensemble. Jennifer's long blond hair was braided into a wide weave down her back. The pearl earnings were the finishing touch. Duane thought to himself, the actress certainly knows how to dress the part.

"Jennifer, do you have any final questions about tonight?"

"I've thought about the role quite a bit. I'll of course allow you and Troy to lead. After all, I'm just an intern."

Troy approached the booth, accompanied by a tall man, well over six feet. Jennifer first noticed the boots. They were ornate and appeared to be constructed out of some rare type of animal skin. Billy was dressed professionally, although the cowboy hat was out of place.

"Good evening, Duane and Jessica. I would like to introduce Billy Landon from El Paso."

Duane and Jennifer exchanged pleasantries. All were seated in the private booth.

"Have you ever eaten at Delmonico's?" asked Troy.

"Can't say I have."

"The dry-aged steaks are world famous," said Duane.

"That's saying something to a man from Texas. We do like our beef in the Lone Star State."

After looking at their menus for a few minutes, a waiter arrived to take their orders. Billy gestured for Jennifer to go first.

"I'd like the petit filet mignon please, cooked medium, with a side of the pan roasted *caulilini*, please."

"Very good, madam."

"I'd like dry-aged porterhouse, cooked medium-rare, with a side of the Delmonico potatoes," said Billy.

Troy and Duane each ordered the boneless ribeye, Troy with a side of brandied mushrooms and Duane with a side of creamed spinach.

"What would you like to drink?" asked the waiter.

"Billy, what are you in the mood for?" inquired Troy.

"A friend of mine introduced me to Samuel Adams' Utopias

last month. You wouldn't happen to have that, would you?"

"Why of course sir. I'll bring the table a bottle."

Troy and Duane glanced at each other, both gesturing that they had no idea of what that beverage was.

Observing this, Jennifer interjected, "Mr. Landon, you certainly have fine taste. The complex aging for that beer renders it both unique and quite delicious."

"Glad you agree, Jessica, and please feel welcome to call me Billy."

Troy then began his sales pitch.

"Billy, we were so pleased to hear that you were going to be in Manhattan and available to have dinner with us."

"I don't get out of Texas that often. There's a lot of Texas to see and enjoy."

"We also appreciate your being receptive to having Jessica join us tonight. She completes her internship at Huffman Brothers tomorrow. After rotating through most of the other departments, she's finishing this week in sales. It's great that she has a chance to see how we build relationships at Huffman Brothers."

"Where are you off to next, Jessica?"

"I've been accepted into several MBA programs in the fall, and I've lined up a couple of other internships this summer. I'm trying to decide what type of career to pursue, and then match the graduate school program with that career."

"Sounds very logical and well considered. My compliments," said Billy.

"Thank you."

Troy then tried to bring the conversation back to Billy's bank doing business with him and Duane.

"We spoke on the phone about the many advantages of establishing an account with Huffman Brothers. Our depth of inventory, our range of markets, and the variety of supplemental services we make available to our clients."

"Yes, I remember those points. Not unique among your competitors."

"What is unique is our focus on building long-term relationships and doing what is right for the client," added Duane.

"I've heard the same from at least five different investment banks over the past three months."

The waiter arrived with the beer. It came in a specially designed bottle, somewhat similar in shape and size to a champagne bottle. Troy indicated to the waiter that Billy would do the tasting.

"Ah, wonderful, just as I remembered it," said Billy.

With their glasses all poured, Troy proposed a toast, "To a mutually successful future!"

The three New Yorkers were surprised by the unexpected, but delicious, taste of the beer and its 27% alcohol content.

Recognizing that his pitch so far was falling flat, Troy changed gears.

"Billy, the other great aspect of doing business with Huffman Brothers is our pricing."

"We often source bonds below market and pass that benefit on to our clients," added Duane.

"And when you are looking to sell a position, we are connected with all of the top firms. That opens up selling to a much broader audience than solely our customer base, typically resulting in advantageous bid levels," said Troy, with enthusiasm in his voice.

"My bank's been growing so fast, we haven't needed to sell many positions in the past year," responded Billy.

Noting the tenor in Billy's voice, Troy again switched gears to another approach.

"Billy, I should have asked earlier. How is the family?"

"All good. My sons are both playing little league baseball right now. The older one has quite an arm. He may have a future in the sport, at least through the college level."

"Congratulations," said Duane. "You sound like a proud father."

"I am. I only wish my wife did not have to travel so much. She's in marketing for one of the major oil companies. It's not unusual for her to fly 100,000 miles a year."

Jennifer then said, "Would you gentlemen excuse me for a moment?"

As Jennifer left the table, Troy could not help but notice how the skirt hugged what appeared to be a very firm ass. He hoped that Billy was making the same observation.

The waiter then arrived with their dishes. The aroma of the sizzling meat was mouth-watering. By the time the waiter had finished serving the entrees and pouring more of the beer, Jennifer returned to the table. She was carrying the short jacket on her left arm. This exposed how tightly the elaborate blouse fit against her breasts.

The four of them commenced eating.

"Fine piece of meat," said Billy.

"I'm glad you're not disappointed," replied Troy. "The side

dishes also look and smell wonderful."

"Billy, let me be direct," said Duane. "Troy and I think we're a great fit for you and your bank. What would it take to convince you to give doing business with us a try?"

There was an awkward silence at the table, as Billy finished chewing his mouthful of food and looked up at the ceiling.

"I'm just not sure how to answer that. We're well covered by three firms headquartered in Texas. I certainly appreciate your interest and what you have to offer. Let me talk to the CFO when I get back to the office next week."

"We appreciate the consideration," said Troy.

The conversation then flowed to a number of topics, with Billy continuing to communicate in short sentences. This type of talking did not provide many openings for Troy to again attempt to get a business commitment from Billy. As they were just about to finish their meal, Jennifer leaned forward and took control of the conversation.

"Billy, let me say again how I appreciate your being willing to let me sit in tonight. This has been a great exposure for me. Can I ask you a question?"

"Sure."

"What led you to decide on a career in finance, compared to, say, marketing, operations, or sales?"

"Well, Jessica, to be completely honest with you, my grandfather and father were both bankers, so I just followed along in the family footsteps."

"So, you weren't motivated by the professional environment, the intellectual challenges, the opportunity to make a difference in your local community, or the income potential?"

"Can't say that I was."

"Thank you for sharing. The more personal experiences I hear, the better insight for my future."

"I'm sorry I wasn't of much help."

The waiter arrived with the check, which was picked up by Troy. He turned to Duane and said, "Duane, can you call Jessica a cab and ensure that she departs safely?"

"Sure thing."

Duane and Jennifer walked to the front of the restaurant. Duane removed an envelope with $2,500 in $100 bills from his jacket and gave it to Jennifer before helping her into the cab.

Not being willing to admit defeat, Troy turned to Billy and asked, "Would you like to get a nightcap at one of Manhattan's famous establishments?"

"No thank you. I'm good. Thank you for a fine dinner."

Troy and Billy walked to the front of the restaurant. Troy and Duane shook Billy's hand, and placed him in a cab back to his hotel. As they waited for another cab, Troy's cell phone rang.

"Don't feel bad. You didn't have a chance."

Duane mouthed, "Who is it?"

Troy whispered back, "Jennifer."

"How did you know Billy would already be gone?" asked Troy?

"I've been on enough auditions to know when there simply isn't a match."

"You're right."

"I didn't witness a single motivation that would have led Billy to doing business with you. Not bank profit, not image, not ego, not personal income, etc."

"Very perceptive of you."

"I also observed that Billy is apparently devoid of vices. He didn't ask for dessert, nor for more beer. He also didn't give me much more than the minimal attention to be polite, despite my efforts. I doubt he does drugs."

"Again, very perceptive of you."

"Well, thank you for the opportunity. I've got to pay the cab driver. Good-bye."

After Troy returned his cell phone to his pocket, he turned to Duane.

"My bad. I was so eager to advance our strategy that I didn't perform adequate advance screening. Jennifer has the right idea. We need to identify a motivation or a vice that can lead the candidates to do business with us. Lesson learned."

"At least we enjoyed a delicious steak dinner."

"And watching Jennifer."

Chapter 31

Tuesday May 12, 1998
Santa Maria, California

At noon, with an hour to go in the trading day, Troy signaled Duane to meet him in the hallway.

"I had an initial call with Santa Maria on Friday. Cordial. The CFO, a guy named Joel, seemed to genuinely care about his bank and doing a good job. He came across as a really nice guy. However, I couldn't get him to commit to opening an account with us."

"You want to try the 'I've got a customer' routine?"

"Spot on. My read is that will work with Joel. Based upon the regulatory and shareholder reports for his bank, he likely has a portfolio of FNMA 8.00% Coupon Pass-Through MBS. How high can we bid him without causing an internal problem?"

"The dollar roll market for pass-throughs is tight right now, so we can include the financing advantage in our pricing. I could justify paying half a point above TBAs if he has product seasoned at least a year."

"Sounds good."

The investment bankers returned to their desks. Troy dialed Joel.

"Hello, Joel Johnson speaking."

"Hello Joel, this is Troy Helmsley from Huffman Brothers. We spoke last week."

"Yes, I remember. What can I do for you?"

"I have a client trying to find matchers for his existing positions in FNMA 8.00% Pass-Through MBS. He's trying to bundle like securities to structure a financing. Might you have any such securities? Our client is offering an excellent price."

"Well, I wasn't planning on selling anything today."

"I understand. I just wanted to bring this opportunity to your attention. My client is willing to buy even a small position and, as I mentioned, he's offering a high price."

"I guess I could consider selling a $1.0 million current face position in one of our seasoned bonds. Our loan pipeline is very strong right now. We'll probably need the funds soon. What is the offer price?"

"101-2/32, plus accrued interest of course."

"Wow. That's more than a point over my basis. But we don't have an account established with you."

"That's not a problem. We would settle delivery versus payment through a third party, such the Federal Home Loan Bank. You would not have any settlement or operational risk."

"Well, we do need to raise liquidity for lending. The gain on sale would help our second quarter income. Okay, I'll sell the following specific CUSIP and original face to you at 101-2/32..."

Troy and Joel completed the specifics of the transaction. Troy and Duane then processed the security purchase on their system.

A half-hour after the market closed, Troy and Duane met in the lunch room.

"We got our foot in the door at Santa Maria," said Troy.

"Great teamwork. Let's grab a drink downstairs and discuss

how to continue to pump Santa Maria, plus also share the latest information on Flagstaff and Tacoma."

The men shared a high five.

Chapter 32

Monday May 25, 1998
Santa Maria, California

"Linda, can you please bring me a large mug of coffee?" asked Dale.

"I'll get you one right away; just the way you like it, with two sugars and cream."

Dale was a little hung over this morning. After being burned by his escapade on the beach with the ecologist, Dale had at first attempted to curtail his sexual adventures. However, his predisposition and addiction simply did not allow for this. The best he could do was to limit his partners to less risky and better-known individuals.

Dale's wife, Anne, was returning from an art exhibition in Denver today. This allowed Dale to spend last night at his condominium with Veronica Sharp. She enjoyed drinking champagne, sensually eating strawberries with fresh whipped cream, and oral sex. Dale had enthusiastically shared in these pleasures.

After consuming a large gulp of the fresh coffee, Dale asked Linda, "What's on the agenda for today?"

"You have your regular executive team staff meeting at 9:00 AM. Then, lunch with George Anderson to prepare for Wednesday's Board of Directors meeting. Nothing booked after that."

"Excellent. I may make an early exit this afternoon."

"I'll call you on your cell phone if anything significant

arises."

"Linda, what would I ever do without you?"

"Dale, where would Carl and I be if you hadn't helped him get that job after recovering from his prostate cancer treatment?"

Later that morning, Dale called the meeting of the Green Valley Community Bank executive team to order just after 9:00 AM.

"As usual, let's start with the financial update. Joel?"

"Our loan funding volume continues to run well ahead of budget. Our account officers are doing a great job of bringing in checking accounts and lines of credit for local businesses. As but one example, we boarded all of the new accounts for Veronica Sharp's retail business in the past week."

Dale raised his mug of coffee to his lips to obscure his grin.

Joel continued, "To help meet the liquidity demand for our loan funding, we sold one Agency MBS earlier this month. Should loan demand continue to be this robust, we may repeat that process in order to avoid too rapidly growing our balance sheet."

"Good point. We want to moderate our pace of balance sheet growth in order to keep our regulatory capital ratios high. Joel, what was the gain or loss on the sale of the security?" asked Dale.

"Almost a one and one-half point gain."

"Excellent. That will contribute to our earnings this quarter, which is already shaping up to be a good one for our shareholders."

Traci Horst, the Director of Human Resources, motioned to speak. "Joel, how is Angela Falcone integrating into the Accounting Department?"

"I think very well. She's bright and hard-working, and also friendly. I spoke with her after receiving an introductory call from an investment bank about buying or selling securities. It was actually Angela who pointed out the benefit of swapping assets in order to support our regulatory capital ratios."

"I knew I liked that woman!" added Kelli Tang, the bank's Regulatory Compliance Officer.

"Dale, if it's okay with you, I'd like to open an account for the bank with the new securities broker / dealer. They were able to source a strong bidder for our security."

"What's the name of the firm?"

"Huffman Brothers. They work out of the Financial District in New York City."

"I've heard of them. Mid-sized investment bank. They do business with some of the community bankers I've met at the conferences. Just gather the usual company and broker information for our files. Then, fine with me to proceed."

"Thank you, Dale."

"Now, who's next to report?" asked Dale.

Chapter 33

Friday July 31, 1998
New York City, New York

Troy and Duane had made a reservation at Gino's for dinner tonight, after ensuring that Jennifer was covering her usual section. The past two months had been a whirlwind. Troy's book of business was almost up to the size expected of seasoned brokers, including six of the Pump and Dump candidates. Troy, Duane, and Jennifer had shared a dinner with Flagstaff similar to the one with El Paso, but with much better results. The CFO at Flagstaff was 35, in his first CFO position, and recently divorced. Jennifer charmed him with her questions and attention. It also turned out that the CFO loved Italian red wines, a subject with which Jennifer was exceedingly conversant.

By about the end of June, Jennifer came to the realization that she was unlikely to land any mid-sized parts on Broadway. She read the body language of the directors and producers, observing that they seemed predisposed to pigeonhole her into understudy or background roles. Over the past couple of weeks, Jennifer had changed her focus to television, both commercials and shows. She had received some favorable preliminary feedback, and was eager to further explore those opportunities. In the meantime, the 'acting fees' from Troy and Duane had helped her rebuild her life after the devastation from the apartment fire.

Upon arriving at Gino's, Troy and Duane made a beeline for their favorite booth. After a few minutes, Jennifer came over and greeted them.

"How are my two favorite investment bankers?"

Troy answered, "Doing well, in part due to your superb performances. Flagstaff is actively trading with our firm."

"Good to hear. It sounds like that poor man exited from a very bad marriage. I hope he continues to turn his life around."

"With our help, his earnings are up and he should be in line for a nice bonus this year," added Duane.

"When you get a chance, can you email me your schedule for August?" said Troy. "Spokane may be coming into the city. We'd like to have another dinner with our intern. Spokane is an excellent prospect."

"Will do. What are you in the mood for tonight for dinner?"

"You tell us."

"Gino just took a pan of baked *manicotti* out of the oven. The smell was heavenly."

"Yet another Italian dish I've never heard of," said Duane.

"Gino's version of *manicotti* are large pasta tubes, stuffed with ricotta, spinach, leaks, Swiss chard, and ground, seasoned veal. Plus, of course, spices. The pasta is then covered in bechamel sauce and *Parmigiano-Reggiano* cheese."

"Sound delicious. We'll each have a plate of that," said Troy.

"I assume you know the perfect wine for pairing?" inquired Duane.

"Perfect is a strong word in the culinary business. That said, I'd recommend a *Sagrantino* red wine from Montefalco. That's located in the Umbria region of Italy. Umbria is commonly referred to as the 'green heart' of the peninsula."

"We'll look forward to tasting that," concurred Troy.

As Jennifer was placing the orders, Troy and Duane recapped where they were with their Pump and Dump plan.

"We have six candidates doing business with us already, plus nine more potential ones in the hopper. We do need to be careful to space out the cherry-picked trades, so that our boss does not become suspicious," advised Troy.

"Agreed. We've already conducted regularly priced trades with three of the first six candidates, plus our overall transaction volume has been quite high. The allocated trades should get buried in all of the activity. Remember, we also have approval to do some break-even or small loss trades in order to attract new accounts," replied Duane. "Who are we planning to work on in August, besides Spokane?

"I'd like one more shot at Tacoma. We should also make initial runs at Hartford and Eugene."

"Okay. Anything else?"

"I'm thinking that Santa Maria is one hell of an opportunity for us. Joel seems like a nice guy, probably attends church with his mother every Sunday. Not very bright, but earnest. His bank is growing and doing well. Could be a superior target for a large Dump," noted Troy.

"Have you thought about how we could further grease that wheel?"

"He mentioned liking to watch basketball. Once the NBA pre-season starts, maybe we could arrange a VIP experience."

"Great idea. If Joel sees us as friends in addition to competent investment bankers, that only further lowers the potential barriers to getting Dumped," opined Duane.

Jennifer arrived with the wine. She poured an initial taste for both men. As usual, her recommendation was superior.

Before she left the table, Troy asked, "Jennifer, are you okay with continuing to play our intern? You've done a marvelous job, but we don't want to overstep things."

"One more dinner and I should have the role totally nailed. Where else can a poor actress meet people from all over the country, partake in interesting conversations, eat a top-quality meal, and earn some much-needed money? Please continue to count me in."

Troy and Duane both relaxed and smiled at Jennifer's answer. They recognized how fortunate they were to find her. This perception was reinforced later in the evening when the steaming plates of *manicotti* were served. The investment bankers left their usual generous tip after downing the last of the *Sagrantino*.

Chapter 34

Wednesday August 19, 1998
New York City, New York

Jennifer returned to the apartment just after 8:30 PM, following an eight-hour shift at Gino's. As she entered, she immediately saw Mandy lying down on the futon which served as the primary piece of furniture in their small sitting room. Mandy had an ice pack on her right cheek, and was developing a black eye.

"What happened? Are you okay?" asked Jennifer.

"In hindsight, I made a very painful decision earlier today."

"How can I help?"

"It's over now, nothing for you to do. I had an early morning audition for a thirty second television commercial. The commercial is for a national auto parts company. The role was for a clerk at an auto parts store, maybe a total of ten seconds of screen time."

"I've never fully understood why the automobile industry, from manufacturing to racing to parts, always seems to need an attractive girl, more often than not in a bikini or short shorts, to market their products. So, what happened?"

"At the end of the auditions, it came down to me or two other young women. The director pulled me aside and said I was first choice, but would only get the role if I agreed to have sex with him after the shooting."

"Did you agree to that?"

"I felt like I had no choice. Remember, I had the flu the first week of this month and didn't work for six days. I wasn't going to be able to pay my half of the rent and utilities at the end of the month without some extra income. The auto parts job paid really well for a one-day gig."

"Oh, Mandy, you know that I would give you every dollar I owned if you needed it."

"I know, Jennifer. But you've already bought most of the replacement items for our apartment. I didn't want to take further advantage of your good graces."

"Don't ever think that way again. How were you hurt?"

"The director conveniently had a fold-out sofa in his office. Based upon his personality, that wasn't a coincidence. He's a big guy. I'd estimate about six feet, four inches tall and at least 250 pounds."

"That's more than two of you!"

"Not only was he a big man, but he liked his sex rough. He started missionary, pounding and squeezing me. Then, he flipped me over like a pancake and entered from behind. When he orgasmed, he thrust forward so hard that my face crashed into the wooden headboard."

"I'm so sorry."

"He wasn't. Not even an apology. What an asshole!"

Jennifer then knelt down next to Mandy and quietly held her. After a good while, Jennifer rose, got two aspirin from the bathroom, and poured Many a glass of water. As Mandy downed the medicine, Jennifer racked her brain thinking about how the two of them could become more financially stable and also progress in the entertainment business --- all without succumbing to the misogyny inherent in the industry.

Chapter 35

Thursday August 27, 1998
Santa Maria, California

At 3:00 PM in the afternoon, Angela Falcone, the Financial Analyst, dropped by Joel's office at the bank.

"Joel, do you have a few minutes to discuss an idea I have?"

"Sure, Angela, please have a seat. By the way, those cookies you brought in this week were delicious. What are they called?"

"*Brutti ma buoni*. That translates to 'ugly but good'. The secret ingredient is fresh hazelnuts."

"I brought a couple home to my mother. She also really enjoyed them. Thank you for sharing them with the Accounting Department."

"My pleasure. Joel, I know I've only been on board a bit more than three months, but I think I've figured out a way for the bank to make more money without taking on more risk."

"Sounds interesting. Please tell me more."

"The bank is receiving quite a few applications for fixed rate commercial real estate loans right now."

"Agreed. I saw the latest loan pipeline report."

"If we simply add a significant volume of fixed rate loans to the bank's balance sheet, we'll skew our interest rate risk profile."

"Please continue."

"If the bank has too many fixed rate assets, and the Federal Reserve raises interest rates, our asset yield will remain roughly constant, but our cost of funding, primarily deposits, will increase. This will result in a narrowing of our net interest margin and a likely decline in overall profitability."

"I understand what you're saying. However, the bank would not want to decline high quality commercial real estate loans from local customers simply because they were fixed rate. That type of behavior would quickly get around our community and hurt the bank's image."

"Agreed. That's why I think we should consider selling the Agency fixed rate pass-through MBS in our investment portfolio. That would take a lot of fixed rate assets off our books, and therefore increase our capacity to make fixed rate loans without skewing the overall interest rate risk profile."

"I see what you're getting at. However, our deposit balances are continuing to increase, bringing more liquidity into the bank. If we sell the Agency fixed-rate pass-through MBS to raise liquidity for fixed rate lending and we also obtain more liquidity from deposit inflows, we'll end up with too much extra cash not earning us much income."

"Good point. Could you potentially swap the Agency fixed-rate pass-through MBS into a shorter life fixed rate investment or a floating rate investment?"

"Maybe. I'd have to discuss that with our investment bankers. There might be a give-up in security portfolio yield if we did that. We need to be careful not to reduce income."

"I'm just learning about the collateralized mortgage obligation markets. We didn't get much education in that regard through the MBA program," noted Angela.

"From what I understand, it's not that established a market, and some of the investment products are relatively new. Tell you what, I'll discuss this with Huffman Brothers tomorrow. I'll let you know what they think."

"Sounds good. Joel, thank you for giving me the opportunity to discuss this topic. I appreciate it."

Angela exited Joel's office and returned to her desk.

Chapter 36

Friday August 28, 1998
Santa Maria, California

Joel arrived at the bank early this morning. He wanted to call Troy at Huffman Brothers before the markets opened for trading.

"Hello, Troy Helmsley speaking."

"Joel Johnson from Green Valley Community Bank calling."

"Good morning, Joel, how are you today?"

"Fine. I wanted to ask you a few questions and get some advice."

"Certainly. How can I help?"

"If our bank sold some or all of our Agency fixed rate pass-through MBS, what could we reinvest the funds into, while also taking less interest rate risk?"

"So, the motivation in selling is to reduce the duration of the investment portfolio?"

"Can you explain that a bit more?"

"Sure. Duration is a weighted measure of the average life of the cash flows of a bond. It is also a measure of price volatility for fixed rate securities."

"Then, yes. We've got a good pipeline of fixed rate loans we want to fund for customers, but we also want to avoid skewing our interest rate risk profile."

"How much yield or interest income are you willing to give

up in conjunction with the swap of securities?"

"Ideally, none. As little as possible."

"Hmmm... Thus far, the only Agency CMO's we've sold you are the top tier, super-defined PAC-1 classes. In other words, all of the other tranches in the CMO structure are designed to support the PAC-1's."

"The PAC-1 securities have worked out well. They've paid a regular stream of principal and interest, without much variation from month to month."

"You could about match the yield on the pass-through MBS by purchasing lower tranches in the CMOs, at least Sequential tranches and maybe a few Z-Support tranches. The Sequential tranches would likely have lower duration than the pass-through MBS. Principal and interest would still be guaranteed by the Agency issuing the CMO. The timing of the principal payments would just be less certain than with the PAC-1 tranches."

"When you have a chance, could you email me some examples?"

"I'd be happy to. Probably after the market closes. Fridays can be quite hectic on the trading floor."

"I understand. Thank you."

"Good-bye."

Troy signaled to Duane to follow him into the men's room. After ensuring they were alone, Troy said, "Great news. Santa Maria called me this morning seeking my advice and also initiating consideration of lower-priority CMO tranches. We couldn't ask for a better setup."

"Agreed. If we can get the candidates to rely on our advice, that will ease our eventually executing the Dump. Great news, indeed."

"I'll need your help after the market closes to generate some illustrations for some SEQ and Z tranches. We'll want to cherry-pick through the inventory to select the very best-looking ones, and to run the illustrations at the lowest price you think we could get away with."

"Gotcha. Come over to my position about a half-hour after the market closes and we'll put our heads together."

Chapter 37

Thursday September 3, 1998
New York City, New York

Ben Cohen called out for everyone's attention on the trading floor about thirty minutes before the markets were to open. Once the room fell relatively silent, Ben began speaking.

"We've got a position we need to liquidate today if at all possible. It's $10.0 million in corporate bonds issued by a technology company that specializes in communications hardware. The bonds are currently rated BBB, investment grade. The trailing twelve-month ratio of debt to EBITDA for the issuer is about 3.0, on the higher and riskier side due to the debt associated with an acquisition last year. Our equity analyst has heard rumors that the new product cycle for their hardware has some technical issues. If the company misses out on the next upgrade cycle in their line of business, the ratio of debt to EBITDA may hit 5.0. If that occurs, the ratings agencies will be highly likely to downgrade the bonds by several notches into Junk Bond territory."

The Huffman Brothers employees on the trading floor quickly grasped what was at risk. A downgrade to Junk Bond status would crater the price for the bonds, creating a large loss for the firm if they were not sold beforehand.

Ben continued, "Our basis is 97-16/32. You are pre-approved to sell as low as 97-00. Any loss on the sale of this position will not be counted against the bonus pool for this year. In addition, any team selling all or part of this position by the close of business today will receive a gross commission at triple the usual rate for Junk Bonds."

There were several gasps in the room. That would be a 0.75% commission on a $10.0 million transaction, or $75 thousand. The employees looked at each other and mouthed 'seventy-five thousand'.

Ben concluded, "Thank you for doing your best." He then walked off the trading floor.

Troy immediately walked over to Duane and whispered, "First Dump?"

Duane nodded affirmatively, and then motioned for Troy to follow him into the hallway.

Duane spoke first. "Which of the Dump candidates has the balance sheet size to buy a $10.0 million position, plus buys corporate bonds in the first place?"

"I'm thinking Tacoma and Spokane."

"Of those two, who is the bigger yield whore?"

"Frank from Spokane. He was also enthralled by Jennifer."

"Let's give it a shot. You make the call and I'll be ready to assist as needed," said Duane.

The men returned to their stations. Troy made the call.

"Frank Simpson."

"Good morning, Frank. This is Troy Helmsley from Huffman Brothers."

"Good to hear from you. How did Jessica do with her internship?"

"One of our better interns this year. Kind of you to ask."

"My pleasure. What can I do for you?"

"We've picked up a $10.0 million position in a BBB rated

corporate bond. We bought in at an excellent price, really more reflective of a debenture at the bottom investment grade of BBB-."

"What's your offer and spread over Treasuries?"

"We can deliver the whole piece at 97-24/32. That's 300 basis points above Treasuries and about 75 basis points wide of the BBB average."

"Email me the CUSIP and the latest credit ratings agency report and I'll take a quick look."

"Will do."

After Troy hung up, he sent the email and then called Duane on the internal line.

"I offered him the whole position at 97-24/32. Frank likes to bid us back, so I gave us some room."

Fifteen minutes later, Troy's phone rang.

"Frank from Spokane here."

"Hello, Frank. What do you think?"

"I'll offer you 97-16/32 for the whole piece, standard settlement."

"Can I put you on hold while I call the trading desk?"

Troy then placed Frank on hold, but made no such call. He was already authorized to sell as low as 97-00/32, but he wanted Frank to perceive that he was driving a hard bargain. After about three minutes, Troy again picked up the line.

"I had to arm-wrestle. You buying the whole position helped. You're done at 97-16/32."

"Send me the trade ticket and settlement instructions as usual."

"Will do."

Troy hung up the phone and buzzed Duane on the internal line.

"Done at 97-16/32, whole piece."

Duane entered the trade onto the system and gave a thumbs up to Troy.

The two men met in the lunchroom later that day while getting their sandwiches.

"Troy, we've got to now plow as much business as we can through Spokane while he's feeling like a genius and before his corporate bond tanks. Might as well harvest every dollar we can before flushing the relationship down the toilet."

"I agree, but we have to be careful not to overdo it. Our equity analyst could be wrong. The technology company could have a successful new product cycle, which would result in the bond trading higher. We could actually look like heroes on this one."

"We could, but that's a low probability. We should act as if we've just robbed him blind."

The men returned to their desks and completed their workday. At the market close, Troy received a phone call.

"Troy, this is Ben Cohen. Can you and Duane please come to my office."

"Yes, sir. Be there soon."

Troy grabbed Duane and shared the content of the call. They agreed to play it cool regardless of what Ben said. Upon arriving upstairs at Ben's office, he waved them in.

"Gentlemen, hell of a trade today. You beat out the entire desk and sold the whole position in one transaction. And, on top of that, you sold above the minimum price and actually achieved a break-even for the firm. Let me shake your hands. Great work!"

"Thank you, Ben. We were fortunate to have a client who fit the position."

"You're too modest, but well spoken. I will follow-up with the Payroll Department and ensure that you receive the promised commission."

"Thank you, again."

Troy and Duane took the stairs down to their floor. In the stairwell, they fist-bumped. Step number one on the Pump and Dump plan successfully completed. Many more steps to go in their scheme to retire comfortably by age forty.

Chapter 38

Tuesday September 22, 1998
Santa Maria, California

Joel was having a cup of coffee in his office at 8:30 AM when the phone rang.

"Hello, Joel Johnson here."

"Hello, Joel, this is Troy from Huffman Brothers."

"Thank you again for those trades last week. My boss was happy to see the gain on sale of the Agency pass-through MBS and also the projected yields on the Sequential CMO tranches."

"That's what we're here for."

"What can I do for you today?"

"I seem to remember that you like to watch basketball."

"You're right. The skills of the NBA players are amazing."

"Our firm has an extra ticket for the pre-season game in Oakland on Thursday October 1. The Lakers are traveling north to start the exhibition season against the Warriors. Would you like to attend?"

"Yes, but I can't miss two days of work right now driving up and back. Oakland is about a six-hour trip from Santa Maria, depending on the traffic."

"You wouldn't miss any work. I'm going to be in San Diego meeting with a client that morning. I've got one of the corporate jets for the trip. I could pick you up at private aviation at the Santa Maria Airport at 4:30 PM on Thursday. The Oakland

Airport is adjacent to the Colosseum. We can be courtside at 6:00 PM. The game tips off at 7:00 PM. You would be back in Santa Maria by 10:30 PM."

"Wow. I've never been on a corporate jet."

"It does make travel much more convenient."

"Okay. That sounds great. I'll look forward to it."

"Good-bye."

After Troy hung up the phone, he smiled broadly. If he could convince the candidates that he was their friend, in addition to a trusted financial advisor, they would be even more receptive to being Dumped.

Chapter 39

Thursday October 1, 1998
Oakland, California

Joel spent almost the entire flight from Santa Maria to Oakland talking about the rosters of the two NBA teams. Since this was the start of a new pre-season, each team had roster changes from the prior year, including the addition of their top draft picks out of college. Troy listened intently, asking follow-up questions and feigning enthusiasm about the matchup. The corporate jet was met by a car service for the short drive to the Oakland Colosseum. Displaying a 'diamond' parking pass, the car drove right up to a rear entrance. Troy advised the driver that he would call him at the end of the game for pickup at the same spot.

Joel followed Troy into the rear entrance. Troy displayed their tickets to a security guard, who welcomed them and then escorted them down a hallway. The hallway emerged right at courtside. An usher took over from the security guard and sat Troy and Joel on seats directly behind the players.

"Wow! I've only been to a couple of basketball games in my whole life, and never had seats like these!" exclaimed Joel.

"Huffman Brothers buys quite a few tickets for each season, as part of our client relationship program. That entitles us to a couple of courtside seats. I noticed that they were available a couple of weeks ago and gave you a call."

"Thank you again, Troy. I'll remember this evening for a long time."

A well-appointed woman wearing a Warriors blazer approached Troy and Duane.

"What would you like to eat and drink?"

"That's right. I didn't even think about dinner. Can I get a hot dog?" asked Joel.

Troy stood up and took control of the conversation.

"I'd be pleased to help with this." He then turned to the woman and said, "We'd both like the beef tournedos, cooked medium rare, with a side of buttered whipped potatoes. To drink, please bring us glasses of Veuve Clicquot."

"Excellent choice, sir. I'll be back with your request."

Joel stared at Troy, indicating a state of confusion.

"Joel, these are diamond level seats. That entitles us to dinner prepared by the facility chef, plus access to substantially any beverage of our choosing."

"I never knew that was possible at a basketball game. By the way, what is Veuve Clicquot?"

"It is a delicious champagne, among the best in the world."

"I do like champagne. My mother always keeps a bottle for celebrating special occasions."

The Warriors cheerleaders were on the floor, warming up the crowd with their various dance and gymnastics routines. Troy signaled to the usher, and pointed to Joel. The usher approached Joel, took him by the arm, and walked him onto the court. The cheerleaders surrounded Joel in formation, with a woman on each side of him leaning in and pouting their lips as if for a kiss. A photographer clicked away. The usher then returned Joel to his seat.

"I certainly did not expect that!" said Joel.

"Another perk of being a diamond seat holder. I'll ensure

that you receive the framed photo once it's developed."

"That will be a conversation starter at the office!"

The well-appointed woman with the Warriors jacket arrived carrying two trays which clipped onto the sides of the seats. The beef smelled wonderful. The food was served on fine porcelain, and the glasses were crystal. Troy thanked the woman and gestured to Joel to enjoy his dinner.

"Try the champagne," said Troy.

"Mmmm... That's much smoother than what my mother usually buys."

"Glad you like it."

The men discussed the rosters and the prospects for each team during the upcoming season while eating their dinner. They finished and had the trays removed at about 6:30 PM. Just then, the two teams exited their locker rooms and commenced shooting warm-ups. At about 6:40 PM, the usher approached them accompanied by the biggest person Joel had ever seen. It was the all-star center for the Warriors, a man standing over seven feet tall.

He inquired of Joel, "What's your name?"

The usher handed a color photo of the Warrior team to the center, who wrote on the bottom, 'Joel, glad you could cheer us on'. He signed and dated the photo, and handed it to Joel. Joel was speechless.

"Just a souvenir to help you remember this evening," said Troy.

"As if I could ever forget this!" replied Joel.

The two men enjoyed the basketball game. Each team played their entire roster, as this was the beginning of the pre-season. Half-time included a refill of the champagne, plus chocolate truffles for dessert. At the closing buzzer, an usher appeared to escort them back to the reserved parking area. The car service was waiting as planned.

Once in the car, Troy turned to Joel and said, "I'm going to be dropped off at a nearby hotel. I have meetings tomorrow morning in Oakland and tomorrow afternoon in San Francisco. The driver will take you to the airport for the corporate jet. It needs to be at LAX tomorrow morning, so dropping you off on the way south won't be any inconvenience."

"Troy, I can't thank you enough for this evening. It's been an awesome experience. In fact, it's been the most fun I have ever had. I'll think back on this with a smile for the rest of my life."

"Joel, thank you for being a good client of the firm; and a friend."

Chapter 40

Friday October 16, 1998
Santa Maria, California

Dale and Anne Huffington arrived at the community center at 6:30 PM. The facility had been dressed up for tonight's festivities, a major fundraiser for the local homeless shelter. Green Valley Community Bank was a major sponsor of the event and one of the larger financial contributors to the shelter. Dale was to give a speech as the bank's President and representative.

As Dale and Anne walked to the front door, Dale admired his wife. Despite being short and thin, without much of a figure, she had selected a silver-shaded gown that made her look elegant. She had her hair done this afternoon, and wore matching earrings and necklace, both comprised of opals.

"Anne, you look especially beautiful tonight."

"Thank you, dear. And you look dashing in your tuxedo. I've been so looking forward to tonight. I hope we can achieve our fundraising goal. The shelter desperately needs updated facilities and more beds."

As the Huffington's entered the main floor, they were greeted by George Anderson IV, Chairman of the Board, and his wife. After exchanging pleasantries, they found their seats at a table at the front of the room.

The Master of Ceremonies announced over the PA system for everyone to be seated. He welcomed the two hundred or so attendees, explained the silent auction in the adjoining room, detailed how the raffle tickets could be purchased, and reviewed the agenda for the evening. There would be a three-course dinner, followed by the raffle and dancing to a live band. The silent auction would close at 10:30 PM, at which time winners would be announced.

The MC then broadcast loudly, "Please join me in welcoming Dale Huffington to the microphone. As most of the you know, Dale is the great-grandson one of the founders of Green Valley Community Bank and serves as its current President. The bank has been instrumental in supporting our homeless shelter, donating money each year and countless volunteer hours by the bank's employees. Dale?"

The crowd broke into applause. Dale beamed in the moment. He loved the attention and position of honor in the community. Stepping up to the microphone, he began to speak.

"Thank you very much. We're here tonight on an important mission. Despite the booming economy, some members of our community have been left behind, often through no fault of their own. When life turns against them, whether due to poor health or loss of a job, the one place that is always there for them is our homeless shelter. In addition to providing lodging, showers, food, and other services, our shelter, through mostly volunteers, reaches out to the clients with offers of long-term assistance. That help can take many forms, from applying for government programs to obtaining medical care to leads for jobs. We also help the children enroll in school so that they don't fall behind in their education. I can't think of another organization that does more for our community than the homeless shelter. Our mission here tonight is to raise $250 thousand to fund an update and expansion of the facilities. With more room, more assistance can be offered, including connecting clients with Section 8 housing and with local dentists and opticians who have agreed to volunteer their time and services. Won't you join me in this mission tonight, buying raffle tickets, bidding at the silent auction, or simply making a donation. I am proud that Green Valley Community Bank is so rooted in our local community. As one example of that, I'm pleased to announce that the bank will match all donations tonight on a dollar-for-dollar basis, up to $25,000."

The crowd again erupted in applause. Dale smiled and soaked in the adulation. He then turned the microphone back to the MC and sat next to Anne.

Later that evening, Dale noticed his wife, full of her usual energy, working the room at the silent auction. Anne had directly witnessed the good accomplished by the shelter during her volunteer hours teaching art to the children. She eagerly shared that vision with tonight's attendees. Her empathy and zest for life were what originally attracted Dale, and what continued to appeal to him today. It was a shame that she couldn't come close to meeting Dale's sexual needs.

Chapter 41

Wednesday October 28, 1998
Santa Maria, California

George Anderson IV called the meeting of the bank's Board of Directors to order at 3:00 PM. He welcomed the attendees, including nine Directors, Dale, and Joel.

"First up on the agenda is a presentation regarding the bank's third quarter results. Joel?"

"Thank you, Mr. Anderson. The bank enjoyed a record-breaking quarter. Loans outstanding reached a new high, facilitated by our interest rate risk management efforts allowing for more fixed rate commercial real estate loans. Deposit inflows were also favorable. We generated the greatest quarterly net interest income in the bank's history, with strong levels of interest income on both the loan and the investment security portfolios. The gains on sale we generated from the securities were icing on the cake. In summary, our shareholders should be very pleased."

A short man at the end of the table raised his hand. George acknowledged him, "Yes, Director Miller."

"I saw on the reports that the bank has purchased new types of securities in recent months. Are we taking on too much risk in doing so?"

Joel responded, "All of the new types of securities are issued by U.S. Agencies like Fannie Mae and Ginnie Mae. As such, they are guaranteed by those institutions, meaning that the bank will definitely receive principal and interest payments from the underlying collateral, which is residential mortgages. The residential mortgages are similar to what the bank originates itself."

"Thank you, Joel."

"If there are no other questions on this topic, let's move on to the next agenda item," said George.

At this point, Joel was excused from the meeting and returned to his office. Upon entering, he saw a large Fed Ex box on his desk. Ripping it open, he removed a professionally matted and framed photo of himself with the Warriors cheerleaders. There was a note inside which read:

To help you remember a great event!
Your friend,
Troy

Chapter 42

Friday December 31, 1999
New York City, New York

The Huffman Brothers office emptied quickly following the ringing of the closing bell. The facts that New Year's Eve was on a Friday and tonight would welcome the commencement of the 2000's resulted in an array of galas being held throughout Manhattan. Troy and Duane were meeting their dates at one of the premier events, being held in Midtown and adjacent to Central Park. As the men jumped into a cab to take them up to Midtown, they discussed the past year.

"Our 1998 bonuses were good, but our 1999 bonuses should be enormous," said Duane.

"Yeah, the firm had a great year, and the trading volume for our specific clients was through the roof," replied Troy. "Not to mention the commissions we earned from our four very successful Dumps this year."

"Flagstaff could not stop asking us about Jennifer. I think it took him a couple of months to realize that the Z-tranche we sold him wouldn't pay out for twenty years."

"We did a really good job on all four Dumps. Spreading them out at a pace of one per quarter is perfect. That's enough volume to soon make us rich, when added to our salary and bonus income. But not so much similar activity as to draw attention to ourselves. Losing one client a quarter is about par for the course in this business."

"I think the number we pulled on Gainesville was great, getting him to pay that high premium on a single-asset commercial MBS that soon paid off."

"Yeah, that was masterful. We can thank Jennifer for also warming Gainesville up. Remember how she accidentally left the top button of her blouse undone when returning from the restroom?"

"I don't think Gainesville heard a word we said afterward," laughed Duane.

"Colorado Springs and Sacramento were more work, but we got both of them over the finish line."

The two men fist-bumped each other.

"Let's bask in our success tonight. Nothing but the finest food and wine," said Troy.

"And dancing with two beautiful women from the London office."

"Working at Huffman Brothers does have its privileges."

....

Meanwhile, in their small apartment in the Theater District, Jennifer and Mandy were dressing for the evening. The past year had been a better one for both of them. They each landed some commercial spots. The booming economy led to packed restaurants and generous tips. The extra cash from Jennifer's work as an 'intern' allowed her to make the apartment more livable, with better furniture and electronics. While by no means wealthy, the two women finally had some savings set aside.

"Who's your date for tonight, Jennifer?"

"A Vice President from one of the large commercial banks. Tall and good looking."

"You should be able to impress him with your knowledge of

the financial markets after all of your hours working as an intern," laughed Mandy.

"Such a tease! And who's your date?"

"I was invited to attend a dinner and dancing event at one of the museums by a very nice fellow who works for one of the non-profits specializing in the arts."

"High society!"

"Hardly, but a nice change from the actors I dated over the past year."

The women each inspected the hair, make-up, and accessories of the other. With mutual approval, they set out for their evenings.

....

Since it was three hours earlier on the West Coast, Joel was still at the office, working down the checklist of accounting entries and reports needed for the year-end financial statements. He picked up the phone and dialed an internal extension.

"Melvin speaking."

"Hi Melvin, it's Joel. Have you finished recording the December security payments?"

"Every debit to the safekeeping account was offset by a credit to the investment portfolio."

"Great. I'll forward the safekeeping reports to you as soon as they arrive in the mail."

"Standard operating procedure. Good-bye."

Joel's phone rang right after he hung up with Melvin.

"Joel speaking."

"Hi, honey, it's your mom."

"Hi, mom."

"Did you get a date for New Year's Eve tonight?"

"I asked one woman, but she was already busy."

"I'm sorry, dear. Tell you what, I'll pick up a bottle of champagne on the way home and we can watch the festivities on television."

"Sounds great. I should be home by 7:00."

Chapter 43

Monday May 1, 2000
New York City, New York

Ben Cohen entered the Huffman Brothers trading floor before the markets opened and asked for everyone's attention.

"Good morning. I would like to bring one of our positions to your attention. One of our traders, who is no longer with our firm, last week purchased a 10.00% coupon FNMA interest only or IO strip CMO tranche at 21-00. The nominal face is about $40 million. Our chief economist is forecasting a downward trend in interest rates over the coming quarters, so we don't want to be holding this position in inventory any longer than we have to. Recognizing that this is a difficult piece to market, the firm has preapproved selling as low as 18-00. Any loss on sale on this security will not be counted against the annual bonus pool. In addition, any sale at 20-00 or better will result in a 1.50% sales commission, to be allocated as usual between the sales desk and the trading desk. Any sale below 20-00 will still receive a 1.00% sales commission. As always, only market this security to accredited and eligible investors. Thank you for your efforts on behalf of our Huffman Brothers team."

Once Ben left the floor, Troy walked over the Duane's workspace.

"I'm one step ahead of you. Let's look at this CMO," said Duane.

"Wow, higher than average loan balances, a concentration of mortgages from California, low loan to value ratios, and a high weighted average mortgage interest rate for the 10.00% coupon securitization. All of those characteristics are associated with rapid prepayments from refinancing of the underlying mortgages. If interest rates drop, this baby is going to self-liquidate in a flash. And we own it at 21-00. No wonder the trader got fired," added Duane. "This bond is as close to toxic waste as you can get without actual radiation being present."

Troy signaled for Duane to follow him into the stairwell. After the door was shut and the men verified that there were no other people above or below them, Troy spoke. "A 1.50% gross commission on about $8.0 million! That's $120 thousand."

"I already did that calculation. Acknowledged, but who would be naïve enough to buy that piece of shit?"

"We Dumped on Tacoma last quarter. Too bad, he would have been a good candidate for this position," commented Troy.

"We've got Boise and Buffalo in the hopper, but I can't see either of them buying that security, even with our most persuasive efforts."

The two men paused and thought. Troy then raised his eyebrows and said, "I had Santa Maria teed up in late 1998 after the NBA game. We didn't Dump on him then, as other opportunities presented themselves. We've continued to give him good trades over the past year and a half, but haven't otherwise devoted much attention to him."

"Do you think he'd feel obligated to take our advice on this IO strip?"

"That would be a new type of investment for Santa Maria. I've only spoken with him a few times in the past year. I think we'd need to first re-up the friendship and stoke his motivation."

Troy and Duane each then said simultaneously, "Jennifer."

Chapter 44

Tuesday May 2, 2000
Santa Maria, California

Joel's phone rang at 2:00 PM in the afternoon. The capital markets had been closed for trading for an hour.

"Joel Johnson speaking."

"Hello Joel, Troy Helmsley from Huffman Brothers."

"Oh, hello Troy, good to hear from you."

"How's the investment portfolio been running?"

"Our Financial Analyst, Angela, reported to me yesterday that our bank ranks in the top fifteen percent of similar community banks nationally in terms of security portfolio yield relative to duration. Angela analyses the quarterly data from the bank regulators every three months."

"I'm very happy for you. And glad to know that Huffman Brothers played a role in that result."

"Yes, I've much appreciated your advice and trades."

"Joel, are you going to attend the annual bankers' convention in Las Vegas at the end of the month?"

"Yes. This will be my first year. Our President tells me that it is an excellent opportunity to meet industry vendors, get educated on the latest technology and other evolving matters, plus meet some of my peers. In addition, Las Vegas is a quick and cheap flight from Santa Maria."

"I'd like to invite you to Huffman Brother's client appreciation dinner on the final night of the conference. It's one way we say 'thank you' to our customers. You'd also have the chance to meet some other CFOs in a social setting, and add to your professional network."

"Sounds terrific. Sign me up."

"I'll email you the details as they are finalized. Good-bye."

As Troy hung up the phone, he flashed a 'thumbs up' down the trading desk to Duane.

Chapter 45

Wednesday May 3, 2000
New York City, New York

Mandy completed her waitress shift at 8:00 PM. She had a hair styling appointment the next morning, and realized that she was out of cash. Stopping by an ATM down the street from her restaurant, she withdrew $200. The salon preferred cash payments in order to avoid taxes, plus Mandy needed some walking around money. As Mandy turned away from the ATM, a tall and heavy man wearing a hoodie and mask knocked her to the sidewalk. She extended her arm to try to break the fall, and heard her wrist snap. The man grabbed the $200 and ran. With her wrist in searing pain, she used her other hand to dial Jennifer on her cell phone. Three hours later, the women were leaving the emergency room together.

"That's quite a cast. Are you still in pain?" asked Jennifer.

Mandy groggily replied, "I think they gave me enough drugs to keep me pain-free for quite a while. I also have the prescription for a narcotic."

"Do you want me to help you file a police report?"

"I don't see how that will do any good. He was wearing a hoodie and mask. All I saw was a large and somewhat rotund man, which isn't much of a description. Why bother?"

"Well, we can talk about that more tomorrow. Let's get you home. Here's a cab."

"The doctor said six to eight weeks for the cast. I don't think I'm going to get many commercial gigs, unless the hospitals are advertising. I hope the restaurant will give me some back-office work until I can waitress again. No tips for that work, though."

"Don't worry Mandy. We both have some money saved. I can try to work a few extra shifts at Gino's. We'll pull through this together."

"You're always there for me, Jennifer. In your next life, you'll need to find a larger roommate who knows karate."

Arriving at their apartment, Jennifer helped Mandy up the stairs and got her into bed, using a pillow from their futon as a resting place for the heavy cast.

Chapter 46

Friday May 5, 2000
New York City, New York

Troy bumped into Duane in the lunch room while he was getting a morning cup of coffee.

"Are we all set for Gino's tonight?" asked Duane.

"Yeah. I emailed Jennifer. She is working her normal station and will get a break at 6:30 PM as usual."

"I'll follow your lead in selling our plan."

The men arrived at Gino's just after 5:00 PM and sat in their usual booth. Jennifer approached and welcomed them.

"Troy, you mentioned another acting opportunity in your email. I look forward to discussing it with you. The timing is good. I can use extra money right now."

Troy and Duane both tried to restrain their smiles.

"What should we have for dinner tonight?" asked Troy.

"Gino spent the entire afternoon making *polpette*, or Italian meatballs."

"That doesn't sound as sophisticated as usual," chimed in Duane.

"These are *polpette* prepared in the Tuscan tradition. They are large, about the size of a baseball. They are made with three types of seasoned meat, a variety of vegetables, and grated, aged cheese."

"Now *that* sounds like one of Gino's dishes," said Duane.

"For an appetizer, I recommend the *caponata*. It's a complex dish comprised of about a dozen ingredients, including eggplant."

"I don't usually think of eggplant as a 'go to' food, but we'll trust you as always. And what wine?" asked Troy.

"You have a lot of intense flavors in your dishes tonight, so you'll need a similarly robust wine to avoid being washed out by the food. I'd recommend the *Dolcetto* from the Piemonte region of Italy."

"Our stomachs are in your hands," smiled Troy.

When Jennifer returned with the *Dolcetto*, Troy asked her, "Can you be available for, say, three days at the end of the month?"

"Yes. I haven't signed up for any shifts yet that far out."

"Might you be willing to make an all-expenses paid trip to Las Vegas?" inquired Duane.

Jennifer thought about the question as she poured the wine.

"I could do that. There are frequent flights out of JFK. I need to serve the next booth. Tell me more when I bring the *caponata*."

Ten minutes later, Jennifer paused at their booth as the men tasted the appetizer. "Delicious," opined Troy.

"Agreed," added Duane.

"You would still be playing your intern role. However, the venue would be a banking conference in Las Vegas. You would attend the Huffman Brothers client appreciation dinner and sit next to one of our clients. We would pay for the airfare, cab fare, your hotel room, and any incidentals."

"Sounds doable. Must be a big client to warrant that much

expense," noted Jennifer.

Later in the evening, as the men were about half-way though their *polpette*, Jennifer again swung by their table.

"Everything okay with your dinner?"

"Another culinary masterpiece," responded Duane.

"Jennifer, there is a bit different aspect to the Las Vegas role. This is an existing client, so you would not need to help sell him on doing business with Huffman Brothers. Rather, we're aiming for you to provide him with a 'girlfriend experience' of sorts.

Jennifer frowned at this information. "I'm not willing to prostitute myself. We can talk about this later at the bar."

After the men finished their meals and left the usual large tip, they met Jennifer at the end of the bar on her break.

"Jennifer, we didn't mean to in any way imply that we're asking you to have sex with the client. He's a really nice fellow, not too bright, naïve, who still lives with his mother despite being in his late thirties," said Troy.

"That sounds better. Tell me more."

"We believe that he hasn't had much success with women in his life, and probably zero experience with a woman as attractive as you are. We're simply asking that you provide him with some extended attention at the convention, plus perform a small gaslight treatment. Our objective is to leave him with an overwhelming desire to see you again, which of course would have to be arranged through us," explained Troy.

"That's more complex than the usual intern dinner. Would you be able to provide an in-depth bio on the banker and greater details on my role?"

"Certainly. And, in addition to covering your expenses, we'd provide $2,000 for wardrobe and pay double the usual fee."

"I could certainly use the $5,000. What are the dates?"

"May 26 through 28."

"Okay, I'm in," said Jennifer.

"I'll follow up with you," said Troy.

"Thank you," added Duane.

Chapter 47

Thursday May 25, 2000
Las Vegas, Nevada

Joel arrived at the hotel hosting the banking conference at 7:30 PM following the short flight from Santa Maria. The event was being held at one of the mega-resorts on the Strip. The conference schedule commenced with breakfast tomorrow morning.

As he was checking in, the hotel employee advised, "Mr. Johnson, we're pleased to provide you with one of our premier suites. No extra charge."

Joel didn't know what to say, other than 'thank you'. Joel also didn't know that Troy had arranged the room upgrade with the concierge. The bellman helped Joel with his baggage, exiting the elevator at the 35th floor. Upon opening the door to the suite, the bellman gestured for Joel to enter. He gasped. The entrance hall to the suite was half the size of Joel's house, and included a baby grand piano. The bellman entered, placed Joel's luggage in the appropriate spot, and opened the double French doors to the bedroom. Joel remained speechless while the bellman showed him the various features of the suite, including automated curtains that either provided privacy or allowed for a view down the entire Strip.

"Mr. Johnson, there is a butler on call 24 / 7. Simply pick up the room phone and press one. Room service is similarly available around the clock. Do you have any clothes which you would like cleaned or pressed?"

Still stunned at the opulence of the suite, Joel simply replied, "No". He handed the bellman the $5 bill he had in his pocket and accepted the room key.

Chapter 48

Saturday May 27, 2000
Las Vegas, Nevada

At 5:45 PM, Duane and Troy were busy setting out the name cards for their client appreciation dinner. Duane and Troy reserved a table for twelve at the upscale steak restaurant located at the top of the casino. Joel's name card was placed at the far end of the table. Jennifer was seated next to and on the inside of Joel. Troy placed his name tag across from Joel. Duane's name tag was positioned at the other end of the table. In addition to Joel, eight other CFOs or Treasurers from Huffman Brothers banking clients had confirmed their attendance.

Troy turned to Duane.

"All set for tonight?"

"I'll work the other guests while you primarily monitor Jennifer and Joel. I checked the CMO inventory last night. That piece of IO crap is still on the books."

"I didn't think there'd be much internal competition to sell that," opined Troy.

Jennifer arrived at 5:50 PM, having spent the last hour in her room rehearsing the lines she had written following a review of the advance material Troy provided. Both Troy and Duane took a deep breath at her entrance. She was wearing a royal blue skirt, this one split up the sides about half-way between the knee and the hip. The white, silk blouse clung to her tightly and had a scooped neck that displayed about an inch of cleavage. The matching blue jacket was well tailored. Jennifer's hair was wound on top of her head, with wisps down both sides.

The earrings and necklace with blue topaz stones completed the ensemble.

"All set as planned?" asked Jennifer.

Troy nodded affirmatively.

The guests commenced arriving at 6:00 PM. Troy and Duane greeted each of them warmly, thanking them for taking the time to share a dinner. Jennifer gave her name as Jessica and explained her position as intern now completing her time with Huffman Brothers, following the usual script.

By 6:15 PM, everyone was seated. Troy tapped on his glass and stood at the end of the table.

"On behalf of Huffman Brothers, we would like to thank you for joining us tonight and for your business. In these days of enhanced technology, we have too few opportunities to spend time with our customers in person. I hope you enjoy tonight's meal. While we've selected a number of wines and champagnes to be served, please feel welcome to ask the wait staff for anything particular you would like."

As Troy sat down, the wait staff appeared with bottles of wine and champagne.

Joel was happy to see that he was seated near Troy. He didn't know any of the other attendees, and was unsure of how such events proceeded. Joel accepted a glass of the champagne. He drank it quickly out of nervousness.

"I don't believe we've met. My name is Jessica."

"Pleased to meet you. I'm Joel."

"Where are you from Joel?"

"I live in Goleta, just north of Santa Barbara, but I work in Santa Maria, all on the Central Coast of California."

"I've never been there. Please tell me about it."

Jennifer continued to ask Joel open-ended, leading questions throughout the appetizer course, while periodically speaking to the individuals to her left and across from her. She was careful not to tip her hand. This was made easy by the fact that Joel failed to ask any questions about her. Instead, he simply responded to each of her queries and comments.

As the entrees were being served, Jennifer turned to Joel and continued.

"This champagne is delicious."

"Champagne is my mother's favorite drink. We have it on special occasions."

Joel then commenced a five-minute description of his mother and her line of work. By the end of Joel's comments, Jennifer came to fully understand Troy's plans for the evening. At this point, Troy proposed a toast, one of several that Troy utilized during the evening to encourage Joel's consumption of alcohol.

As they were eating their entrees, Jennifer again turned to Joel and inquired, "What do you enjoying doing outside of work?"

"I work a lot of hours, since this is my first CFO position. I guess my answer would be attending church with my mother on Sundays and playing the piano."

Jennifer smiled, but worried that her performance would not be successful if she could not redirect Joel's focus from his mother.

"I love the piano! I think it's among the most expressive of musical instruments, and able to play such a wide range of music. What's your favorite type of music to play?"

"For the classics, I'd say Chopin. For more contemporary, my mother and I both like playing Billy Joel songs."

"*Piano Man*, *The Longest Time*, *Just The Way You Are*, and *Uptown Girl* are some of my favorites!" said Jennifer.

As the dessert course was being served, the wait staff delivered bottles of port to the table. Jennifer poured a full glass for Joel, and then a much lesser amount for herself.

"A toast to a successful conference," said Jennifer to Joel.

They clinked glasses and Joel downed the port.

Following dessert, Troy again tapped his glass and announced, "I hope you all enjoyed our dinner tonight. If anyone is interested, Duane and I will be over at the bar afterwards, happy to share cordials."

Jennifer turned towards Joel and said, "I'd like to hear more about what it's like to be a Chief Financial Officer. Accounting is a potential career path for me. Won't you join me for a cordial?"

"Well, okay."

Seeing Jennifer and Joel approach the bar, Troy ordered them each a glass of Frangelico. Troy distracted Joel while Jennifer poured hers into a used glass from another patron.

After about twenty minutes during which Jennifer strained to keep up a conversation with Joel, she said, "It's still early. I'd love to hear you play some Billy Joel. If only there was a piano available."

"I have one in my suite."

"That's great! Let's go."

Jennifer followed Joel to the suite, noting his impaired balance and coordination. Upon entering, they saw that the table in the foyer was topped with fresh strawberries, whipped cream, and a bottle of Veuve Clicquot (arranged in advance by Troy).

"This hotel certainly knows how to treat its guests," said Joel.

"Let's have a glass. That is excellent champagne."

As Joel sat down at the piano to play *Uptown Girl*, Jennifer poured him a full glass of the champagne. She then encouraged him to sing as well as play the piano, as a means of increasing his thirst.

Four songs and another toast later, Joel hit the wall. Jennifer guided him over to the bed, helping him lie down after she pulled back the sheets. Joel passed out.

Jennifer undressed Joel. It was evident that Joel hadn't recently seen the inside of a gym or, for that matter, much sunshine either. She tucked the pale, flabby man into bed. Making a well-educated guess, she neatly folded his clothes and placed them on top of the dresser. Opening her purse, she removed two condoms. She carefully opened each wrapper, removing the condom and placing the wrapper on the nightstand next to Joel. Taking the condoms to the bathroom, she filled each with a squirt of hand lotion and placed them in the waste basket.

Surveying the situation, she could think of nothing else to do, so she set the alarm on Joel's side of the bed for 6:00 AM, hung her clothes and lingerie in the closet, and climbed into the other side of the bed. As she fell asleep, she congratulated herself on a fine performance, and then thought through the final scene for tomorrow morning.

Joel groaned at the blaring alarm clock. He groggily reached over and turned it off. His head was pounding. As he rolled back towards the bed, he realized that he was naked and not alone. Sitting up next to him was Jennifer, her breasts just inches from his face. They were the most beautiful breasts Joel had ever seen. They were also the only breasts Joel had ever seen.

Jennifer spoke, "Joel, can you please make a pot of the in-suite coffee? I've got an early flight out this morning."

Joel watched as Jennifer calmly exited the bed, walked over to the closet, collected her clothes and lingerie, and entered the large, marble bathroom, turning on the shower.

His head still pounding, Joel racked his brain. What had happened last night? He did drink much more champagne than usual. He couldn't remember anything after playing *Uptown Girl*. It was then that he noticed the two opened condom wrappers on his nightstand and his clothes folded on the dresser, just as he usually did at home.

"I'll need a to-go cup for the coffee," Jennifer called out from the shower.

While somewhat dizzy, Joel made his way to the bar area in the foyer and started the coffee maker after finding the packets and the cups.

Jennifer emerged from the bathroom, now fully dressed, but with her long, blonde hair hanging down over her shoulders.

"You were quite the lover last night, Joel. I'm a bit sore this morning, but the night was well worth it."

While Joel stood there stupefied, Jennifer poured the coffee into one of the 'to go' cups, picked up her purse, kissed him gently on the lips, and walked towards the door.

"I'm sorry to have to run, but I've got an 8:00 AM flight. Thanks again."

Alone in the room, his head pounding, Joel collapsed into the bed and slept for three more hours. Upon waking, he used the toilet, glanced down, and saw the used condoms in the trash can. Despite his best effort, he could still not recall what had transpired the night before.

Chapter 49

Tuesday May 30, 2000
Santa Maria, California

Joel arrived back in Santa Maria on Sunday night. His head did not completely clear until Monday afternoon. By Tuesday morning, he felt like his old self, sipping a cup of coffee at his desk early in the day. Today would start the usual month-end closing entries on the accounting system. The phone rang.

"Joel Johnson."

"Good morning, Joel, this is Troy from Huffman Brothers. Thank you again for allocating some time at the conference to attend our client appreciation dinner. It was great to get some in-person time."

"Thank you for the dinner invitation. I do have a question."

"Okay."

"What was the last name of your intern who sat next to me? I never did get that."

"Jones. Jessica Jones."

"Thank you. Any chance you have a phone number or email address for her?"

Troy made noises as if shuffling through his desk. "She was only with our department for a week, and concluded her internship at the conference. I can't find any contact information at my desk."

"Can you do me a favor and look into that?"

"For a friend like you, I will. We're not supposed to divulge employee information, but I'll ask around and ger back to you."

"Thank you. I appreciate it."

Joel was eager to learn more about how he lost his virginity and exactly what transpired in his suite at the Las Vegas hotel. He also wondered if he could see Jessica again.

"Joel, I also called this morning to tell you about a new position we brought in that might be right up your alley."

"We have continued to experience strong deposit inflows and do have money to invest right now. Our Business Development Officers are doing a great job."

"The security is a Fannie Mae CMO. This particular tranche is the interest-only portion of the securitization. I think this would be a great bond for you for two reasons."

"I'm taking notes. Please go ahead."

"First of all, the yield is very attractive. The coupon is 10.00%, more than you could get on a pass-through in the current market."

"I understand."

"You'd need to amortize the purchase price against the coupon, just like you amortize a PAC-1 CMO purchased at a premium."

"That makes sense."

"I'll email you some runs off Bloomberg, but at an annual prepayment rate of, say, eight percent, the average life is around seven years and your yield to maturity would be around 7.00%, with of course monthly payments and no credit risk due to the Fannie Mae guaranty."

"That yield sounds attractive."

"There's a fringe benefit. If I remember correctly, in your bank's last earnings release, it was mentioned that Green Valley has been funding quite a few fixed rate commercial real estate loans."

"You have a good memory. Yes, that's true."

"Those fixed rate loans aren't as attractive if interest rates rise and funding costs increase. On the other hand, higher general market interest rates typically lead to a slowing of mortgage refinancing and prepayments. If that were to happen, the average life of the IO would extend, resulting in less purchase premium amortization and a higher effective yield. So, this bond is a natural, partial hedge for your fixed rate loans."

"That was a lot of information. Tell you what, email me the runs off Bloomberg. I'll look at them, think about what you said, and call you back."

"Sounds good. That will give me an opportunity to ask around about Jessica."

As soon as he hung up, Troy teamed with Duane to generate the runs on the Bloomberg system, based upon a purchase price of 21-00. They only modeled the IO Strip at annual prepayment rates of six, eight, and ten percent. This avoided showing that the IO Strip performed poorly, from a rate of return perspective, at higher prepayment rates. Troy then ensured that the runs had the standard wording inserted at the bottom:

These projections are illustrative only and are not a guaranty of future performance.

Troy emailed the pages to Joel, along with the page out of the Fannie Mae prospectus that addressed the Agency's guaranty against credit losses.

After reading the email (and attachments) from Troy, Joel was still uncertain about the investment. He decided to call Al Cook at his home number.

"Hello." A woman's voice answered the phone.

"Hello. This is Joel Johnson from Green Valley Community Bank. I'm calling for Al Cook."

"My father's traveling somewhere through Europe right now. I'm his daughter, Chelsea. I'm house sitting for my parents."

"Oh. I didn't know that Al was still overseas."

"He does call me periodically when he has access to a local phone and the time zone difference is workable for both of us. Can I take a message?"

"No, thank you."

Joel hung up. He again reviewed the email from Troy, after which he decided to call him to further discuss the potential investment.

"I read the email and material that you sent. I've never purchased an interest-only strip CMO before. Is there any other aspect that I should be aware of?"

"It's just another tranche within the overall CMO structure, like the PAC and SEQ bonds you've done so well with."

"Well, that yield is attractive," said Joel, "plus the hedging benefit for the fixed rate loans."

"That's why I gave you a call. The security is about $40 million in current face, so you'd be looking at investing about $8.4 million."

"Could I make an offer below 21-00?"

"My job is to present any offer you'd like to make."

"Do you think I could purchase it at 19-00?"

"Wow, that's almost ten percent below the offered level. That's a big discount for an Agency security. I'll offer it if you want, but I doubt the trading desk would agree to that."

"I understand what you're saying. Could you do your best and see if I could buy the bond at, say, 20-00. That would be an even $8.0 million investment."

"I'll twist arms for you. Can you give me a few minutes? I'll call you back after I wrestle with the trading desk and likely the Department Manager."

"That's fine. By the way, did you find any information yet for Jessica?"

"She didn't leave any contact information with the team on the floor here. One person said she was hired out of one of our other offices. I'll have to do some more digging."

"Thank you for all your effort. I'll look forward to your call back."

After Troy hung up the phone, he buzzed Duane on the internal line.

"Santa Maria is willing to purchase the entire IO piece at 20-00."

"That will line us up for the higher commission rate."

"Exactly what I was thinking."

"Call him back and confirm the trade. I'll input it right now on the system. Don't let the fish off the line!"

Troy waited fifteen more minutes before calling Joel. He wanted to ensure the appearance of his fighting for the purchase price was convincing.

"Joel Johnson."

"Troy here. I won't be able to use my right arm for a week, but we got you done at 20-00. Standard settlement, delivery versus payment. I'll send you the trade ticket and confirm the settlement instructions."

"Thank you, Troy. I really appreciate it. Whenever you get some information on Jessica, please give me a ring."

"Will do."

Troy got Duane's attention down the trading desk and gave him a thumbs up signal. Duane responded by imitating swallowing a shot of whiskey. Troy nodded affirmatively.

After the market closed, the two men walked over to bar nearest the office.

"Two shots of Macallan 30-year-old," ordered Troy.

The bartender replied, "Glad to. Just so that there are no surprises, that is $200 a shot, cash or credit card up front."

Troy handed over his gold card.

The men savored the aroma of the scotch, aged 30 years in select oak barrels.

Before taking a sip, Troy raised his glass and made a toast. "To a fantastic Dump!"

Duane clinked with his glass, grinned from ear to ear, and followed with, "To the financial initiation of Joel Johnson!"

"We certainly popped his cherry!" added Troy.

Chapter 50

Tuesday February 27, 2001
Santa Maria, California

The Federal Reserve commenced a policy of monetary policy easing on January 4, 2001, when it cut its target rate for overnight funds one-half of one percent. This was followed by a similar decrease on February 1, 2001. The capital markets anticipated a further one-half percent reduction at the upcoming March 21, 2001 meeting of the Federal Open Market Committee. In response to the words and actions by the Federal Reserve, bond market investors and traders bid down the yield on the 10-year Treasury Note from about 6.40% when Joel purchased the FNMA IO Strip CMO to under 5.00% in early 2001. The lower interest rate environment ignited a tidal wave of home mortgage refinancing, as borrowers rushed to replace their higher rate mortgages with significantly lower rate ones.

By the end of February 2001, Joel began to realize that he had a problem. The monthly payment amount received on his IO Strip CMO was decreasing rapidly. This was because the pool of residential mortgages in the CMO structure was paying off quickly with the refinancing wave. Fewer mortgages meant less interest flowing into the CMO. Not yet understood by Joel, the refinance impact on the CMO was particularly large relative to other, similar CMO tranches because of the multiple adverse characteristics of the underlying loans. Joel called Troy.

"Troy speaking."

"Hello Troy, it's Joel from Green Valley."

"Oh, hello Joel. What's up?"

"I noticed that the monthly payment amount the bank is receiving on the IO Strip CMO is quickly getting smaller."

"It's not unusual to have a few spiky months of a high level of prepayments at the start of a refinancing wave."

"Do you think I should sell the CMO?"

"There isn't really a market for IO Strips when the Federal Reserve is aggressively cutting interest rates. There probably would not be a bid, or, if there were a bid, it would be super low."

"Is there anything I can do?"

"Well, some investors credit the entire monthly payment to their basis in the bond during spiky prepayment months. In other words, recording all of the cash flow as a cost recovery."

"But that means showing no income for the security for the month."

"That's right. I'm just sharing what some other investors do. Not recording any income for a month or two on an investment that has been providing high returns isn't the end of the world."

"Thanks for the advice, Troy. I appreciate it."

"Good-bye."

While Joel input a journal entry on the bank's accounting system to do as Troy mentioned, it was akin to closing the barn doors after the horse had run away. The Federal Reserve continued its program of cutting interest rates. In addition to the widely foreseen one-half percent rate decrease on March 21, 2001, similar rate reductions were made about every six weeks through October 3, 2001. As a result, the target rate for overnight funds fell from 6.50% in May 2001 to just 2.50% in early October 2001. In response, the mortgage refinancing wave grew and grew, eventually becoming enormous.

By early June 2001, Joel finally had the revelation that he was in serious trouble with his IO Strip CMO investment. The monthly payments of the interest from the underlying mortgages were decreasing at such a high rate that it was now apparent that the bank would not even receive back its original investment of $8 million. Joel decided to collect and organize all of the relevant information, and then schedule a meeting to discuss this with his boss, Dale Huffington.

Chapter 51

Thursday June 14, 2001
Goleta, California

It was 7:00 AM on a typical workday. Joel and Cheryl Johnson were finishing their breakfast in the kitchen of their small house. Joel had his head down reading the local newspaper when he suddenly heard a crash. He looked up from the newspaper and saw his mother slumped over the table. Her coffee cup had smashed on the floor. Running over to her, he quickly recognized that, while she was breathing, she was non-responsive. Joel grabbed his cell phone from his pocket and dialed 911.

"What is the nature of your emergency?"

"I need an ambulance immediately."

"Please confirm your address."

Joel did so.

"What is the nature of the injury?"

"I'm not sure. Maybe a heart attack or a stroke. My mother is still breathing, but she is not moving and not able to speak."

"Keep monitoring her breathing and unlock the front door to your house. Paramedics should arrive within five minutes. An ambulance should arrive shortly thereafter. I will stay on the line with you until the first arrival."

The paramedics soon arrived and performed an initial medical assessment. They commenced supplying oxygen and carefully moved Cheryl to the sitting room couch, laying on her back. About this time, the ambulance arrived. That team loaded Cheryl onto a stretcher.

Joel heard one of the paramedics tell the ambulance team, "Possible stroke."

The ambulance driver replied, "We'll call ahead to the hospital in Santa Barbara to have the clot-busting drug ready for immediate application."

As Joel watched his mother being loaded into the ambulance, one of the paramedics advised him to drive his own car to the hospital. His mother would be treated in the Emergency Room ICU.

At 11:00 AM, a doctor walked into the waiting room and called out "Johnson". Joel walked over and introduced himself as Cheryl's son.

"Joel, your mother has had a stroke. A blood clot in her brain was the cause."

Joel breathed heavily, not knowing what to do or say. The doctor continued.

"It was fortunate that you called the ambulance immediately. We were able to timely administer a clot-busting drug. While it's still too early to tell, in cases like this, the patient often achieves a full or near-full recovery. We'll be keeping her in the hospital for a couple of days, providing more treatment, and also evaluating the location and scope of the brain damage. With physical and / or speech therapy and a continued course of blood-thinners, your mother should have a positive prognosis."

"Thank you, doctor. When can I see my mother?"

"Likely tomorrow afternoon. I'll have the nurse station call your cell phone as soon as your mother is in a condition to have a visitor."

Joel again thanked the doctor and walked out of the hospital to a garden sitting area on the grounds. He called Melvin on his cell phone.

"Melvin Needham speaking."

"Hello, Melvin, it's Joel."

"Hello Joel."

"Melvin, could you please tell the Accounting Department team and Linda that I won't be in the office for a couple of days? My mother had a stroke and I need to stay down south here, close by in case something happens."

"Will do, Joel. Take all the time you need. It's the quiet time of the month. I'll ensure that the mid-month checklists are being completed."

"Thank you, Melvin."

"Good-bye."

After hanging up, Joel looked up at the blue sky and then dropped his head into his hands. First, the loss on the IO Strip CMO. Now, this. How would he ever handle everything? The more he thought about things, the worse he felt. His mother's insurance coverage from the department store was a thin plan with a high deductible and a large out-of-pocket maximum. She would not be able to work for a while. That thought reminded him to call the department store and update them regarding events. At least his mother was out of danger in terms of dying. Joel could not imagine his life without the woman who had always been there for him and whom he loved dearly.

Chapter 52

Tuesday June 26, 2001
Santa Maria, California

Dale arrived early at the restaurant for his lunch meeting with Joel. This was one of his favorite restaurants, constructed next to a working winery and fields of grape vines. Grape and wine production were booming areas of business for the valley, as consumers shifted their tastes from hard liquor to wine and craft beers. As Dale sipped on a glass of iced tea, he thought how unusual it was for Joel to ask him out to lunch. As he thought back over the years, he could in fact not remember ever having lunch with Joel out of the office. Joel arrived and took a seat at the table.

"Good afternoon, Dale."

"How's your mother doing?"

"Thank goodness the emergency room was able to apply the clot-busting medication within an hour of the stroke. My mother has been home now for about a week, with on-site physical and speech therapy. The latest medical report I have indicates that she should be able to achieve a full recovery in about two months."

"I'm so very happy to hear that. I know you two have always been close."

Joel's demeanor now changed somewhat.

"Dale, thank you for taking the time to have lunch with me out of the office."

"My pleasure, Joel. I was just thinking that we haven't done this before."

"I wanted us to be able to talk privately, without the risk of another bank employee hearing us."

"That sounds ominous. What's the matter?"

"Dale, I'm not sure exactly how big a problem we have, but I *am* sure it is quite large."

"Can you be more specific?"

"Do you remember that $8.0 million purchase I made in the Fannie Mae IO Strip CMO?"

"Let me see... Yes, that was, what, about a year ago?"

"Close enough. I'm afraid we're going to take a loss on that investment."

"Joel, you've produced some very nice gains on the securities portfolio over the past several years. It's only logical to expect a loss now and then. No one bats one thousand percent."

"But, Dale, I think this loss may be in the millions of dollars."

Dale gasped. He wiped his brow with his napkin, took a deep breathe, and sipped some more of the iced tea.

"How many millions of dollars?"

"I'm not sure, but perhaps in the range of $3 million to $5 million."

"Fuck! How could that have happened!" Dale leaned back and again inhaled deeply. That was a huge loss for Green Valley Community Bank. The bank's net income for the year could turn negative. That would be the first time in the bank's one-hundred-year history.

The waitress arrived to take their orders. Joel also requested an iced tea. After the waitress departed, Dale assumed control of the conversation.

"Okay, let's take this one step at a time. Joel, please tell me how we could lose that much on a U.S. Agency issued and guaranteed security."

Joel then explained that the IO Strip CMO simply entitled the bank to receive the interest payments on the underlying pool of residential mortgages. If most those mortgages paid off in the refinance wave, there would not be enough interest paid for the bank to even recover the initial $8 million investment.

"Is it possible that the refinance wave will slow or end, thereby improving the prospective cash flows from the security?" asked Dale.

"It's possible. However, everything I've read indicates that the Federal Reserve is likely to continue cutting interest rates in order to support the U.S. economy."

"So, things could actually get worse?"

"Unfortunately, yes. Look at our bank's loan pipeline. We have a record volume of refinance applications in process right now."

"Fucking shit! Just stick a broom handle up my ass."

The waitress arrived with their lunches. Each of them only took a few bites. Dale racked his brain trying to think of what to do. He was a Huffington, a descendent of one of the bank's founders. He was also President of the bank. Such a huge loss would impair his personal and professional images. How could he walk around town when everyone would know that it was on his watch that the bank suffered its only loss in a century? Would the Board of Directors fire him for allowing this to happen? And what would be the response from the bank's regulators? The various regulators were highly focused on banks regularly operating in a safe and sound manner. A huge loss would be proof positive that Green Valley was not being managed accordingly.

After he managed to somewhat calm himself, Dale continued, "Joel, let's agree on some initial steps. First of all, do not talk about this with anyone but me. Do not include this information in any email, note, or fax."

"Okay, Dale. I can keep quiet."

"Second, contact a brokerage firm other than the one that sold you the CMO to try to get an idea of its true market value. We need some hard facts. Do this as soon as you return to the office."

"Good idea."

"Third, bring all of the information you have in this regard to my condominium this evening after work."

"I didn't know you owned a condominium."

"Here's the address."

Dale wrote the address on a napkin, and paid the check. Upon returning to the bank, he told Linda that he was not feeling well and to reschedule his afternoon appointments. He then departed for his condominium, seeking a quiet and private place to think.

Joel arrived at the condominium at 5:30 PM. Dale let him in and gestured for him to sit at the dining room table. The table was strewn with sheets of paper, the result of Dale's calculations throughout the afternoon.

"Did you get an independent opinion of the market value of the IO Strip CMO?"

"Sort of. The other investment banks told me that the market for high coupon, IO Strip CMOs was virtually non-existent at this time given the orientation of the Federal Reserve.

However, they were kind enough to generate some cash flow models for me. Bottom line, the best guess is that we'll incur about a $4 million loss. That would reflect our crediting one hundred percent of the incoming cash flows from the CMO to principal."

"So, we'd report no income from the security and also take a $4 million loss on the investment principal?"

"Correct."

"What a fucking terrible situation. Do we have any recourse against the investment bank that sold us this pile of shit?"

"I'm not a lawyer, but I doubt it. I bought the security over a year ago, before the Federal Reserve commenced loosening monetary policy and cutting interest rates. You can't blame an investment bank for the actions of the Federal Reserve."

Dale paused at this point. That size loss was at the outer bound of what might be possible to cover up. That size loss was also sufficient to ruin Dale's life. The valley was the only life he had ever known, other than the years away at college and grad school. Many of the prominent families and many of his friends were shareholders in the bank. Reporting a loss of that size would brand him with a scarlet letter. His life would never be the same.

"Joel, I think we have two options. Under the first option, we disclose the loss in the upcoming quarter-end financials and regulatory reports. I would have no choice but to fire you. I suspect the Board of Directors would similarly have no choice but to fire me."

Joel gulped at this realization. How could he support his mother without a job? The bank was his only full-time work experience, dating back about a decade and a half. What else would he do with his life and how would he earn a sufficient living for both of them? He also understood that he would likely be banned from the banking industry, either formally by the regulators or informally by word of mouth. On top of all that, his mother would be ashamed of him.

"Did you mention that we have a second option?"

"Yes, but it's not attractive either. I've been racking my brain all afternoon. I think it's possible that we could cover up the loss, eventually making the bank whole."

"Wow! How do we hide and then recover $4 million?"

"I think the best pathway is through a series of small steps, each action not so large as to draw undue attention."

Dale then gathered some of the pages off the dining room table. He organized the pages with a circled number at the top.

"Here are the twelve steps to what I'll call the master plan. I'd like you to evaluate each step at your home over the next couple of days. None of this at the office, and certainly not on any bank computers. We'll meet again Friday night in Paso Robles to make a final decision."

"Understood."

"Joel, do you think you could keep something like this quiet and carry out a long-term plan in secret?"

Dale knew that he himself would have no problem keeping things secret. Decades of extramarital affairs had honed his skills in that regard.

Joel took a deep breath.

"Yes, since the alternative is having my life ruined and not being able to take care of my mother. I can't let her return to work too quickly. She deserves all the time she needs to recover. Even then, she shouldn't be working such long hours at her age and given the condition of her health."

Joel gathered up the twelve sheets of paper and departed for his house in Goleta. On the drive home, he thought through the dozen steps. Could any of them be improved? Were there other actions which could be added? He didn't like step 12. What could possibly replace that? As he approached his house, he thought about how important it was to keep this entire matter from his mother. She had sacrificed her entire life for him. He could not let her down.

Chapter 53

Saturday June 30, 2001
Santa Maria, California

Joel arrived at the bank's headquarters building at 8:00 AM. He was still tired from yesterday, after having driven about three hours roundtrip through the intense rainstorm to meet with Dale in Paso Robles the night before. He brought his laptop from home to avoid doing certain work on the bank's computer system. The first step in the coverup plan was for Joel to be able to generate false estimates of market values for the IO Strip CMO. The safekeeping bank that held the bank's securities and collected payments thereon typically provided market prices for all of the bank's securities at each month-end. The exception was the IO Strip CMO. The safekeeping bank did not provide a market value for the IO Strip CMO because it was a somewhat unusual security, subject to significant volatility in value, and without a liquid trading market. As a substitute, Joel had been soliciting estimated market values from three different investment banking firms, and then averaging those figures in calculating the bank's (unrealized) gain or loss on the investment.

Joel purchased some high-end editing software over the Internet last night, installing such on his personal laptop. Joel took the March 31, 2001 (previous quarter) estimates of market value and performed a high-resolution scan of each of them on one of the bank's new, digital copiers. He then transferred the scanned files from the bank's network to his laptop. After several tries, he succeeded in mirroring the font, typeface sizes, and coloration of the documents from the three investment banking firms. He then generated fictitious estimates of market value from the three investment banks dated June 30, 2001. Joel was careful to report a small loss on the investment, consistent with the prior quarter (but actually far less than the actual loss was at June 30, 2001). The last step would be to provide printouts of the fictitious documents to Melvin for use in the usual accounting entries and financial reporting. Because providing the market value estimates to Joel was a one-off activity for the three investment banks, they would not notice Joel's failing to prospectively contact them in that regard. In addition, if anyone noticed the lack of inquiry, Joel could simply tell them that the bank had sold that security.

This first step of the coverup plan would hide the loss and not draw attention to Joel's keeping the IO Strip CMO on the bank's books for a much greater value than warranted.

Joel next turned his attention to step two. The bank's accounting system recorded information for the investment security portfolio in numerous distinct categories. For example, separate general ledger accounts were maintained for U.S. Government T-bills versus Notes, different types of U.S. Agency debentures, and various kinds of mortgage-backed securities and collateralized mortgage obligations. Following the general instructions from Dale's sheet, Joel designed a new recordkeeping system that only used three categories of securities. This new approach would result in the securities being accounted for in just a few buckets, each of which would contain large balances. This tactic would facilitate the coverup by obscuring the impacts of their activities. Joel planned to explain to Melvin that having fewer general ledger accounts would streamline their operations.

The third step in the coverup plan was for Joel to credit all of the incoming cash flow from the IO Strip CMO to the bank's basis. This would result in no interest income being recognized and therefore constrain the bank's revenue. However, it was better to report lower revenue than to record a loss on investment. Joel would explain this to Melvin by stating that he wanted to be conservative in the accounting for the new type of investment given the prevalence of mortgage refinancing.

Now that the first three steps were lined up, Joel collected his laptop and began the drive home. He would await Dale's confirmation of several events prior to performing additional tasks under the master plan.

Chapter 54

Tuesday July 3, 2001
California Central Coast

Dale had spent much of Sunday collecting a phony driver's license and social security card; plus developing the fake documents necessary to implement the next stages of the master plan. The Santa Maria Valley needed farm labor to harvest the various crops, especially those that required picking by hand. A portion of that labor had been provided over the generations by illegal immigrants, primarily from Mexico and Central America. There was an underground cottage industry in the valley that produced a wide variety of fake documents, which in turn facilitated the hire of the illegal immigrants. As a longtime resident of the valley, Dale knew exactly where to obtain a phony driver's license and social security card. The identity on the documents was that of a recently deceased widower named Don Martin, born the same year as Dale. The widower had been a longtime customer of the bank. Dale knew that the man did not have any children, nor any relatives in the area. This profile facilitated the utilization of perfectly accurate information for the documents, with the exception that Dale's photo was utilized on the driver's license. Being an experienced banker, Dale also knew precisely what legal documents he would need for the new entities he was about to create. He copied the wording from similar documents utilized by comparable bank clients.

On Monday, with the preparation from Sunday completed, Dale created three new limited liability companies, or LLCs, through the California Secretary of State. They would be used as conduits for funds transfers under the master plan. The ultimate owner of the new business entities was The Fesler Trust. The Fesler Trust contained the founder's ownership interest in the Blue Pacific Ventures partnership. The Fesler family had excelled at procreation over the succeeding four generations. A total of 47 heirs now shared in the 22.5% of the partnership owned by the Trust. None of these heirs was involved in the partnership, nor even lived in the Santa Maria area any longer. The 47 individuals simply received and cashed quarterly checks representing their share of the earnings of the partnership. The sole trustee of the Trust was Dale Huffington, having assumed that position following the death of his father, Henry.

Dale started his Tuesday by driving to south Santa Barbara. Once he arrived at the local Bank of America branch, he opened the first business checking account, utilizing the fake documents and posing as Don Martin. As a non-interest-bearing account, there would be no annual tax information reporting performed. The address listed for the company was a post office box Dale had rented in Santa Barbara under the name of the LLC. As an extra layer of precaution, Dale had also filed a change of address form with the United States Post Office in Santa Maria for Don Martin. Any mail addressed to the deceased Mr. Martin would be forwarded to the Santa Barbara post office box.

Dale then drove further south to Carpinteria and repeated the process for a second of the LLCs. His final stop for the day was still further south in Ventura, where he opened a third business checking account. Dale had selected Bank of America branches due to the bank's huge size, meaning that his planned activities would likely not be noticed in the enormous volume of transactions processed by the large bank each day. By opening the checking accounts in separate branches, he also reduced the probability of his activities being noticed by anyone. Bank of America was also chosen because it was distinct from the safekeeping bank utilized by Green Valley Community Bank. As a final icing on the cake, Dale opened the checking accounts on July 3, when the various employees would be focused on the upcoming holiday and therefore less likely to ask questions.

Upon returning to Green Valley Community Bank late in the afternoon, Dale simply walked by Joel's office and quickly flashed him a thumbs up. Step four of the coverup plan was now complete. Steps five through twelve could now proceed in rapid succession.

Chapter 55

Thursday July 5, 2001
Santa Maria, California

Joel arrived at the office at 5:30 AM so that he could implement step 9 without being observed. He was fairly sure that no one would take the time to review the low level, detailed changes he was making to the bank's computer system. It was an arcane aspect of the bank's accounting, something only someone who had worked at the bank for so many years might even know about, much less understand. By 8:00 AM, step 9 was completed.

Dale arrived at the office at 8:30 AM. Linda greeted him as usual, soon entering his office with a mug of coffee, just the way Dale liked it.

"Good morning, Dale. How was your 4th of July?"

"Excellent. Anne and I drove to the beach early, had a picnic dinner, and watched the fireworks. How about you?"

"Carl and I enjoyed dinner at our favorite restaurant."

Dale then looked down at his desk and found the piece of paper he was looking for.

"Linda, with the Federal Reserve having cut rates again at the end of last month, we should adjust the deposit rates on our large trust accounts, to keep such in line with the market. Here's a list of accounts I'd like you to update with the deposit operations staff today."

"I'd be happy to."

Dale handed her the document.

Looking at the information, Linda asked, "Should we decrease the deposit rates that much?"

"I have to be judicious in that regard. As both the President of the bank and the trustee of the trusts, I have to be careful to not to show favoritism to the accounts I control. That would be a red flag to the regulators."

"That makes sense. They're so lucky to have you as trustee in the first place, they shouldn't complain about earning less interest."

With Linda downstairs unknowingly working on step 8, Dale shut the door to his office and pulled down the shade to the glass wall. He now had the privacy he needed to complete the research necessary for step 11.

Chapter 56

Thursday August 9, 2001
Paso Robles, California

Dale and Joel again met at the Paso Robles Inn, this time for dinner, about six weeks after their initial meeting there. By 7:00 PM, both had arrived and were enjoying their appetizers.

"Joel, the various components of the coverup plan seem to be working well, as far as I can tell. Did you have any trouble with Melvin when he saw the extra security payment arriving in the safekeeping account last month?"

"I did exactly as you instructed. I simply told Melvin that the bank would now be receiving principal in addition to interest each month on that security. He's used to that pattern, as some of our Sequential CMO tranches present a similar profile."

"And he bought that, despite the security being an interest-only strip?"

"Melvin doesn't know much about the capital markets and securities. He certainly does not understand what an interest-only strip is. It made sense to him when I explained that the bank would now start receiving principal payments on a CMO tranche now that the prior, more senior tranches had paid off."

"Excellent."

The men clinked their glasses of draft beer.

"Did Melvin also accept the addition of the new LLCs as vendors for the bank?"

"The thing about Melvin is, as long as you have the right

documents, and debits equal credits, he doesn't ask any questions."

"Great. Everything is looking good. You'll need to be careful with the creation of the false market value estimates. We don't want to show too much variation in the mark to market loss, but we also don't want there to be too little change in that figure. Either extreme might draw unwanted attention."

"I'll double check that work at the end of each quarter."

The entrees were served. Dale took a few bites and then looked up at Joel.

"I haven't seen any results from step number 5 yet. How's that looking?"

"I haven't been able to land anything yet, but I'll keep working on it."

Step five of the coverup plan was for Joel to take every opportunity to book gains on the sale of securities. Those gains would be used to offset recorded impairments, or write-downs, on the IO Strip CMO. However, with Joel cut off from the favorable trade allocations by Huffman Brothers for well over a year now, Joel's true expertise (or lack thereof) with regard to the capital markets had become manifest. In fact, the other investment banks with which Joel conducted trades generally took advantage of him, although nowhere near the extent that Huffman Brothers did with the Dump. Troy and Duane had immediately migrated their allocation of favorable trades to new potential Pump and Dump candidates after selling Joel the IO Strip CMO, recognizing that Joel was unlikely to do more business with Huffman Brothers after figuring out the truth about the toxic waste they had sold him.

As Dale finished his entrée, he spoke further.

"Remember, we need to maintain absolute secrecy about our

actions. There must never be any evidence left at the bank. We should have some large fund inflows lined up soon. Keep your ears open for anyone having any questions about our activities."

"Will do."

"We'll continue to meet periodically at safe locations, and vary those. It's important that no one perceive a pattern. It's going to take a while to bury this pile of crap."

Joel nodded affirmatively. While he suffered occasional bouts of conscience with regard to their coverup plan, he kept reminding himself of what would happen to his mother if they lost his income.

Chapter 57

Thursday December 13, 2001
Santa Maria, California

Dale and Joel arranged to meet at Dale's condominium at 6:30 PM. Their master plan continued to operate flawlessly. While there was still over $3 million in loss to replenish, they were chipping away steadily each month. With luck, in another year, the loss would be small enough to simply recognize on the bank's books without creating a stir. They could then breathe a sigh of relief and return to their normal lives.

After welcoming Joel into the condominium, Dale gestured for them to sit at the dining room table.

"Joel, as you know, the year-end audit by the CPA firm will commence in about a month. That's our next key hurdle."

"Yes, I've been thinking about that. Is there anything else we can do to further reduce the possibility that the CPAs discover our plan when they perform the audit?"

"I believe there is. Since the bank is a relatively small and simple client compared to firms trading on the New York Stock Exchange, etc., the CPA firm will likely assign one bright, experienced accountant to the audit, and then supplement with lesser caliber individuals and maybe a couple of trainees. I'll meet with the team as soon as they arrive and ask enough questions to identify the experienced CPA."

"I'm with you so far. Please continue."

"In addition, the CPAs are always on a tight schedule during the first half of the year, as they move from one audit to the next. The team at the bank will therefore only have so much time available. If we are slow, but not obviously so, in providing them with their requested reports and information, they will have less time to dig around."

"That makes sense. The bank employees are always very busy at the start of a new year, so it's not unusual to be a bit slow in responding."

"I also plan to invite the experienced CPA to dinner one night. He can hardly decline an invitation from the President of the bank. I'll see if I can get him to over-indulge in his preferred alcohol. Nothing like a hangover to slow someone's productivity."

"That's devious, but another good step."

"And, finally, I'll have Linda organize a couple of in-office birthday celebrations with cake and noise. That will constitute yet another distraction."

"Wow, Dale, remind me to never play poker with you," said Joel.

Dale smiled.

"If either of us sees that the CPAs are moving in the direction of uncovering our plan, we signal the other one for an off-site meeting. We'll put out heads together and figure out a way to alter their trajectory."

"Sounds good."

"If we can't think of anything else, our fallback plan will be to schedule fire and earthquake preparedness drills and termite treatments to the building while the CPAs are on site.

Joel nodded his concurrence. He admired Dale's quick mind and analytical skills. If only he had consulted with Dale before buying that damn IO Strip CMO...

Chapter 58

Thursday January 10, 2002
Santa Maria, California

Joel was in his office at 10:00 AM, reviewing the final accounting entries to close the books on 2001. He was also surveying the checklist that his predecessor, Al Cook, had left him. Angela Falcone, the bank's Financial Analyst, popped her head into Joel's office.

"Joel, do have time for a couple of questions?"

"Sure, Angela. How are you?"

"I've finally started eating again after being gorged during my family's Christmas celebrations. Italian families actively celebrate Christmas through Epiphany, which was last Sunday."

"I didn't know that."

"It ties in with the Italian focus on creches and nativity scenes. The arrival of the three wise men from the east completes the holiday and related festivities."

"Did you have a question?"

"Oh, yes. In performing my financial analysis of the bank during the fourth quarter of last year, I noticed an unexpectedly large drop in the yield on our investment security portfolio."

"That was to be expected. Remember that the Federal Reserve continued cutting its benchmark interest rates all the way through the end of the year. Their target overnight funding rate declined from 3.00% in mid-September to 1.75% in mid-December."

Joel had rehearsed that response for the CPAs after discussing it with Dale. In fact, the continued cutting of interest rates by the Federal Reserve only exacerbated the loss associated with the IO Strip CMO.

"Okay. My other question is why our operating costs bumped up during the last quarter."

Joel had also rehearsed this response with Dale.

"The bank turns one hundred years old in 2002. We're taking steps to spiff up our facilities and are ordering supplies in support of planned celebrations in both Santa Maria and San Luis Obispo."

"That makes sense. Thank you."

As Angela departed, Joel was pleased with himself. He had performed well. It was prescient of Dale to have prepared him in advance. The Federal Reserve's continued cutting of interest rates was putting a headwind onto the implementation of their plan. Mortgage loan refinancing activity was soaring, resulting in even more diminished cash flow from the IO Strip CMO. Joel and Dale were effectively shoveling sand against the tide. However, Joel maintained his confidence in the master plan. If anyone could engineer the coverup, it was Dale.

Chapter 59

Monday March 4, 2002
Santa Maria, California

Dale was feeling on top of the world this morning. He hit the gym early and with vigor. His wife, Anne, would be out of town for a couple of days facilitating another art exhibition. Heather Perkins, the former Miss San Luis Obispo, called Dale last night to let him know her availability and desires. This evening would be one to remember.

Dale was also elated that the coverup plan continued to work perfectly, with the exception of Joel's failing to generate gains on the sale of securities. The CPA firm completed the year-end accounting audit without finding any irregularities. Joel had performed excellently in obfuscating the investment security activity and falsifying the market value estimates. More recently, the various actions taken during February all proceeded without a hitch. There was no indication that anyone suspected anything.

Dale greeted his executive assistant, Linda, upon walking into the bank.

"Good morning, Linda."

"Good morning, Dale. Can I bring you a cup of coffee?"

"Yes, and one of the *cornettoes* from Concetta's bakery down the street, if you have time."

"My pleasure."

Dale was reviewing his emails when Linda returned with the coffee and Italian pastry.

He thanked her, and then added, "I bumped into Mrs. Franklin on the way in. She completed the wire request form she picked up yesterday. Here it is. Can you take that downstairs to be processed?"

"Of course. I haven't seen Mrs. Franklin in years. How is she?"

"I'm afraid age has caught up with her. She doesn't get out much anymore."

Linda took the outgoing wire form downstairs to be processed. It wasn't unusual at all for customers to give Dale deposits and other bank documents when they bumped into him in town. For much of Santa Maria, Dale *was* Green Valley Community Bank. Linda glanced at the completed form as she turned it in to the Wire Department. She did not recognize Security Investment LLC, but it sounded like one of the firms typically utilized by bank clients for their stock, bond, and mutual fund investments.

The day passed quickly. At 5:00 PM, Dale departed the bank. He stopped at the local grocery store on the way to his condominium, purchasing two bottles of Louis Roederer NV champagne, a can of synthetic whipped cream (the spray bottle version), a basket of strawberries, a bottle of chocolate sauce, some wheat crackers, and a large wedge of fresh, young brie cheese. These items would serve as both nourishment and stimulation for Dale and Heather.

By 9:00 PM, Dale was spent. Sex with Heather was always energetic and passionate, plus he had started the day early with a heavy workout at the gym. As he fell asleep with a beautiful woman lying on his shoulder, he smiled at his good fortune in living a robust and happy life.

Little did he know what awaited him the next morning.

Chapter 60

Tuesday March 5, 2002
Santa Maria, California

Dale skipped the gym this morning, still somewhat tired from his escapades the previous evening. At 8:45 AM, he was seated at his desk.

"Good morning, Dale. The usual coffee?"

"Please, Linda, and thank you."

When Linda delivered the mug of coffee, she mentioned, "Someone called for you earlier this morning from the Federal."

While Dale greatly appreciated Linda, she could at times be zaftig.

"There are a lot of entities with Federal in the title. Can you be more specific?"

"I'm sorry. I can't. I was distracted by a call on my cell phone at the same time. But don't worry, the gentleman said that he would be sending you an email."

Linda departed the office and Dale started reviewing some loan and deposit activity reports. It wasn't long until his computer beeped, indicating an incoming message. Flipping screens to his email application, Dale saw the email. It was sent by a Mr. Matthew Trentino, from the Federal Deposit Insurance Corporation (FDIC); and read:

Good morning Mr. Huffington. I am writing to advise that the Federal Deposit Insurance Corporation will commence both a comprehensive safety and soundness examination and a full regulatory compliance examination of Green Valley Community Bank commencing on Friday June 24, 2002. That is the day the examination team will start reviewing the advance information, listed in the attached file, that we request you provide by June 10, 2002. We anticipate being on site at your bank on Monday July 8 for a period of between two and three weeks. At this time, I anticipate that the examination team will be composed of ten individuals, led by myself as Examiner in Charge. As usual, we will be reviewing the bank's capital adequacy, asset quality, management, earnings, liquidity, and sensitivity to market risk, along with its financial reporting and all aspects of regulatory compliance, including consumer disclosures. We are providing more advance notice than usual due to the scheduling of two examinations at the same time. Santa Maria is a fair distance from the FDIC's San Francisco office, so it makes sense to conduct both examinations simultaneously in order to most efficiently utilize the FDIC's resources. Thank you for confirming your receipt of this email. Please contact me if you have any questions.

Dale took a finishing gulp of his cup of coffee and leaned back in his chair. How could he accelerate the recoupment of the loss on the IO Strip CMO before the FDIC arrived? Unlike the CPAs, the FDIC examiners were well known for staying on schedule, not fraternizing with the bank's employees, and extending their on-site period if needed to complete all aspects of the examination. At least he had plenty of advance notice.

Steps 6, 7, 8, and 9 of the coverup plan were proceeding perfectly, but could not be used to accelerate a large payment to further reduce the bank's carrying value of the IO Strip CMO. Steps 10 and 11 presented more potential in that regard, but

Dale had to be careful not to trigger any alarms. After further pondering the updated situation, Dale decided that he would need to push steps 10 and 11 to the limit, while also activating the final step he had hoped to avoid, number 12. Dale thought to himself, *in for a penny, in for a pound.*

Dale exited his office and walked down to the Accounting Department. He winked as he walked past Joel's office. Joel rose from his chair and followed Dale at a distance. Once they were alone in the stairwell used as a fire exit, Dale updated Joel regarding the email from the FDIC.

"We'll need to activate step 12," said Dale.

"I was hoping to not have to do step 12," replied Joel. "That works against the reason I agreed to pursue the coverup in the first place."

"I understand. But, at this point, I can't see any other option. The good news is that the FDIC will likely review the investment security portfolio as of June 30, so we have three months to work down the internally reported IO Strip CMO balance, hopefully to a small enough level relative to the size of the bank so as to not garner too much attention."

Observing that Joel was still less than completely committed regarding step 12, Dale added, "we can run step 7 a while longer and use those funds to gradually reverse step 12."

"That makes me feel better, for my mother's sake. Thank you, Dale."

The bank officers separated, with Joel taking the stairwell down to the Accounting Floor and Dale walking up the stairs to his floor.

Chapter 61

Monday June 3, 2002
Santa Maria, California

"It's been a pleasure doing business with you, Mr. Huffington," said the Bank of America employee.

"Thank you again for the timely response to my inquiry," said Dale.

Dale walked out of the Paso Robles branch of Bank of America, having completed his portion of step 12 of the coverup plan. He had a drive of about an hour and a half south to the Green Valley Community Bank's headquarters in Santa Maria. He used that time to think through every aspect of the coverup plan, eventually developing one new idea to further his and Joel's cause. He called Joel's personal cell phone from his car.

"Joel Johnson, speaking."

"It's Dale. Before we talk bank business, how did you mother do this past weekend?"

"She worked an eight-hour shift on both Saturday and Sunday at the department store. She was exhausted by Sunday evening, but proud of herself. The department store is limiting her to thirty hours a week on the orders of her doctor, but they really want her there on the busy weekend days."

"Good to hear that she continues to get better. Say, Joel, how long has it been since Melvin has been on vacation?"

"Hmmm... Now that you mention it, I can't remember Melvin *ever* being on vacation. He's like clockwork. Arrives at his desk at exactly 8:00 AM every day, eats lunch at noon on the dot, and departs precisely at 5:00 PM every evening."

"If I remember the bank's Human Resources Policy correctly, all accounting staff have to be on vacation for at least two weeks consecutively every year, as an internal control. In other words, if a member of the Accounting Department is cooking the books, the two-week vacation period provides time for some other employee to perform his duties and perhaps uncover anything adverse."

"Now that you mention it, I believe you are correct. That said, I don't think that Policy has ever been extensively enforced."

"I think you should visit Melvin with a printout of the Policy this afternoon. Explain it to him, while also stating that you would not want him to be an exception to the Policy with the FDIC coming in for a full-scale examination."

"I can do that, but why?"

"If, under your guidance, Melvin takes two weeks off on vacation starting July 8, he won't be available to answer questions from the FDIC's examination team. Therefore, they'll have to approach you with all of their accounting and finance questions. That would give us much better control of the information being shared. You can justify the July 8 date by telling Melvin you need him on site the first week of the month to close the books for the second quarter."

"I see your point. Great idea, Dale. I'll take care of that today."

"I should arrive at the bank in about an hour. I've lined up some more funds under steps 11 and 12. We can discuss that at our next off-site meeting. Good-bye."

Joel printed out a copy of the Human Resources Policy and called Melvin to make an appointment for a 2:00 PM meeting this afternoon. The meeting would take place in Melvin's office, as usual.

The bank's employees were working intensely when Dale arrived at the headquarters building just before noon. There was just one week to complete the preparation of the information for the FDIC, plus residential mortgage applications continued to flow into the bank in response to the low interest rates engineered by the Federal Reserve.

"Hello, Linda."

"Hello, Dale. Would you like me to go out and bring you back some lunch?"

"That would be great. I've got a late start today, and we have so much to accomplish in the next week. I don't deserve such a super assistant."

Linda smiled broadly. She lived for the positive reinforcement from Dale. Her husband, Carl, was by nature a quiet individual, much less evocative than Dale.

"Oh, and I picked up an outgoing wire request from Mrs. Abernathy on my way in. Can you have this processed today?"

"Of course. She must be well into her nineties by now. How did she look?"

"Pretty spry for someone her age. She must have excellent genes."

Dale gave the outgoing wire request form to Linda. The recipient account at Bank of America was in the name of Security Investment LLC. That name rang a bell to Linda, but she could not remember why. Seeing her pause while looking at the document, Dale spoke up.

"Can you bring me back one of those delicious subs from Harry's, no mayo as usual?"

"Got it. I'll be back soon."

As Dale sat at his desk and commenced checking his email, he stopped for a moment and mentally added up all of the funds that would arrive at the safekeeping bank this month designated as a payment on the IO Strip CMO. He had pulled out all of the stops, as had Joel. There was nothing more they could do. The loss was down to about $2.0 million. Now, they just needed to make it through the regulatory examination.

Chapter 62

Monday July 8, 2002
Santa Maria, California

It was a hot, dry summer day on the Central Coast. The usual breeze from the Pacific Ocean was absent, sending temperatures towards ninety degrees. The FDIC examination team started arriving at about noon. The final member of the twelve-person examination team showed up at about 3:00 PM, having traveled from his prior examination site in Reno, Nevada.

The bank allocated the Board Room at the top or twelfth floor of the headquarters building to the FDIC team. It was the largest single workspace in the bank, plus the executive team wanted to show the FDIC staff respect by giving them the best space in the building. Dale knew from his long experience that this would get the examination off to a good start. At the various banking conferences over the years, he had heard about bank's taking the opposite approach, housing the FDIC team in a basement boiler room, for example, as a theoretical impetus to have them quickly leave. Such strategies were rarely effective.

At 3:30 PM, the usual 'Welcome Meeting' commenced. The FDIC team each introduced themselves and provided business cards. The bank's executive and senior staff did the same. The FDIC Examiner in Charge, Matthew Trentino, then outlined which FDIC employees would be working on each of the various component areas of the examinations.

Dale quickly glanced through the FDIC business cards as Matthew spoke. It looked like the team included two trainees.

Looking around the Board Room table, only three of the examiners had grey hair. Dale thought to himself, *so far, so good.* Dale then returned his attention to Matthew, trying to size him up. Matthew was about six feet, three inches tall, thin, and appeared to be in his early thirties. His vocabulary was sophisticated. He was well spoken, focused and on point with each of his statements. After listening further, Dale concluded that Matthew was likely a rising star at the FDIC, which is why he was appointed Examiner in Charge at a relatively young age.

Matthew continued his presentation.

"One of our planned FDIC examiners was involved in an automobile accident over the weekend. He will be okay, but unfortunately will not be able to join us for this examination. As a result, I'll step in and take the lead on the safety and soundness subject of Sensitivity to Market Risk."

Dale kept his cool at this point, despite his gut check. Having a rising star looking at the bank's market and interest rate risk was a most unfavorable development. Quickly processing the situation, Dale turned his attention to identifying any potential weaknesses in Matthew. Based upon his thin frame, food was clearly not a vice. Ditto for alcohol, most of which contains a significant number of calories. Maybe cocaine or one of the popular upper drugs. Some of those users tended to be thin from a lack of appetite. Dale didn't detect any homosexual mannerisms or references. Maybe women would be an avenue to pursue. Dale continued to listen not only to what was being said, but also to the tone and intonation of the voice and the body language. Years of deciphering whether women might be receptive to an affair with him had honed his powers of perception.

Matthew was wrapping up his presentation at this point.

"We'd like to thank all of the bank staff who worked to timely provide us with the advance material we requested.

We've been pouring through that information for the past couple of weeks. We'll start our introductory, high-level follow-up questions tomorrow morning, and then proceed to get more granular throughout the week."

Dale then stood up.

"On behalf of Green Valley, we look forward to working with all of you in accomplishing a timely and complete examination. If you notice any opportunities for us to improve our operations, our technology, or our policies, even if such observations are not of a serious nature, please feel most welcome to share them with us. The FDIC team gets to see how many banks approach the same issues. We want to benefit from your insight into best practices throughout our industry."

Dale then sat down. Matthew announced the conclusion of the meeting and again thanked everyone for their attendance.

As the room emptied, Dale worked his way over to Matthew, greeting him with a warm handshake.

"If there's anything your team needs, even something as simple as where to buy something locally, please feel most welcome to contact my assistant Linda. She would be happy to help you."

"That's kind of you. Thank you," said Matthew.

"Where are they putting up your team?"

"Well, we're constrained to a strict per diem limitation while on the road. So, we're staying at the budget hotel near the airport."

"I understand how government works. If any of your team is thinking about staying over one of the weekends, one of our bank's founding families, the Kehoe's, still owns the elegant hotel located at the downtown crossroads. Entering that building is like stepping back in time for a hundred years. The architecture is unique and the original bar is still being used. One of our local landmarks."

"Thanks for the heads up."

"Would you like a quick tour of the building?"

"That's considerate of you. Yes. However, we'll need to be relatively quick, as I need to cycle through the team before they depart for the evening."

Dale provided Matthew with a fast-moving tour, descending one floor at a time from the Board Room. On each floor, he pointed out the functions performed there and features that might be of use to the FDIC team, such as an employee kitchen or a room with copiers and fax machines. As they walked through the Accounting Department, Dale observed that Matthew's pace slowed a bit when they walked past Angela's office. Dale finished the tour on the ground floor, avoiding the basement, and dropped Matthew off at the elevators, saying goodbye and returning to his office.

About an hour later, as the employees were leaving for the evening, he walked down to Joel's office and whispered, "Meet me at the condo tonight at 6:30."

Joel nodded affirmatively.

By 6:45 PM, Joel and Dale were sitting at the dining room table in the condominium, each drinking a beer to help relax after a stressful day. Dale shared his initial impressions of each member of the FDIC team.

"So, you're saying that our focus should be on Matthew from two different points of view. First, we should each attentively listen for any clues that might divulge any personal weaknesses, with your best guesses at this point being perhaps women and maybe some type of stimulant. Second, we need to be responsive, but not overly helpful, as he works on the analysis of market and interest rate risk. Since Melvin is on vacation for two weeks, I should be able to guide that aspect of our plan," recapped Joel, aiming to ensure that he clearly understood the next steps in their plan.

"Correct. The fact that Matthew is doing double-duty should be to our benefit. The less time he has to look into things, the better. But be very careful. He strikes me as someone who is both intelligent and inquisitive. That can be a dangerous combination from our perspective."

As the men finished their beers, both commented that they just needed to get through the next three weeks. After that, it should be smooth sailing.

Chapter 63

Thursday July 11, 2002
Santa Maria, California

It was Thursday afternoon before Matthew Trentino had a chance to commence his examination regarding Green Valley's market and interest rate risk. The Examiner in Charge role during a combined safety and soundness and compliance examination was extensive, akin to a captain on a sailing ship. The crew needed to be kept coordinated and advancing on the correct heading, almost hour by hour. Having two trainees only increased the demands on his time.

Matthew first reviewed the notes generated by the FDIC analyst who had read the related material submitted in advance by the bank. That reminded Matthew that he needed to send a follow-up email checking on the man's recovery from the car accident. In addition to information supplied by the bank, the FDIC screened the bank's performance and operations by comparing its results to a database of various metrics collected through the regulatory reporting process for similarly sized financial institutions. The FDIC analyst had identified two comparative variances for further research.

Although he was still relatively young, Matthew had already learned from more seasoned FDIC personnel to always start at the bottom of the organization chart and then work one's way upward, accumulating information at each level. There were two benefits to this approach. The first one was that executives often didn't have a detailed knowledge of the operations and technology utilized by lower-level staff in the organization. The second one was that it was more effective to ask questions of the senior leadership team after the examiner had a foundational understanding of the matters of interest.

Picking up the copy of the employee directory the bank had supplied, he dialed an internal extension.

"Hello, Angela Falcone speaking."

"This is Matthew Trentino with the FDIC examination team. Might you be able to meet with me upstairs here at about 4:00 PM? I have a few questions that I'd like to ask you as part of our financial analysis review."

"Certainly. I'll be there then."

"Good-bye."

Matthew was in the Board Room explaining the various risks that banks inherently face to one of the trainees when, out of the corner of his eye, he caught a glimpse of the quite attractive woman he had noticed during the building tour with Dale. Turning his head for a better look, Matthew judged her to be about 5'10" tall, late-twenties, with a toned, athletic body. Most noticeable was the long black hair which extended almost to her waist in the back. He stood up, caught her attention, and asked "Are you Angela?"

"Yes."

"I'm Matthew Trentino, the Examiner in Charge."

"Pleased to meet you."

"Let's use one of the nearby offices. It gets quite loud in here with so many staff working."

As Angela followed Matthew to the office, she first noticed his height at about 6'3", then the fact that he was quite thin, and finally that he possessed an attractive face, with distinct but not overpowering features. Instinctively, she next looked for a wedding ring. There was none. As they sat down at a meeting table in the office, Matthew spoke first.

"As you probably already know, the FDIC uses the information from the bank regulatory reports to build a database of information. That database allows us to analyze a bank's performance and any changes over time, plus also enables us to compare a given bank to a peer group."

"Yes, I'm familiar with the Uniform Bank Performance Report system. I generate financial ratios and other metrics for the bank as part of my job. Many of those measures are the same as or similar to the ones generated through that system."

"Good to hear. I'd like to first ask you about the decline in the bank's investment portfolio yield over the past couple of years."

"Yes, that has been significant. Of course, the fact that the Federal Reserve cut its target rate for overnight lending from 6.50% in May 2000 to just 1.75% today certainly had a lot to do with it. As our older fixed rate bonds amortized and matured, replacement security purchases were for much lower yields. In addition, our position in adjustable-rate securities delivered progressively lower yields as the Federal Reserve kept easing monetary policy."

"That makes sense. We've seen those impacts across substantially all of the banks we've recently examined. However, there's one aspect I don't yet understand."

Angela kept listening politely, although she did catch herself looking into his hazel eyes for an inappropriately lengthy amount of time at one point.

"For the year 1999, Green Valley ranked at the 85th percentile of banks of similar size in terms of investment portfolio yield relative to duration. That means only fifteen percent of the peer banks in the entire country had a better relative performance. That ranking is impressive."

"Yes, the bank enjoyed great financial success in 1999. It was a record year in many regards," replied Angela.

She did not know that mid-1998 through mid-2000 was when Huffman Brothers was exerting a maximum Pump on Joel, sending him the very best, cherry-picked security trade allocations.

"However, Green Valley dropped to the 75th percentile for the year 2000, the 45th percentile for the year 2001, and then down to the 10th percentile during the first quarter of this year. I'm trying to figure out why there was such a dramatic and rapid change in relative performance."

Angela pondered for few moments and then responded, "I'd have to do some specific analysis to answer your question. I know that, in addition to the macro factors I previously mentioned, the bank sold many mortgage-backed pass-through securities in order to free up capacity for new, fixed rate commercial real estate loans to our clients in the area. That was a prudent reallocation of duration within the balance sheet in maximizing the amount of return relative to a targeted interest rate risk profile."

While Angela's response was financially astute and well grounded, what Matthew most heard was the fact that this woman is intelligent in addition to being beautiful. He glanced at her left hand, noting the absence of a wedding ring. With a deep breath, he pulled himself back into the conversation.

"Your analysis would be helpful. The way the bank has organized its accounting for securities renders it difficult for someone outside the organization to identify much causality."

"I'll circle back to you as soon as I can. We're still working on the quarter-end financial and regulatory reporting right now, but I'll put in some overtime."

"Thank you. Oh, Angela, please keep my information request between us right now. I don't want to excite or worry any of the bank executives over a simple inquiry."

Matthew had already well-learned the lesson that needlessly raising the blood pressure of executive officers often slowed the progress of regulatory examinations. He was on a tight schedule at Green Valley given the two concurrent examinations and the loss of the experienced FDIC employee involved in the car accident.

Angela was perplexed. She was raised with a robust ethical foundation in her parent's strongly Catholic household. She did not want to be placed in a position of potentially having to lie to her boss. She remembered her father's speaking at the dinner table, often quoting from the bible and famous historical figures, such as Thomas Jefferson:

Honesty is the first chapter in the book of wisdom.

On the other hand, Angela acknowledged the authority of the FDIC and did not want to initiate an issue with the examination team, as that might reflect negatively on the bank. She concluded that Matthew's request was a modest one, not worthy of creating either a moral dilemma for herself nor a situation with the regulators.

"I understand. Will do."

Angela then rose to depart the conference room. As she glanced one last time at Matthew, she confirmed that, yes, he was one handsome man. How had he not been taken before now?

Chapter 64

Friday July 12, 2002
Santa Maria, California

At 3:00 PM in the afternoon, Matthew Trentino and the three grey-haired FDIC examiners met in a conference room with the bank's executive team. A recap meeting at the end of each week was standard practice during a regulatory examination. This provided an opportunity for the collective attendees to discuss preliminary findings and also gave the bank the chance to fix minor issues before the conclusion of the examination, and thus keep those matters outside of the subsequent regulatory follow-up process.

Matthew opened the meeting.

"Thank you all for attending this first end of week recap meeting. I'd like to begin by thanking the bank for the hospitality and assistance throughout the week. Your employees have been helpful and responsive, which makes our job much easier."

Matthew continued, "Thus far, we have identified one regulatory compliance violation with regard to the wording and content on one of your consumer loan disclosures."

Matthew then distributed copies of the offending document and explained the compliance issue.

After Matthew finished his explanation, Dale said, "Thank you for pointing that out to us. I believe we have the ability to dynamically update that document on our computer system. I will contact our Regulatory Compliance Officer, Kelli Tang, to initiate that correction as soon as we complete this meeting.

I will also have Kelli follow-up with your team on this next week, confirming the correction."

"That sounds good. The more findings that can be corrected while we're on site, the better it is for everyone. Your customers benefit more quickly, and the regulatory team has less follow-up work to perform. Thank you for volunteering to have that addressed so timely. We also identified three opportunities for adoption of 'best practices' in various areas that we would like to pass along."

"I'll be happy to work on those," said Gene Phillips, the bank's Chief Operating Officer.

Matthew passed the documentation down the table to Gene. Matthew again took the floor.

"We should have much more to discuss at the similar meeting a week from now. Our team spent most of this first week entering the information provided by the bank into our regulatory reporting system, making introductions to key personnel, and identifying additional data we will need to complete the examination. We'll be performing much more analysis next week. Thank you again for your time this afternoon."

As the meeting was breaking up, Dale felt a whiff of relief. One week down, two to go. Despite Anne's being in Los Angeles this weekend, he had passed on scheduling a tryst. Rather, he had a meeting set up with Joel for Saturday afternoon in a seldom visited portion of a local state park. They had planned this in advance to share notes, observations, and even any rumors associated with the regulatory examination. Dale's only frustration was that he had not yet firmly identified a vice in Matthew Trentino that might be exploited.

Chapter 65

Wednesday July 17, 2002
Santa Maria, California

The FDIC team was having a good morning, spurred by the 'do it yourself' *cannoli* bar that was set up on the side table of the Board Room when they arrived that morning. The tubular shells were pastry dough that had apparently been fried in some type of seasoned oil. The squeeze bags of stuffing were chilled, ready to be deployed into the shells. This ensured that he shells would be crisp while the filling soft, adding a tactile aspect to the dessert. Matthew knew enough about *cannoli* to identify the ricotta filling, but could not recognize the other components that produced such an astoundingly delicious taste.

As Matthew licked the last of the *cannoli* off his fingertips, he dialed the internal extension for Angela.

"Angela Falcone speaking."

"Good morning. It's Matthew from the FDIC. Might you come upstairs at your convenience so we can have a follow-up conversation about the investment security portfolio?"

"Yes. I'll be there in just a bit."

After they were seated in one of the offices, Matthew began speaking.

"The *cannoli* were scrumptious. Do you know where the bank got them? I'll need to visit that bakery before we finish the examination."

Angela blushed.

"That bakery would be my kitchen."

Matthew's face flushed a bit in response before saying, "You have quite the culinary skills."

"Taught to me by my *nonna*. After her first heart attack, she admitted her mortality and started sharing her secret recipes with me, wanting them to be passed down to future generations."

"I'm of Swiss-Italian heritage. Both of my parents' families were originally from the far northern part of Italy and into southern Switzerland. However, that was three generations ago."

"My father's family was from Tuscany and my mother's family was from Sicily. My grandparents were the first generation born in America."

"Well, thank you again for the treat this morning. We rarely get very good food while on the road, given the work hours and the small allowable per diems."

This was music to Angela's ears. She loved cooking. She also had a genetic predisposition to immediately start feeding anyone as thin as Matthew. After a couple of deep breaths, she was able to put those thoughts aside and focus on Matthew's questions.

"Were you able to discern the causes of the relative decline in the bank's investment portfolio performance?"

"Not specifically, as I don't have access to a Bloomberg system. However, I was able to develop a time series chart."

Angela removed the document from her folder and handed it to Matthew. She then continued.

"It appears that the relative performance decline commenced in the fourth quarter of 2000 and then accelerated at a curvilinear rate quarter by quarter through the first quarter of 2002. In addition, I researched the investment portfolio yield during the second quarter of 2002, although the bank has not yet filed that regulatory report. The portfolio yield for the second quarter of this year appears roughly consistent with the first quarter."

"Interesting. Can you have the Controller provide me with a copy of the safekeeping reports for the bank for each quarter-end from the fourth quarter of 2000 to the recent June 30th? How about also bringing me a copy of the consolidated general ledger trial balance for each of those quarter-end dates? Come to think of it, might you also copy the monthly general ledger transaction reports for the investment securities accounts for me, for the same time period?"

"The Controller is on vacation this week, but I can copy the safekeeping reports from the orange files and the general ledger reports from the green files in his office and bring them to you later today."

"That would be great. Thank you."

As Matthew watched Angela walk away, admiring her lustrous black hair, he thought back to her statement about the orange and green files. That sounded odd. He decided to let it pass and see what the reports looked like.

Chapter 66

Wednesday July 18, 2002
Santa Maria, California

Matthew spent the morning looking through the investment security safekeeping reports and the general ledger reports in between answering questions from his team and responding to emails and phone calls from the San Francisco office. The safekeeping reports were produced by a large commercial bank. That entity electronically held the bank's securities and received the associated payments each month. The safekeeping bank also segregated the bank's securities based upon whether they were pledged or not. Certain counterparties to Green Valley Community Bank required that collateral be pledged for various types of financial positions.

As he ran through the reports, everything matched up perfectly. The payments received by the safekeeping bank were exactly matched by the entries into the general ledger accounting system. As he came to the end of the safekeeping report, he did, however, notice that there was one security without a reported current principal balance and without an estimated market value. He decided to make a quick call to the FDIC's Capital Markets Division.

"Hello. David Morgan speaking."

"Hello David. It's Matthew Trentino from the examination team on site here in Santa Maria."

"Oh, yes. We've met once or twice. How can I help you?"

"I'm going to email you a CUSIP for an investment security. Can you look it up on your systems and email me back a description of the security?"

"Will do. Give me until after the markets close and I'll take care of that for you."

"Thank you."

At 2:30 PM, Matthew received the incoming email from David. The security was a collateralized mortgage obligation issued by Fannie Mae. The particular tranche owned by Green Valley Community Bank was the interest-only strip. Matthew had seen this type of security a couple of times before, but was not intimately familiar with it. He called Angela on the internal phone system.

"Angela Falcone speaking."

"Hello Angela. It's Matthew from the FDIC team. Do you have time for a question?"

"Of course. How can I help?"

"I see that the bank owns an IO Strip CMO. We don't see that type of security too often. Do you know why the bank purchased it?"

Matthew had been trained through the FDIC's professional education program to question anything out of the ordinary.

"I'm not directly involved in the security purchases, so I can't give you a definitive answer. There is, however, one financially logical reason I can think of."

"Please continue."

"As I mentioned in an earlier conversation, the bank experienced a high demand for fixed rate commercial real estate loans over the past couple of years. If market interest rates climbed, those fixed rate loans would be less financially attractive. In comparison, an IO Strip CMO would become increasingly attractive as interest rates rose due to the implied slower prepayments and longer life; and, therefore, a more significant aggregate incoming cash flow."

"I think that makes sense, at least from a big picture perspective."

Angela then interjected, "On the other hand, the correlation between fixed rate commercial real estate loans and 30-year fixed rate residential mortgages is less than ideal due to the differing optionality. So, the IO Strip CMO might not be the most effective way to hedge the interest rate risk."

"You're losing me now. I'm not a financial expert. Might you please come upstairs and perhaps draw me some graphs to help me understand?"

"I'll be there soon."

Angela first ran to the women's restroom, combed her hair, and rinsed with the small bottle of mouthwash she kept in her desk. She then returned to her office, grabbed some graph paper and some colored pens, and took the elevator up to the Board Room floor.

After about fifteen minutes of drawing yield curves, prepayment curves, and various financial metrics, Angela succeeded in having Matthew understand her comments.

"Thank you for being so patient with me. I've received basic capital markets and security analysis training, but nothing this advanced."

"My pleasure. You know, I did have one more thought while running through this with you."

Angela had actually had two other thoughts, only one of which was about business.

"Please, go ahead."

"I suppose if the IO Strip CMO was purchased at a really

attractive price, the extra associated yield could more than compensate for the lack of correlation with the fixed rate commercial real estate loans."

"I see what you're getting at. There's often a sufficiently attractive price to allow a perhaps second choice alternative to become a primary selection."

Angela smiled and nodded.

Matthew stood up to indicate the conclusion of their meeting, saying "Thank you again for keeping this confidential. I'll follow up with the Chief Financial Officer soon, but I want to ensure I understand everything well before taking up his time."

As Angela approached the door to the office, she stopped, turned, and said, "We're having a pot luck lunch on Friday throughout the bank. I'm making *gnocchi*. Do you prefer the traditional Genovese green sauce with the basil, olive oil, and pine nuts, or the red sauce with the tomatoes, onion, and garlic?"

"I must admit to not being familiar with either. My family's culinary focus was often more Swiss than Italian. Whatever you recommend."

Angela grinned, said "Okay", and departed.

Matthew, out of the corner of his eye, watched Angela's firm form as she walked away. Returning his focus to work, he decided to send a follow-up email to David Morgan. In it, he asked for the IO Strip CMO's payment history and a PDF of its offering circular.

Chapter 67

Thursday July 19, 2002
Santa Maria, California

Joel walked into the employee lunch room to grab a cold soda and overheard Angela speaking with Michelle, one of the accountants. They were seated at a table at the far side of the room, facing away from Joel.

"He's so handsome," said Angela.

"I agree. Could use some more muscle for my taste, but definitely worthwhile material. Have you had a chance to speak with him?"

"A couple of times."

"Well?"

"Definitely smart, well spoken, Swiss-Italian family."

"Do you think he might be interested?"

"I'm not sure yet. That would of course have to follow the conclusion of the examination."

"I can tell by that look in your eyes. You're highly interested in conducting an exam of your own."

At this point, Joel exited the lunchroom and returned to his office. He texted Dale's personal smartphone: 'condo at 6:30?'

Within minutes, he received a 'Y' reply.

When Dale and Joel met that evening, Joel shared what he had overheard in the lunch room.

"Hmmm... I noticed Matthew's potential interest in Angela during the introductory tour," said Dale.

"Do you think we could use this to our advantage?" asked Joel.

"There are a number of potential alternatives. We could explore if Angela might be able to simply distract Matthew, and therefore reduce any potential focus on the IO Strip CMO."

"Okay. What else?"

"We could also explore if Angela might be willing to be a sort of spy, seeking information on where Matthew and the examination team might be heading in terms of any adverse conclusions."

"I can see that as an opportunity."

"The extreme option would be for us to engineer Angela to convince Matthew to do something he would not do otherwise, out of desire for her."

As Dale finished his sentence, an overwhelming wave of perception engulfed Joel. His mind was quickly filled with flashbacks to Las Vegas. He turned white and began perspiring profusely.

"Joel, do you need a drink? You're suddenly looking somewhat ill. How can I help you?"

"It's okay, Dale," said Joel, slowly regaining his composure. "How should we approach Angela?"

"Let me think about that some more and leave it to me. The FDIC team will be digging deep next week as they try to wrap things up. Plus, Melvin will be back from vacation. We'll need your full attention on the Accounting Department."

On the drive south to his home in Goleta, Joel reviewed

everything he could remember about Jessica and the period immediately following their encounter at the banking conference. Yes, it was just days after waking up in his hotel room next to a beautiful and naked woman that Joel had been convinced to purchase the IO Strip CMO. Joel finally realized that was not a coincidence. He had been set up by Troy and Jessica. Why was it only now, far too late, that he remembered the answer to one of the questions from the final examination in Professor Krakaris' Philosophy 101 class:

> *There are three principal ways to lose money: wine, women, and engineers. While the first two are more pleasant, the third is by far the more certain.*
>
> *Baron Rothschild*

Chapter 68

Friday July 20, 2002
Santa Maria, California

As the second week of the regulatory examination was drawing to a close, the FDIC team worked intently, trying to reach preliminary conclusions in a number of areas. By the end of the examination next week, they would need to grade about ten distinct components, plus develop two overall grades: one for regulatory compliance and one for safety and soundness. The FDIC employees were very pleased to be able to partake in the bank's pot luck lunch, as that saved time versus going out to eat. In addition, the food was generally well prepared. Two steaming bowls of Italian soft dough dumplings were consumed almost immediately, one bowl covered in a savory green sauce and the other in a robust red sauce. Matthew was fortunate enough to arrive just in time to get one of the last servings of each.

Finally, at 2:00 PM, Matthew had a chance to open and review the latest email from David Morgan. The Fannie Mae Offering Circular for the CMO seemed quite standard for such, to the extent of Matthew's ability to understand that 120-page document. The description of the IO Strip tranche also appeared unremarkable. The owner of that particular tranche would receive the interest payments (as differentiated from the principal payments) on a defined pool of residential mortgages within the aggregate CMO, less the usual fees for servicing and the Agency guaranty. He next reviewed the payment history provided by David Morgan from the Bloomberg system. It didn't take Matthew much time to realize that the payments from the Bloomberg system were much lower than the ones he had seen on the safekeeping reports. Putting such side by side, he was able to match up half the payments. He observed that there was a second payment each month on the safekeeping reports that was not present on the information from David Morgan. He thought about this for a while, trying to think about why the bank would be receiving a second payment that was not reported by the CMO servicer. The most likely answer was that somewhere in the processing chain, a payment for another security was being miscoded to the CUSIP of the IO Strip CMO. Many CUSIP numbers were similar, so mistyping even one digit on input could have generated the observed pattern.

He made himself a note to visit with the bank's Controller first thing on Monday morning to explore the potential payment miscoding. As he mentally prepared for the upcoming afternoon meeting, Matthew was somewhat comforted that at least there was *more* money than expected. In his years with the FDIC, he had already been involved with several instances of there being less money, which was all too often correlated with theft or embezzlement.

The standard end of the week status update meeting commenced at 3:00 PM. The FDIC staff reported that most topics evaluated thus far appeared to be in good shape, consistent with the bank's century of profitable operation. A couple of relatively minor errors were identified in some of the periodic regulatory reports. Joel accepted responsibility for the errors, pledged that they would be timely corrected, and that associated procedures would be updated to prevent a recurrence in the future. A second consumer disclosure violation was identified, this time in the bank's home equity line of credit documentation. Gene Phillips acknowledged the shortcoming and promised that it would be corrected by the middle of next week. Throughout the meeting, Dale sat quietly, listening to the voices and watching the body language of the participants.

Nothing he observed raised concern.

At 6:30 PM, Dale and Joel were again in the condo.

"Joel, did you hear or see anything that would raise an alarm?"

"No. I haven't spent much time with the Examiner in Charge, though."

"They usually do the executive interviews during the final week. I didn't see or hear anything that made me nervous, either. The FDIC staff seemed focused, but also comfortable, as they shared in the pot luck lunch. If they were concerned about a major issue, their behavior would almost certainly have been different."

"Were you able to determine if and how we might use Angela to our advantage?"

"I asked her several leading questions and made a number of 'open to interpretation' comments to her the past couple of days. She didn't bite on any of the bait. I don't think we could get her to intentionally work to our benefit."

"Unlike Jessica," Joel mumbled to himself.

"I didn't quite hear that."

"Oh, I was just talking to myself. I do have one idea."

"I'm all ears."

"I'll keep Angela's workload as light as possible next week. With more free time, she may take that opportunity to at least flirt with, if not actively pursue, Matthew."

"Sounds good. Let's both keep alert each day next week, and signal to the other one if we become aware of any risk."

"Agreed."

Chapter 69

Sunday July 22, 2002
Santa Maria, California

Matthew decided to drive south to Santa Maria on Sunday, although this was outside of normal FDIC protocol. He couldn't check into the usual hotel at the airport without arousing suspicions regarding his early arrival, so he took Dale's suggestion and booked a room at his expense at the historic hotel located at the crossroads of Santa Maria.

Upon entering the hotel at 3:00 PM, he immediately appreciated what Dale had mentioned. The ornate architecture and appointments from early in the last century were impressive. The lobby was large, with seating areas on both sides, and a scent of well-seasoned wood. After checking into his room, he was pleased to see that the hotel had been upgraded with Internet service. He used his laptop to send an email to Sally McIntyre, one of the FDIC team members on the examination. He requested that she make an appointment with the Controller upon her arrival Monday. Matthew had three motives in this regard. First, Sally's making the appointment would attract far less attention and concern than if the Examiner in Charge made such. Second, he wanted a second FDIC employee present in the interview to corroborate any findings that might develop. And, finally, he had found throughout his career that having a woman present often softened the atmosphere, leading to more candid and thorough responses to questions.

After taking a shower, Matthew walked downstairs and asked if he could get some food in the hotel. The receptionist replied that the restaurant would not open until 6:00 PM, but that the bar served some delicious plates. Upon entering the bar, Matthew was immediately impressed with the wooden bar itself. It was evidently assembled from one of the nineteenth-century sailing ships that plied the California coast. The room contained just a handful of patrons. Matthew took a seat at the bar. He soon caught the eye of the bartender, a burly man with large sideburns, about 60 years old by Matthew's estimation.

"What can I get for you?"

"The receptionist mentioned that you have some tasty bar plates. What would you recommend?"

"Well, I may be biased, but I think we serve the best Santa Maria tri-tip in the valley."

"What's that?"

"A local specialty. It's a marinated meat with an outstanding flavor. Our dish accompanies the steak slices with a fresh-baked buttermilk biscuit and butter."

"You've convinced me. That sounds good. What should I drink with that?"

"My family is friends with the Cook family. They have a pinot noir that is grown on some of their premium acreage. Matches well with the tri-tip."

"That also sounds good. I'll take a glass of that."

The bartender, with not much to do, started a number of conversations with Matthew as he drank his wine and ate the sliced steak. Both items were excellent. The biscuit was soft, rich, and flavorful. As Matthew was finishing up, the gregarious bartender again approached.

"You seem like a good fellow. How would you like to join me

in a glass of French brandy, on the house?"

Still anxious about what tomorrow might bring, and not wanting to insult the bartender, Matthew agreed. The bartender placed two snifters on the counter, and then reached far down under the bar. He eventually emerged with a bottle of Armagnac, showing the label to Matthew.

"Ever had this before?"

"Can't say that I have."

"It's a family favorite, and also somewhat of a tradition."

He poured Matthew a regular serving, and then a much healthier one for himself.

"I don't believe I ever asked your name."

"Matthew."

"Matthew, a toast to another blessed Sunday in our Santa Maria Valley. To paraphrase a famous quote by George Bernard Shaw: *Those who are looking for paradise on Earth should come and see the Central Coast of California.*"

They clinked their glasses and each savored the Armagnac, from the initial aroma, to the entry taste, to the lingering finish. The bartender indulged in fairly rapid and sizable gulps.

"It sounds as if you're extremely well acquainted with the valley. I don't believe I got your name."

"Brendan Kehoe."

Chapter 70

Monday July 23, 2002
Santa Maria, California

Melvin was at his desk at 8:00 AM as usual. The two weeks away from the bank had not resulted in any changes to his daily pattern. At 9:00 AM, the phone rang.

"Hello. Melvin Needham speaking."

"Hello, this is Sally McIntyre. I'm a member of the on-site FDIC examination team. I'd like to make an appointment this morning to ask you some questions."

Before he could answer, Sally's memory flashed back about 15 years.

"Did you say Melvin Needham?"

"Yes."

"Dewey, it's me, Sally McIntyre. I sat behind you in geometry class in high school. I was the tall girl with the long red hair."

"Oh, yes, I remember you."

"Dewey, how have you been all these years?"

"Fine. I like my job and have everything well set up."

"I look forward to seeing you again. What time can we arrive at your office?"

"Would 10:00 AM work? I have a couple of things I need to do right now."

"That's fine. Matthew Trentino will be joining me. See, you

then, Dewey."

"Good-bye."

As Melvin hung up the phone, the pains of his high school years resurfaced. During the first semester of his freshman year, some smart-aleck jock senior had bestowed the nickname 'Dewey' upon him. It stuck like glue. Even the teachers referred to him as Dewey, apparently unaware that his given name was Melvin.

Sally emailed Matthew with the time of their appointment. They met a few minutes beforehand, when Matthew showed her the discrepancies in the payments associated with the IO Strip CMO. As Sally went to use the restroom, it dawned on Matthew that he had never seen the Controller's office during his trips to the Accounting Department the past two weeks. He called Angela on the internal extension.

"Angela Falcone speaking."

"This is Matthew from the FDIC."

"Good morning. How are you?"

"Just fine. By the way, were you the chef for those potato dough dumplings last week?"

"The dish is called *gnocchi*. Guilty as charged."

"Absolutely mouth-watering. I was lucky to snag one of the last scoops of each variety."

"I'm glad you enjoyed the food. Which *sugo* did you prefer?"

"*Sugo*?"

"Excuse me. Sauce. Did you prefer the green or the red?"

"Both were great. By the narrowest of margins, I'd vote for the green."

"Just like a northern Italian!"

While Matthew would have liked to continue the social conversation, he didn't want to be late for the appointment with the Controller.

"Angela, I have a question. Where is the Controller's office?"

"Oh, you want to see Melvin. His office is in the basement. Take the stairwell to the left of the elevators on the first floor. Don't turn on the lights."

"Thank you."

"Good-bye."

Sally returned and joined Matthew. He picked up the documentation he had prepared. They took the elevator down to the first-floor lobby, soon finding what was evidently the door to the basement. Matthew opened the door for Sally. Sally looked down a long and steep flight of stairs, illuminated by what must have been a 25-watt light bulb. At least there was a sturdy metal handrail. Sally walked ahead of Matthew down the steps. Upon reaching the bottom of the stairs, Sally could just barely make out a hallway in front of them, as the area was without illumination. She instinctively felt around for a light switch. Finding one, she flipped it. A bank of overhead fluorescent lights along what was now clearly a long corridor flickered on.

"Argh! The lights! The lights!" A blood-curdling scream echoed down the hallway.

Sally jumped backwards toward Matthew. He caught her; then quickly remembered the instructions from Angela. He let go of Sally and turned off the lights.

The words 'thank you' echoed down the hallway, followed by the appearance of a dim glow from the far end. Matthew led

Sally down the dark corridor, barely able to make out the electrical rooms, storage rooms, and janitor's closet along the way. They were better able to see as they approached the end of the hallway and the source of the modest illumination.

"Hello. I'm Melvin Needham, the bank's Controller. Please come into my office and have a seat."

Both Matthew and Sally were speechless. Melvin's office was illuminated by just the light from his computer screen and an incandescent bulb that appeared to match the one in the stairwell. The office was roughly square. One side of the square contained the door and Melvin's desk, facing the wall. The other three sides were completely populated with file cabinets of various shapes and sizes. Each file cabinet drawer was labeled with a laminated page of colored construction paper, with the contents of the drawer printed onto the sheets prior to the lamination process. There was a folding table, deployed, in the center of the office.

Melvin produced two folding chairs from behind one of the file cabinets and gestured for Matthew and Sally to use them. He then took his desk chair, turned it around, and sat down.

Still agog, Matthew quickly concluded that Melvin likely did not get many visitors.

"I apologize for screaming about the lights. The frequency of the fluorescent lights interacts with my retina to produce terrible migraines. I thought everyone in the bank knew that."

"We apologize, Dewey. Thank you for setting aside some time this morning to meet with us. We've identified a couple of items where we have some follow-up questions that we thought you could help us with," said Sally.

"Please call me Melvin. I am happy to help."

Matthew did not understand the Dewey reference, but

quickly moved on.

"Melvin, we noticed that the safekeeping bank processes two payments each month for the FNMA IO Strip CMO investment security owned by the bank. Here's the CUSIP."

Upon hearing the word 'CMO', Melvin stated, "Yes, just as with all of the bank's CMO investments. One payment for the interest and one for the principal. The bank began receiving the principal payments a while back now. The bank owns several securities that are similar."

Matthew paused. It didn't appear that Melvin understood the nature of an IO Strip CMO. He decided to probe a bit deeper.

"Are you sure that one of the payments attributed to the IO Strip CMO is not for another security owned by the bank, perhaps with the CUSIP having been entered incorrectly? Or, perhaps, that one of the payments actually belongs to another client at the safekeeping bank and has been mid-coded to Green Valley?"

"In response to your first question, I don't believe that is the case. All of the payments for the other investment securities match up perfectly each month. I make sure of that. Would you like me to show you the latest reconciliation from the orange file?"

Not sure of what to say, Matthew nodded in agreement.

Melvin walked over to the file cabinet with the orange colored, laminated label that read 'Investment Securities'. He pulled out a similarly orange colored file folder that was labeled 'June 2020' and opened it to an orange file label with the CUSIP of the IO Strip CMO. He handed the folder to Matthew. Matthew slid his chair closer to Sally, so that they could both review the documentation. Looking at the various pages, Melvin was clearly detailed in ensuring that the deposits to the safekeeping account exactly matched with the credits to the general ledger accounting system. Both Matthew and Sally thought to themselves that this was the most meticulous reconciliation they had ever seen.

Matthew decided to again ask about his second hypothesis. "Thank you for walking us through the orange files, Melvin. Quite impressive. Let me circle back to my earlier comment. Might one of the payments received for the IO Strip CMO actually belong to another client at the safekeeping bank, and perhaps has been miscoded to Green Valley?"

"I guess that could be possible, but highly unlikely. We've been receiving the two payments like clockwork each month for quite a while. If any of the money belonged to another bank, it would have been discovered long ago when the Controller at the other bank did his or her orange file work."

Matthew had one further thought. "Melvin, when the CPAs conducted their attestation audit for December 31, 2001, did they ask you any questions similar to those I presented to you this morning?"

"Not exactly. They never visited me in person. I did scan and email them some of the same documents I showed you."

"Melvin, thank you for your time this morning. We may have some other questions as we finish the examination process. Would you mind if we called you as we develop new questions? We're on a short timeline to complete the examination this week."

Melvin briefly showed a bit of disappointment. He did like getting some visitors on occasion, especially if the event allowed him to show off the organization of his accounting and recordkeeping system.

"Certainly. Please call anytime. I am at my desk from 8:00 AM to 5:00 PM daily. I eat lunch at noon."

With that, Matthew and Sally stood up and began the slow walk down the long, dark hallway, not wanting to bump into any of the pipes and conduits that lined the corridor. Once they arrived back at the Board Room, they simply stared at each other for a minute. Sally eventually spoke first.

"We can audit some more time periods, but I think it's apparent that everything running through Dewey is balanced to the penny and thoroughly documented."

"Agreed. By the way, why do you refer to him as Dewey?"

"That's what everyone called him in high school."

Matthew had a quizzical look on his face.

Sally noticed this and slowly enunciated each syllable, "Dewey Needham."

Matthew gave a small laugh and shook his head. This morning's events would need to be carefully edited if eventually incorporated into the examination report. He did not want to become legendary within the FDIC for the Dewey Needham story. Matthew thanked Sally for her assistance and returned to his laptop. He emailed David Morgan, inquiring about the likelihood of a payment for another bank's investment being sent to the wrong financial institution month after month. He then emailed his boss, Elaine Harmon, at the FDIC. The safekeeping bank account statement indicated that the second payment each month for the IO Strip CMO was received via wire from Bank of America. Given the size of Bank of America and its importance to the US economy, the FDIC maintained a permanent staff there. He briefly explained to Elaine that he was tracking some funds flows, and wondered if the FDIC staff could research details about the wires from Bank of America to Green Valley's account at the safekeeping bank. This was not an unusual request, as the various regulators often tracked funds flows in pursuit of identifying money laundering by criminals or nations adverse to US interests.

After sending the second email, Matthew got a cup of coffee and began checking in with each of his examination crew, aiming to keep the process on target for conclusion by Friday afternoon.

Chapter 71

Tuesday July 24, 2002
Santa Maria, California

As soon as Matthew awoke, he reached over and launched the email program on his laptop. Looking down the list, which included the usual broadcast emails to all FDIC employees, he found the return email from David Morgan. David replied that he had never seen a security payment being misdirected for more than one month. The electronic system was well designed, plus banks maintained a practice of reconciling payments to both their accruals and the information reported by the servicer for each security. Matthew was perplexed. Why would Bank of America be sending the extra money to Green Valley Community Bank every month? The cumulative amount was by now quite substantial.

After making himself an in-room coffee, he continued scrolling through the emails. Just then, one arrived from Elaine Harmon. Matthew quickly opened it. The FDIC on-site team at Bank of America identified Security Investment LLC as the originator of the extra monthly wires to the safekeeping bank. Matthew was now even more confused. That name sounds like an investment banking firm that could very well be servicing a security like the IO Strip CMO. Could that firm have continued to err for so many months?

Matthew quickly dressed and drove over to Green Valley's headquarters. Upon arriving in the Board Room, he gestured for Sally to join him.

"Sally, can you run a comprehensive set of inquiries on a firm named Security Investment LLC? All databases the FDIC has access to. Please bring me a summary of the information you find as soon as possible. I'm looking for their location, contact information, ownership, line of business, etc."

"Will do."

About ninety minutes later, Sally approached Matthew.

"I'm afraid not much to report. The California Secretary of State information shows the address is a PO Box in Santa Barbara. That database also shows that the LLC has a sole member, or owner, The Fesler Trust. I could not find a website for the LLC. There is no listing in the Santa Barbara phone book. We could initiate records requests from the California Franchise Tax Board and the IRS."

"The tax agencies take forever to respond. Let's hold off on that. Thank you for your help. Let me think about this for a while."

Matthew began to feel highly stressed. The examination was scheduled to conclude in three days. He had a lot of work to do on all of the many other aspects of the examination, and this pursuit of the unusual information associated with the IO Strip CMO was burning a lot of his time. After thinking some more, he sent a follow-up email to Elaine asking if the FDIC team at Bank of America could forward any information on the Security Investment LLC checking account and regarding The Fesler Trust. He then returned to his other duties.

Just after lunch, a return email arrived from Elaine. Matthew knew that she had pull as one of the longest serving FDIC employees, but this turnaround was still impressive. The return email included copies of the Bank of America checking account statements for Security Investment LLC for the past two years. Elaine said that there was no information at Bank of America available on The Fesler Trust. Matthew again called Sally over.

"Can you start a spreadsheet comparing the outgoing wires from the Security Investment LLC checking account to the extra payments received by the safekeeping bank? Can you then analyze what deposits to the checking account funded the outgoing wires? Finally, can you run a comprehensive database search on The Fesler Trust?"

"Will do."

At 4:30 PM, Sally approached Matthew with her findings.

"First of all, no information whatsoever regarding The Fesler Trust."

Matthew shrugged his shoulders and exhaled loudly.

"Second, no question that the source of the extra IO Strip CMO payments into the safekeeping bank is the Security Investment LLC checking account at Bank of America. The figures match-up exactly."

"I thought that might be the case. Good information."

"Finally, the funds inflows into the Security Investment LLC checking account vary each month, but do roughly approximate the outgoing wires. The checking account receives regular cash deposits, internal transfers from other Bank of America accounts, plus periodic incoming wires. There is no paper trail of deposited checks."

Matthew clenched his fists in angst. This matter was like peeling an onion. Every time he pulled back one layer, there was another one waiting for him! He again thanked Sally and politely dismissed her. What should he do next? This matter was risking a delay in the completion of the examination, which was heavily frowned upon by the FDIC. If he continued to send more and more emails to Elaine, she would eventually question whether he knew what he was doing. It was widely known within the agency that it was not wise to disappoint

Elaine. Thus far, all he had discovered were extra payments coming into the bank – not exactly headline news.

As Matthew watched the FDIC team pack things up for the day, he made a rash decision. Peeling the onion one layer at a time was going to take far too long. He had to find a shortcut. He picked up the phone and dialed Angela's internal extension.

"Angela Falcone speaking."

"Hello, it's Matthew from the FDIC. I don't want to come across as improper in any way, but might you be available to join me for a drink this evening? I have some questions about the bank that would be best asked outside the office."

While Angela was surprised at the request given the typical regulator protocols, she had also prepared herself for such an opportunity. Last weekend, she sorted through her wardrobe and selected all of the best outfits for wearing during the final scheduled week of the examination. Her aim was to at least open up the possibility of continued communication with Matthew after the examination concluded.

"I can meet you in the ground floor lobby in about ten minutes."

"Sounds good."

Angela was waiting for Matthew as he emerged from the elevator. He again noticed her long, soft black hair, flowing over an indigo suit jacket, which in turn partially covered an azure blouse.

"Angela, thank you again for meeting me on short notice."

"No problem at all."

"Shall we walk down to the historic hotel?

"Good suggestion. They serve great bar food."

The bar was thinly populated at 5:15 PM. Matthew guided Angela to a table near the end of the long wooden bar, trying to avoid anyone's potential notice.

"Thank you again for agreeing to meet with me offsite. Our examination team has bumped into a couple of curiosities. I need the knowledge of someone familiar with the bank to assist us."

Angela nodded, indicating her understanding.

"I need to ask you up front if you are comfortable keeping this conversation absolutely confidential, including from your superiors at the bank."

Angela's conscience rattled. She did not like having to keep secrets from her superiors. However, she had been regularly assisting Matthew for a couple of weeks now. It would be awkward to suddenly change her behavior. Plus, the examination was scheduled to end in just a few days, so everything would soon be revealed to the bank's executive team and Board of Directors. In addition, Angela experienced a flashback to early in her professional career.

"While that's not how we usually operate at Green Valley, I can appreciate the FDIC's needing to have confidential conversations in conjunction with an examination. You have my word."

Angela then paused, with her body language clearly indicating that she wished to speak further.

"Your last question is bringing up a bit of déjà vu for me. While I was working as a consultant for one of the big eight accounting firms, I was assigned to a team which eventually uncovered a substantial embezzlement engineered by a small group of employees. The company ultimately declared bankruptcy and was liquidated, with the loss of hundreds of jobs, not to mention the impacts upon the suppliers and customers. If only our consulting team had been brought in a year or so earlier, the company might have been saved."

"I assure you that, while we have identified a number of unusual transactions, we have no evidence of embezzlement. Are you sure you're okay with helping us further?"

After a short pause, Angela replied, "Yes."

"Thank you. My first question is, have you ever heard of Security Investment LLC?"

Angela thought long and hard before responding, "I don't believe so. That doesn't ring a bell, neither in my experience at the bank nor living in the area."

As Angela was finishing her sentence, Brendan Kehoe approached the table. The bar hostess did not come on duty until 6:00 PM.

"What can I get you folks?"

Angela replied, "I'd like a glass of the local chardonnay produced from the grapes grown in the Fesler Ranch vineyard. That's one of my favorites."

Matthew jumped to attention upon hearing this, but managed to keep quiet for the moment.

Brendan replied, "An excellent choice. That's one of our valley's premier estate white wines. Say, I've seen you in here before. I never forget a face as pretty as yours. My name is Brendan Kehoe, one of the proprietors of the hotel."

Angela smiled and slightly blushed. Matthew took a slight offense at not being recognized despite having dined in the bar just a few days ago. He quickly calmed himself, acknowledging that he would also remember Angela far more readily than the stout bartender.

"And what will you have?"

Matthew replied, "Make it a second glass of that chardonnay. And please bring us the cheeseboard plate to share."

"I'll be right back."

Matthew turned his focus back to Angela, staring somewhat too intently into her dark brown eyes.

"Angela, you mentioned the Fesler Ranch. Please tell me more about the name Fesler."

Angela pondered for a few moments, then said "Let me think for a minute." Afterwards, she continued, "I don't know a great deal. The Fesler family was one of the original founding families in the valley in the second half of the 19th century. There is a Fesler Avenue in town, and a small Fesler railroad museum at the old train depot. I only know of the Fesler Ranch because of the labeling on the chardonnay."

Brendan arrived with their wine and food just as Angela was finishing her sentence. He joined the conversation without invitation.

"We had a regular customer with the last name of Fesler, must have been about twenty-five years ago. Nice fellow. Always had money in his pocket, tipped well, and dropped in to the bar three or four times a week."

"Do you know any Fesler family members in town today?" asked Matthew.

"No. The fellow I mentioned was the last Fesler I can remember. Now that I think some more, I believe there was a Fesler in the class ahead of me in high school, but that was over forty years ago."

"So, you've lived your whole life in the valley?" inquired Matthew.

"Proudly. The Kehoe family was one of the original founders of Green Valley Community Bank just after the turn of the twentieth century. My family helped build this town, along with several others including the Phillips' and the Huffington's."

Matthew's ears again perked up at this comment. He decided to first speak some more with Angela before asking additional questions of Brendan. After Brendan returned to the bar, Matthew turned to Angela.

"Is the Huffington family that the bartender referred to the same one as the bank's President?"

"Yes. I've heard Mr. Huffington mention several times over the years that his great-grandfather was one of the bank's original founders. I believe that's one reason he's been putting so much planning into the 100th anniversary celebration later this year."

They both tasted the chardonnay, which was superb, with a smooth entrance and a rich finish. After allowing Angela to take a few bites of the cheese and crackers, he continued his line of questioning.

"Who do you think would be the most knowledgeable person regarding the Fesler family?"

"I'm not really sure. I know from other employees that George Anderson, the Chairman of the Board, is also a descendant of one of the valley's founding families. In fact, I think I heard that his legal name is George Anderson the fourth. Mr. Anderson might be able to provide you with more information regarding the Fesler family."

"Thank you. I'll give him a call first thing tomorrow morning."

They both sipped some more of the chardonnay, after which

Matthew added, “Angela, I may need to ask you over the next several days to perform some internal research for me at the bank. I don’t want to needlessly raise alarms or suspicions, but there are some accounts we need to examine more closely.”

Angela was familiar with the federal agencies’ focus on money laundering, or the effort to disguise the source of illegal funds by integrating the money into legitimate accounts in the financial system.

“I understand.”

“Thank you.”

At this point, Matthew relaxed. He had a lead for The Fesler Trust, the owner of Security Investment LLC, the source of the extra payments into the bank’s safekeeping account. He also had a bright (and attractive) insider to assist his investigation. Satisfied with his professional efforts for the evening, he enjoyed accompanying the second half of his glass of chardonnay with a pleasant and social conversation with Angela.

As they were about to depart the hotel bar, Matthew deviated from his usual considered behavior and impulsively asked, “Angela, I don’t want to sound inappropriate in any way. I was wondering if you might think about whether we might stay in touch following the conclusion of the examination.”

Angela’s heart skipped a beat. She then gathered in her emotions and allowed her intellect to take over. The examination was still in process, and she was performing confidential research for the Examiner in Charge. She needed to avoid creating an issue for herself and also for the bank. She also wanted to sidestep indirectly generating a problem for Matthew.

She replied, with a bit of a mischievous smile, “I’ll analyze that possibility and get back to you.”

Chapter 72

Wednesday July 25, 2002
Santa Maria, California

At 8:00 AM, Matthew called George Anderson IV from one of the offices near the Board Room. He had obtained Mr. Anderson's phone number from the bank's corporate secretary.

"Good morning. This is George Anderson."

"Mr. Anderson, this is Matthew Trentino, the FDIC's Examiner in Charge at Green Valley Community Bank."

"Oh, yes. I have on my calendar to attend the closing meeting this Friday afternoon."

"I'm actually calling about something else. I was hoping that you might be of assistance."

"Glad to."

"Are you aware of an entity named The Fesler Trust?"

"Yes. I'm quite familiar with that entity."

"How so?"

"I'm the General Partner of the Blue Pacific Ventures partnership. The Fesler Trust is one of the primary limited partners within that partnership, owning 22.5% of that entity."

"When was The Fesler Trust established?"

"I'm not certain off the top of my head. Something like seventy years ago. Daniel Fesler was one of the founders of Blue Pacific Ventures, along with my great-grandfather. Daniel was also a member of one of the founding families of our valley, circa 1860's or 1870's. I believe Daniel established the trust to hold his interest in the partnership upon his passing, for the benefit of his heirs."

"That is excellent information. Do you know who the beneficiaries of the trust are?"

"Not precisely. Daniel had, I think, seven children. Those seven children in turn had more progeny. The trust's stake in the partnership has never changed. The partnership distributions to the trust must be being shared across multiple dozens of individuals by now."

"Much appreciated. Do you know of any Fesler heirs currently living in the area?"

"I can't remember meeting a Fesler for decades now. So, none that I am aware of."

"Might I inquire about the magnitude of the partnership distributions to the trust?"

"The distributions vary from year to year based upon the cash flow from the multiple business interests owned by the partnership. That said, The Fesler Trust has been receiving annual distributions north of seven figures for years now. The partnership has been quite successful."

"Thank you."

As Matthew was about to conclude the call, he thought of one additional question.

"I do have just one more question."

"Glad to oblige. I'm also a shareholder in the bank. I'm happy to do anything I can to benefit the bank."

"Do you know who the current trustee is or trustees are for The Fesler Trust?"

"Members of the Huffington family have served as trustee for decades. The current trustee is Dale Huffington, whom you've undoubtedly spoken with at the bank over the past couple of weeks."

"Yes. Dale's been most gracious and helpful to the FDIC team. I won't take any more of your time, Mr. Anderson. Thank you again."

Upon hanging up the phone, Matthew thought to himself, finally, I've peeled away enough layers to approach the core of the onion. The trustee of The Fesler Trust is the President of the bank. The Fesler Trust owns Security Investment LLC. Security Investment LLC has been sending extra payments into the bank. But why? Matthew kept thinking about all of the training he had received to identify funds being withdrawn improperly from a financial institution. He had never attended a class regarding the contribution of excess funds *into* a bank. There was no direct evidence that the President knew anything about the extra payments. Matthew knew that he was in no position to make any accusations. He also recognized that he needed to tread cautiously because the valley was such an incredibly closely knit community. My gosh, even the local bartender was tied in to the dominant families. He had to be careful not to tip his hand, or risk potential evidence being destroyed.

After further thought, he decided that it was time to have a live conversation with Elaine Harmon. Elaine was somewhat famous within the agency for her work during the savings and loan crisis of the 1980's and 1990's, having been directly responsible for sleuthing out the malfeasance of multiple high-ranking thrift officials. He made the call, carefully and systematically presenting Elaine with all of the information he had collected to date. After he had finished, Elaine took control of the conversation.

"Matthew, I concur that what you have discovered warrants further investigation. Let me think through the logical next steps."

After a couple of minutes, Elaine presented her plan.

"First, I'm going to contact our on-site team at Bank of America and ask them to research all incoming deposits to the Security Investment LLC checking account and to search for any accounts in the names of any of the bank senior officers. Second, you are going to announce tomorrow the extension of the examination for one more week. Simply explain that the FDIC team has not yet been able to complete reviewing all of the information and drafting the required reports. Third, I am going to send you one of our examiners who specializes in investigation of potential improper or criminal behavior. He will be on site with you on Monday. Fourth, you are going to use your trusted inside source to generate a couple of analyses. Based upon my prior experience, have her look at all of the previously dormant deposit accounts that were not escheated to the State. Also have her produce an analysis of all of the new vendors added to the bank's accounts payable system over the past three years, plus develop a report comparing payments made to vendors in each of 2000, 2001, and 2002 year-to-date. Fifth, have a member of your examination team audit all of the outgoing wire transfers over the past two years. We are looking for wire transfers to either Security Investment LLC, The Fesler Trust, or to any bank senior officer. Did you get all that?"

"Yes. I was furiously taking notes as you were speaking."

"One more idea. Do we know where The Fesler Trust banks?"

"Not at this time."

"Have one of the examination staff run an audit within Green Valley to see if there are any accounts with Fesler somewhere in the title."

"Got it."

"Finally, you need to stay calm and approach the additional investigation simply as part of the normal examination process. Do not keep overly early or late hours at the bank. We want to avoid the destruction of evidence, fleeing by any guilty parties, and, heaven forbid, violent action by anyone associated with this situation."

"All understood. Thank you for the support, Elaine. I'll keep you well informed."

"That's what I'm here for."

"Good-bye."

As soon as he hung up, Matthew began drafting an email to both the FDIC staff and the bank's senior management regarding the extension of the examination for one more week. Once that was sent, he called in Sally to request that she commence the detailed audit work. Since it was now almost noon, Matthew called Angela on the internal extension and asked if she would be available for lunch. They again met in the lobby of the headquarters building and quickly exited.

"Do you know a nearby place where we can get a decent sandwich and likely not be observed by other bank staff?"

"Yes. Tony's Bar is a dive. Most bank employees would not want to be seen going into a bar at lunchtime. It's a small town."

"I'm appreciating that more and more."

"The good news is that Tony imports his *prosciutto* directly from Parma, Italy. Similar for the *Bel Paese* cheese. He gets his rolls from the only Italian bakery in town."

Matthew was again impressed with Angela's culinary knowledge. It wasn't long until they sat down at a less than spotless table at the rear of Tony's Bar. He had been so preoccupied with the pending investigation that he had, until now, failed to notice that she was again smartly, but professionally, dressed in a well-tailored, burgundy skirt and matching jacket with a fuchsia blouse and matching semi-precious stone earrings. He thought to himself: here's a very attractive woman who knows how to dress well, could compete with the chefs in many of the San Francisco restaurants that he had frequented over the years, and who is quite intelligent. How can she still be available?

After they each ordered the same *prosciutto* and *formaggio panini* along with a glass of iced tea, Matthew conveyed the analyses he wanted Angela to generate on a confidential basis.

"I know where to gather the information for both of those studies. I should be able to have them to you by Friday afternoon."

After taking another bite of the sandwich, enhanced by the use of extra virgin olive oil rather than mayonnaise, Angela said, "You know, I brought up the increase in the bank's operating costs a while back to Joel. The bank's ratio of non-interest expense to average total assets has risen slightly over the past couple of years, in contrast to the gradual decrease reported by our peer group."

"And what response did you receive?"

"Now that I think about it some more, just a generic comment about preparing for the celebration of the bank's 100th anniversary later this year."

"And you didn't press further for a more detailed answer?"

"Well, no, for two reasons. First, I was relatively new to the organization and did not want to ruffle any feathers before better understanding the operational and political landscape."

“Not unusual for a new employee. And second?”

“To be polite, let me just say that Joel is not an Einstein. I soon learned that it wasn’t productive to push him for analysis or insight beyond his capability. Doing so would only create stress, which Joel would react to by shutting down.”

“I see. I haven’t had that much interface yet with Joel. I’ll have more opportunity in that regard next week.”

After finishing their sandwiches and while waiting for the check, Angela decided that she needed to provide some indirect positive feedback to Matthew in response to his recent inquiry of a personal nature. She asked, “Do you live in San Francisco?”

“Yes, in the Marina District.”

“Do you like living there?”

“Quite a bit. I enjoy the range of cultural and entertainment events in the city, plus of course the restaurants. However, I must admit, I’ve eaten at quite a few that don’t come close to your culinary expertise.”

Angela managed to contain her glee at this comment, simply flashing a broad smile to Matthew. They continued their social conversation on the walk back to the bank. They spaced their entrance to the headquarters building and each took a separate elevator.

Upon arriving back in the Board Room, Matthew focused his attention on the team’s completing the ‘regular’ parts of the regulatory examinations. Whatever the eventual findings associated with the suspicious activity, the usual reports would still need to be timely produced.

At 6:30 PM that evening, Dale pulled into the parking lot for the Paso Robles Inn. He had whispered to Joel that they needed to meet tonight soon after Dale received the email regarding the extra week of on-site presence by the FDIC team. Upon entering the bar, he saw Joel waiting at a table in the rear.

"I took the initiative of ordering us gin and tonics. I hope that was okay."

"That's fine, Joel. I assume you saw the email regarding the extended examination time by the FDIC?"

"I did. What do you think?"

The waitress arrived with their drinks. After taking a large swallow, Dale answered.

"In my experience, the extension is unusual. It's also unusual how little time the Examiner in Charge has spent with the senior officers over the past three weeks. I'm afraid the regulators may have discovered some aspect of our coverup plan, or perhaps the loss on the security, or both."

Joel's eyes widened as his heart rate increased.

"What should we do?"

"Let's not jump to conclusions and in so doing incriminate ourselves. On the other hand, let's assume that they've identified one or more of our twelve steps. I recommend that upon arriving home tonight, we scour our residences for any documents even remotely associated with the coverup and shred or burn such. We should also audit our computers and cell phones for any content that could possibly be related and erase it."

"I've been really careful, but it can't hurt to conduct a comprehensive audit and scrubbing."

"In addition, we immediately shut down all activity related to the plan. We'll have a decision to make next month regarding the usual payment from Security Investment LLC. If we don't transmit that payment, Melvin will notice that it is missing and start asking questions. We'll need to determine whether it is riskier to send or not to send that payment."

"Gotcha."

"One more key point, Joel. If the examiners ask you a question that might divulge some part of our plan, simply state that you can't remember offhand and will need to think about it, or that you need some time to research the answer. Then, signal me and we'll have a private conversation."

"I understand. Just talking about this between us is stressful."

"We should know what the examiners are up to soon enough. It would be highly irregular to extend the onsite time by more than one week. We should have an answer within ten days. We just need to stay strong and relatively silent until then."

With that, the bankers gulped down the last of their drinks, left cash on the table for the check, and drove to their homes to commence information scrubbing.

Chapter 73

Friday July 27, 2002
Santa Maria, California

Matthew took the unusual step of supplementing his usual cup of coffee in his hotel room with a second cup of coffee at the bank this morning. He didn't sleep well last night. The pressure of being the Examiner in Charge of two concurrent regulatory examinations and now a potential fraud investigation was taking its toll on him. He hadn't eaten much yesterday, his stomach tied in knots while awaiting the results of the various inquiries. As he poured his coffee in the lunch room, he noticed a plate of fresh pastry, evidently some type of fried doughnut stuffed with a yellow crème and covered in powdered sugar. Recognizing that he needed more than just coffee as sustenance, he took one of the pastries back to his workstation. After opening his email application, he took a bite. His mouth was overwhelmed with the richness and density of the custard-type filling augmented by the flavor of the fresh dough and the sweetness of the powdered sugar. Coming back to his senses, he concluded that this could only be the work of Angela and that one of these pastries must equate to an entire day's worth of calories. He made a mental note to thank Angela when the opportunity presented itself.

Thus fortified, Matthew turned his attention to his inbox. He quickly identified an email from Elaine Harmon. He opened it and read the content. James Robinson, the FDIC's investigative specialist, would arrive in town Sunday afternoon, staying at the usual hotel by the airport. Matthew was to then meet him and bring him fully up to date. Elaine wanted the two of them to have a plan prepared for implementation starting first thing on Monday morning. Matthew typed up a return email to Elaine, confirming receipt and his understanding of her instructions. Just after he hit 'send', Sally McIntyre approached.

"Good morning, Sally. How are you?"

"I stayed late last night auditing two years of records for outgoing wire transfers. I did not identify any going to The Fesler Trust. Likewise, there were no outgoing wires to accounts of the senior officers. However, I did find five outgoing wires to the account of Security Investment LLC at Bank of America. All five of these wires were requested by different bank customers, and about two to three months apart. The smallest of these five wires was for about $75 thousand and the largest was for about $125 thousand."

"Interesting. Did you notice any other pattern in the five wires?"

"Only that they were all submitted by Linda Morris."

"The President's executive assistant."

"Correct. There could of course be any number of reasons why the wires could be perfectly legitimate. We still don't know what type of business Security Investment LLC conducts. If it is some type of investment firm, the bank clients could be purchasing mutual funds or bonds or similar. In a small town like this, it wouldn't be out of character for customers to speak with the President about withdrawing money to make an investment."

"Thank you for the good research. If you'll provide me with a copy of each of the five wire request forms, I'll take it from here."

"Will do."

After Sally provided the documents and left, Matthew dialed

the internal extension for Angela.

"Angela Falcone speaking."

"Good morning. It's Matthew. Before I ask you some banking questions, were those pastries in the lunch room of your doing?"

"I'll admit to that. I figured everyone could use some extra energy at the end of the week."

"What are those called? I've never had one before."

"They go by different names in various regions of Italy. The most common names are *bombolone* or *bomba* for short."

"Quite apropos. I won't need to eat anything else today. Delicious, and filling."

"Glad you liked it."

"Can I give you five client names and ask you to research them for any commonality?"

"Certainly, and confidentially as usual?"

"Yes."

Matthew then gave Angela the first and last names of each of the customers associated with the outgoing wire transfers to Security Investment LLC.

"Call me if you discover anything and we'll speak offsite."

"Okay."

As he hung up the phone, Matthew used his laptop to pull up the checking account statements for Security Investment LLC which he had earlier received from Elaine. He quickly identified the deposits from the five wire transfers from Green Valley. They matched perfectly with the wire request forms that Sally had furnished.

Sally had previously roughly matched up the aggregate inflows into the Security Investment LLC checking account with the extra payments arriving in the safekeeping account for Green Valley. The next layer of the onion was to track downstream the other deposits into the Security Investment LLC checking account. There were multiple cash deposits each month, which would likely be of limited investigative value. Anyone could deposit cash to any bank account, with minimal records retained so long as the cash deposits were not that large. There were never any check deposits. Matthew did notice a pattern of internal transfers from two other Bank of America accounts. He also observed a recent deposit for $357,500 via internal transfer from yet another Bank of America account. He emailed those three account numbers back to Elaine and requested research regarding ownership.

Thinking through all of the information collected to date, Matthew realized that whatever was going on, the process appeared to have started just over a year ago. That was about a year after the bank purchased the IO Strip CMO based upon the acquisition date in Melvin's orange security file.

Matthew put aside the investigative work to team with his fellow regulators to complete the normal aspects of the examination process. He also needed to carefully prepare his remarks for the usual 3:00 PM end of week status meeting with the bank's senior officers. At 4:45 PM, as the FDIC team was packing up for the weekend, another email arrived from Elaine. The two Bank of America accounts that regularly transferred funds into the Security Investment LLC checking account were titled in the names of Central Coast Maintenance LLC, and Central Coast Supply LLC. According to Elaine's email, both of those entities were single member LLCs owned by Security Investment LLC. Matthew rested his face in his hands. Where did this daisy-chain end? This likely wasn't the work of a single individual. What team of people conspired to establish such an elaborate scheme? And to what purpose? The only objective identified to date was to transfer extra money *into* the bank. After pondering the situation, Matthew sent a reply email to Elaine requesting account statements for Central Coast Maintenance LLC, Central Coast Supply LLC, and the account at Bank of America that had recently made the large transfer into the checking account of Security Investment LLC.

As Matthew finished the latest email to Elaine, a text message arrived from Angela. 'Can you meet me in Melvin's office tomorrow at 9:00 AM and bring your laptop?'

Matthew replied affirmatively. He already needed to be in town on Sunday for meeting Mr. Robinson. He might as well spend the weekend. He called the hotel by the airport and extended his stay.

Chapter 74

Saturday July 28, 2002
Santa Maria, California

At just before 9:00 AM, Matthew opened the door to the stairwell that descended into the basement of the headquarters building. Holding the handrail, he carefully walked down the stairs illuminated by the 25-watt lightbulb. However, unlike his first visit to this part of the building, the fluorescent lights down the long hallway were on. Arriving at Melvin's office, he saw Angela sitting behind a table at the center of the room. Multiple documents were arrayed on the table.

"Good morning, Matthew."

"Good morning. Why are we meeting here?"

"Melvin never works on weekends. Can you think of another place in the building where we would be less likely to be observed?"

"Excellent point."

Lifting his eyes from the table and documents, Matthew noticed that Angela was smartly attired, as usual. Not in a suit, but in a light blue, patterned A-line skirt that had side splits to the knee, complemented by a powder blue blouse and matching blue topaz earrings. Her long black hair was held back by a black hairband. Angela spoke several words before Matthew focused his attention on what she was saying.

"...five accounts appear to have two commonalities besides having transferred funds to Security Investment LLC in the past year. The first factor is that all of the bank accounts are in the name of women in excess of 85 years of age. The second factor is that all of the bank accounts were on the dormant account report and were scheduled to be escheated to the state within a month following the outgoing transfers."

Matthew inhaled and looked up at the ceiling. Financial institutions were required to close accounts with an extended period of inactivity, and, following multiple prior unsuccessful contact attempts by the bank, send, or escheat, the funds to the state. This was a source of cash flow for the state. The account holders could always contact the state and the funds would be returned, but this did not happen frequently. Escheated accounts were typically associated with people who relocated and forgot about the accounts, customers who died without leaving information for heirs, or clients who suffered from serious medical conditions such as dementia.

Matthew talked out loud, "So, about $535 thousand that would have been sent to the state was instead redirected to Security Investment LLC. The bank had been unable to contact the customers for months, and the accounts had no deposit or withdrawal activity, so the customers would likely not miss the funds. At the same time, the state never knew what funds were going to be escheated, so there would be no questions from that source."

"That sounds logical."

Matthew then opened his laptop and showed the scans of the five outgoing wire requests to Angela. "Do you see anything unusual in these wire request forms?"

"Not unusual per se, but I see that Linda Morris initiated all five of them. It would not be unusual for Linda to help clients complete those forms. It does strike me as an amazing coincidence that she was involved in all five of these."

Matthew nodded his agreement.

Angela then continued, "I completed the vendor analyses you requested. The reports are on the table. The two vendors with the largest percentage increase in expenses in 2001 were Central Coast Maintenance LLC, and Central Coast Supply LLC, essentially increasing from zero in 2000 to between $5 thousand and $10 thousand per month each from about mid-2001 through to last month."

Matthew looked like a deer in the headlights. Those were the two LLCs owned by Security Investment LLC and that were regular transferors of funds into that entity.

"Did you happen to make copies of their vendor files?"

"Yes. Those documents are also on the table. The vendor approval and set-up look normal, as do the invoices. Central Coast Maintenance LLC has been charging the bank for parking lot and window cleaning. Central Coast Supply LLC has been charging the bank for a variety of typical office supplies, from toner to copy paper."

"Who approved the invoices?"

"In every case, Joel Johnson."

Matthew took a deep breath, stood up, and walked around the office, being careful not to impact any of the color-coded file cabinet labels.

Angela observed this behavior and said, "It's not unusual for the Chief Financial Officer to approve vendor invoices."

"I understand."

He did not want to explain the other aspects of his findings to Angela at this time.

"Let me collect all of the copies you have made and further review this information tonight. You can do one more thing for me, if you might. Check the signatures on the wire request forms with the account signature cards maintained at the bank. I want to ensure the funds transfers were approved by the account holders."

"No problem. I can access the signature cards on Monday and let you know."

"Angela, thank you again for all of the assistance."

"My pleasure."

After they carefully ensured that Melvin's office was returned to its prior physical status, they separately departed the headquarters building. As he drove back to the airport hotel, Matthew recapped the latest findings to himself. Two new vendors had commenced doing business with the bank at about the same time all of the unusual financial activity started. The bank paid the vendors' invoices by sending funds via the Automated Clearinghouse or ACH system to the vendor checking accounts at Bank of America. Those same funds were then transferred to the checking account of Security Investment LLC. Security Investment LLC then wired the funds into the safekeeping account for the benefit of the bank. In essence, the bank's own funds were making a long round trip. But why? Once back at his hotel room, he emailed Sally to investigate all databases for Central Coast Maintenance LLC and Central Coast Supply LLC.

Chapter 75

Monday July 30, 2002
Santa Maria, California

Matthew and James Robinson, the FDIC Investigator, had spent much of Sunday evening at the airport hotel discussing the various findings to date and planning their course of action for the coming week. They decided to start at the bottom of the organization and initially focus on the most straightforward of the findings. Later in the week, they could investigate the relatively cloudy matters. They agreed to aim for spending Wednesday and Thursday interviewing the senior officers. On Monday afternoon, Matthew would announce a typical end of examination exit meeting for Friday afternoon. Elaine Harmon would drive down from San Francisco to attend. The bank's Board of Directors would also be invited.

Matthew and James arrived at the bank at 8:00 AM. They selected the most remote office on the Board Room floor for the investigation interviews. They brought in three chairs, a pitcher of water, and several glasses. The various documents collected to date were organized into a credenza at the rear of the office. Matthew ensured that the remainder of the FDIC staff was organized to complete the various segments of the standard regulatory examinations. At 9:00 AM, he called Angela on the internal extension.

"Angela Falcone speaking."

"Good morning, Angela. Might you have had a chance to verify the signatures on the five outgoing wire request forms we discussed?"

"Yes. They all matched almost perfectly with the original account signature cards, allowing for some slight variations in signatures from time to time."

"Thank you. I'll call you again later today."

"Good-bye."

Matthew and James discussed the latest information. The signatures on the outgoing wire request forms submitted by Linda Morris to send money to Security Investment LLC were genuine. Why would five bank clients initiate such funds transfers? They decided to first interview Linda before taking any other action in this regard.

Matthew called Linda Morris on the internal extension.

"Good morning. This is Linda."

"Hello Linda. This is Matthew Trentino with the FDIC. There's something we'd like you to help us with. Might you come up to the Board Room floor to assist us, say, in about forty-five minutes, around 10:00 AM?"

"Certainly. I'll see you then."

Linda immediately entered Dale's office and signaled him, interrupting a phone conversation. Dale quickly ended the call. He immediately noticed the stress evident in Linda's face. They had worked so closely together for so many years that he could easily read her body language.

"Linda, what's wrong?"

"The FDIC just called me. They want to see me upstairs in a half hour."

"Okay. Did they say why?"

"Only that they wanted my help with something. Mr. Trentino was really vague."

Dale quickly thought through the situation. The meeting request could be about something trivial. On the other hand, the FDIC could intend to drill Linda in their efforts to discover more about the IO Strip CMO or the coverup plan. In either case, Dale needed Linda to calm down. If she behaved overly emotionally, or, heaven forbid, hysterically, that could only adversely impact him and Joel.

"Linda, I know you get nervous around government officials. That's easy to do, especially with the ones that utilize their positions and the power of their agencies to intimidate others and pump up their egos. We've both seen a number of officials with that profile over the years. However, the on-site FDIC staff has been nothing but professional. Maybe they want to speak with you about something as simple as arranging a late night, working dinner for their team."

"I hear what you're saying. I should be calmer, but you know that it's difficult for me. I keep having flashbacks to that mean IRS auditor who questioned our deduction of Carl's medical expenses. The auditor said he didn't believe that treating cancer could cost that much. The way he looked at Carl, implying that he wasn't worth the expense..."

Linda started to cry. Dale put his arm around her and gave her his handkerchief. After a few minutes, Linda composed herself. Dale used this moment to try to provide her with the best reassurance he could.

"Linda, you're a great bank employee and a good person. You have nothing to worry about. Just be as pleasant and helpful as you always are. If they ask you something you're not sure about, explain that to them. It's perfectly okay to say that you don't know or that you'll need to look something up. I'll be glad to help you with anything. I won't leave the office and will be here waiting for you afterwards."

"Thank you, Dale. You're so good to me."

Dale's offer of assistance was both genuine and strategic. By helping Linda with whatever follow-up might be required, he would gain insight into the knowledge and direction of the FDIC team.

Linda departed for the elevator bank at the appropriate hour. While she had dried her tears and freshened her make-up to improve her appearance, her legs felt weak and her pulse rate was elevated. Matthew met Linda at the elevator at 10:00 AM. He explained that he would like to introduce her to a new member of the examination team. Matthew walked with her to the office where James waited, seated behind the desk with his laptop open.

"This is James Robinson from our San Francisco office."

"Pleased to meet you," said Linda.

Linda quickly concluded that the matter to be discussed was not trivial. She knew that conversations with two government officials at the same time were almost always about important topics.

"Linda, please have a seat."

James gestured to an inside seat in front of the desk, so that Matthew could sit in the outside seat. This positioning subtly communicated that Linda was surrounded, without an avenue to exit.

As an experienced investigator, James immediately began to analyze Linda. Likely in her early sixties, about forty pounds overweight, and with either a slight case of asthma or a deviated septum based upon the pattern and sound of her breathing. She was already a bit flush from some combination of the walk from her office and her anxiety about what was occurring.

"Before we start, it's important that I remind you to answer our questions truthfully and completely," advised James.

"Of course. I understand," responded Linda.

"I'd like to first ask you a few questions about some unusual transactions involving you and Dale Huffington."

Linda turned white. Her pulse rate soared. She began to sweat.

"Okay," mumbled Linda.

"Linda, does Dale have you initiate and / or conduct various transactions for him or under his direction at the bank?"

Linda began to hyperventilate. She had never been in any type of trouble before. Her phobia regarding government officials kicked into high gear. She began to panic, sweat forming on her forehead.

She blurted out, "I know about the red checkbook, the condo, and the affairs. Yes, I made bank deposits and paid the bills."

Now experiencing shortness of breath and dizziness, Linda gasped for air, grabbed her chest, and collapsed. Matthew reacted quickly and caught her head just before it hit the desk in front of her.

Still holding Linda's head, Matthew yelled at James, "Call 911, request paramedics and an ambulance. Give them the address and the floor."

Matthew repositioned himself to best support Linda as James was calling.

As soon as James hung up, Matthew commanded, "Help me get her prone on the floor outside. We need to elevate her head. We've got to try to reduce the strain on her heart and help her breathe."

Matthew had never forgotten his first aid and CPR training from boy scout camp.

James did as Matthew directed. Once they had Linda in the hallway, other FDIC employees observed what was occurring and brought cushions from the chairs in the lunch room. James called the building reception desk to advise them to be ready to direct the emergency responders. The paramedics arrived in less than ten minutes and began administering oxygen while measuring Linda's vital signs. While this was occurring, Matthew had the presence of mind to dial Traci Horst, the bank's Director of Human Resources. Traci quickly arrived at the scene, understood what was happening, and called her staff on her cell phone. Less than fifteen minutes later, Linda, who had not regained consciousness, was loaded onto a stretcher and driven off by ambulance to the nearby hospital. Traci called Linda's husband, Carl, on his cell phone after her assistant texted her the emergency contact information stored in the bank's human resources computer system. Traci followed the ambulance to the hospital in her own car, calling Dale on the way to update him.

After everyone but the FDIC staff had departed, James signaled to Matthew to sit with him in the investigation office.

"I hope she's going to be okay," said Matthew. "We just asked a couple of introductory questions. I hope it wasn't a heart attack, but it did look like one."

"In over a decade of investigative work, that was a first for me," replied James, still shaken from the events.

Both men sat silent for a long while.

James then continued, "Well, we did learn several things. First of all, Linda is clearly very close to Dale. Second, Dale evidently maintains a, shall we say, vibrant social life. And, finally, it may be a while, if ever, before we can secure Linda's testimony about the five outgoing wires to Security Investment LLC."

"That sounds macabre."

"I only meant it factually."

"We shouldn't allow any perception about Dale's social life to influence our investigation," said Matthew. "After all, we regulate financial activity, not virtue."

"I agree completely. That said, there does seem to be a surprising amount of unexpected activity in this valley."

Matthew nodded his agreement. The two examiners then discussed what to do next. They agreed that Matthew would first go out and thank each FDIC employee for jumping in to assist this morning. Matthew would then send an email to Elaine Harmon advising her of the morning's events. James would call the FDIC team on site at Bank of America for an update regarding their search for additional information. Both would be alert to any update regarding Linda's condition.

At 2:30 PM, all of the bank staff and Matthew received the following email from Dale:

> *It is with great sadness that I share the passing of Linda Morris. She was a wonderful person, a dear friend to so many of us, and a loyal employee. She died late this morning in the arms of her husband, Carl. She experienced a heart attack and could not be saved despite the great efforts of the hospital staff.*
>
> *Visitation will be this Wednesday from Noon to 6:00 PM at Rossetti Mortuary. The funeral service will be held on Thursday at 2:00 PM at St. Paul's Episcopal Church. All bank managers are encouraged to schedule their staffing so that as many employees as desire can attend either or both of these events.*

In recognition of Linda's thirty-five years with Green Valley Community Bank, the Board of Directors has volunteered to personally pay for all of her final expenses.

Please join me in praying for Linda's family and providing any assistance they might need.

Dale Huffington

Matthew was racked with sadness and guilt after reading Dale's email. Perhaps he could have spoken to Linda one on one, and more gently. Maybe he and James could have been more direct in the investigation and addressed the questions about the wires to Dale. Linda had offered the FDIC team every assistance since they arrived on site, and always with a smile. Matthew decided he needed some fresh air and went outside for a twenty-minute walk.

After returning to the Board Room floor, he wrote another email to Elaine Harmon. He advised her of Linda's death, requested approval for any members of the examination team who so desired to be able to attend the services on agency time, and suggested that the exit meeting be postponed one week, with just he, James, and Sally remaining on-site next week. All of the regular components of the examination would be completed by the FDIC team by this Friday.

Matthew received a response from Elaine within the hour. She expressed her sorrow. She noted that she would extend her condolences to both Dale and George Anderson IV today. She approved all of Matthew's requests, adding that the FDIC had counseling available to any staff wishing such after witnessing the sad event.

Matthew forwarded the email to James.

Sally approached Matthew and asked if he were available. He responded affirmatively.

"I checked all of the databases for Central Coast Maintenance LLC and Central Coast Supply LLC. Both are fairly recently created single member LLCs, one hundred percent owned by Security Investment LLC, as Elaine advised us earlier. The only addresses are post office boxes in Santa Barbara. There is no other contact information, no phone book listings, and no websites. In summary, the same profile of very limited information we observed with Security Investment LLC."

"Those results are not unexpected," replied Matthew. "Thank you for your good work."

As Sally returned to her workstation, Matthew realized just how exhausted he was. Running two regulatory examinations and a parallel investigation into potential fraud or other criminal activities had taken a toll on both his mental and physical health. He hadn't been eating regularly, nor maintaining anything close to what could be termed a good diet.

Although it was now only 4:30 PM, Matthew walked over to James and asked, "Would you like to get a drink? I know a local spot that also serves great bar food."

"I could certainly use a drink. This has been quite a day."

"Great. There's a friendly bartender who serves at substantially all hours, just down the street."

"Sounds like there's a story there."

"I'll let Brendan Kehoe speak for himself, which he undoubtedly will."

Chapter 76

Tuesday July 31, 2002
Santa Maria, California

Matthew arrived at the bank at 7:45 AM. In light of the events yesterday, he and James had decided last evening to keep as low a profile as possible today. Matthew first sent an email to Dale advising of the change in regulatory examination scheduling, requesting that Dale coordinate with the other senior officers and with the Board of Directors. Matthew commenced the email to Dale by expressing the condolences of himself and the entire FDIC team.

Matthew then penned another email to David Morgan at the FDIC's Capital Markets Division. Over a martini yesterday, James had pointed out that the lack of market value on the safekeeping reports for the IO Strip CMO had not yet been investigated. Matthew requested that David provide the June 30, 2002 market value from his sources.

Matthew and James then revisited their planned sequence of interviews, deciding that the CFO would be questioned on Friday morning and the President on Friday afternoon. Emails calendaring those appointments were sent.

Matthew called Angela on the internal extension.

"Angela Falcone speaking."

"It's Matthew. I apologize for not getting back to you yesterday."

"I completely understand. Poor Linda. She was such a warm and welcoming person, so eager to help and also so focused on pleasing. We're all going to miss her."

"Although I've only been on site a short while, I appreciate what you're saying. The whole FDIC team expresses our condolences. I plan to attend both services later this week. I feel it's the least I can do."

"Carl, Linda's husband, will be touched by the number of people attending. The bank will be on minimum staffing. I've heard through the grapevine that all of the Directors are attending. Mr. Huffington will be giving the eulogy."

"News evidently travels fast around here."

"Many of the bank employees will work their entire career at Green Valley. In addition, you've already heard about the multigenerational families who call this valley home. People are very well connected."

"Angela, I'm wondering if it would be okay to ask you to contact the five customers who initiated the outgoing wires to Security Investment LLC. I suggest a simple approach of stating that you work at the bank and are conducting a customer satisfaction survey. Have five or six general questions about their opinions of the quality of various bank services. Then, include a specific question about wire transfers, such as if they have used the bank for any wire transfers in the past year; and were they satisfied with the service. Stay quiet and allow them to talk as much as they would like."

"I'm a financial analyst, not an actress, but I'll do my best. What am I listening for?"

"We think that it's highly unusual that these five elderly clients would each wire such large sums to the same beneficiary, always spaced between two and three months apart. We're not sure if there might be a case of elder abuse, a scam, or some other nefarious aspect."

"I've read about those types of activities. Elderly people are often targeted. I'll get on the phone soon and then let you know what I learn."

"Thank you again, Angela. We of course need to keep this confidential. We don't want to alert any perpetrators."

"I understand. Good-bye."

After Matthew hung up with Angela, he noticed that an email from David Morgan had arrived. David explained that valuing IO Strip CMO was challenging, as there was not a deep and liquid market for such. In addition, the value fundamentally derived from the present value of the future interest payments on the underlying mortgages, which were subject to curtailment or prepayment at any time. After that preamble, David indicated a likely market value at June 30, 2002 in the range of $250 thousand to $350 thousand. Matthew's heart raced when he read that line of the email. He remembered that the bank's valuation at the same date was approximately $2.3 million. Now he had two significant discrepancies. A second set of monthly payments attributed to the IO Strip CMO and a $2.0 million variance in market value. He typed a quick thank you to David and then met with James in the investigation office to share the latest information. The decided to ask Sally to make an appointment with the Controller for 1:00 PM.

At 12:45 PM, Sally met with Matthew and James. They briefed her on the upcoming line of questioning. On the ride down in the elevator, Sally reminded the men to avoid turning on any light switches. As they exited the elevator on the ground floor, Sally signaled that she wished to go first. Sally opened the door to the stairway leading down to the basement. The 25-watt light bulb was still working. The long corridor at the bottom of the stairs was dark, as before, with just a glimmer of light at the far end. Upon reaching the bottom of the stairs, Sally removed a small flashlight from her briefcase and activated it. At this point, James was dumbfounded by what was occurring, but decided it was best for him to simply follow at the rear. Matthew made a mental note to recognize Sally for her effective preparation in conjunction with the examination.

Once they arrived at Melvin's office at the far end of the corridor, Sally turned off the flashlight and said, "Good afternoon, Dewey. Good to see you again."

"Please call me Melvin. Please come in and sit down."

The folding table was in the same location as before. However, Melvin had his desk chair on the same side of the table as the two folding chairs. A large wooden box was placed on the other side of the table, upon which Melvin sat.

"I've never had more than two visitors at one time."

"Melvin, my name is James Robinson. I'm also an FDIC employee on the examination team. I understand that you already know Sally and Matthew."

"Yes, we've met before, and I attended high school with Sally."

"Small world," said James.

"We're here to ask you about the market values for the investment securities," advised Matthew.

"Okay. I take those from the safekeeping report for every security except the one you asked me about earlier. The safekeeping bank provides that report to us each month. Because the safekeeping bank does not provide a market value for that one particular CMO, Joel obtains market value estimates from three investment banks in determining a final value for accounting purposes."

"When do you receive the safekeeping reports, and the market value estimates from the investment banks?"

"After Joel brings them down to me. It's usually about the fourth of fifth day of the month."

The three FDIC employees raised their eyebrows at this response. It was a standard internal control procedure in banking for someone other than the individual purchasing and selling securities to receive the associated reporting. Melvin's comment raised a large red flag.

"Why don't you receive the safekeeping reports and the market values estimates directly?"

"The mail clerk won't deliver anything to my office. All my interoffice and outside mail goes to Joel, who brings it down to me every day, or has someone else do so."

On the one hand, Matthew understood why the mail clerk might not want to traverse the dark basement corridor to deliver items to Melvin. On the other hand, the practice did open up the possibility of report falsification.

"Melvin, can you show us the folder that contains the reconciliation between the market values on the safekeeping report, plus the market value estimates from the three investment banks, and the journal entries into the bank's accounting system?"

"Of course."

Since that was another matter related to investment securities, Melvin retrieved an orange folder from the file drawer with the laminated orange label. The accounting work was the neatest James had ever seen. The market value estimates from the three investment banks for the IO Strip CMO as of June 30, 2002 were about $2.0 million higher than the information Matthew had received from David Morgan. Matthew returned the folder to Melvin and looked at James. James indicated that he had no further questions. Observing this, Sally spoke up.

"Melvin, can you please email me a copy of the pages we just reviewed for our files, plus the similar pages for each quarter-end over the past two years?"

"Yes. They finally let me have a copier with a scanner down here last year."

Sally continued, "Thank you again for helping us. Your accounting and record-keeping system is quite impressive."

Melvin beamed with pride on the inside, but simply replied, "Thank you."

The three FDIC employees departed Melvin's office, again led by Sally and her flashlight. Once they were back on the Board Room floor, Matthew excused Sally and met with James in the investigation office.

"Since the market value estimates for the IO Strip CMO all came from large investment banks with no source or contact information, we really can't investigate that aspect without alerting the CFO to our concerns," opined Matthew.

"Agreed. Let's save that topic for our upcoming interview with the CFO. We want to keep this as quiet as possible as long as possible."

"Why don't I ask David Morgan if he is sure about the recent IO Strip valuation and if he can estimate the historical values over the past couple of years. I'm wondering if there might be some type of trend we can identify."

"Good thinking," replied James.

Matthew returned to his workstation to compose the email to David Morgan. Just after hitting 'send', an incoming email arrived from Elaine Harmon. It contained copies of the last two years of account statements for the checking accounts associated with Central Coast Maintenance LLC and Central

Coast Supply LLC, plus information on the third account at Bank of America that had recently transferred funds to Security Investment LLC. Also attached to the email were the PDFs of the customer information that Bank of America had on file for the three LLC accounts. Matthew forwarded the email to James and suggested that they meet again in the investigation office in about an hour.

Wanting to keep things as quiet as possible, Matthew started a spreadsheet to reconcile the bank's invoice payments to the two new vendors with the activity in the LLC checking account statements. He soon realized that the numbers matched perfectly. Matthew had now confirmed the flow of funds, from the bank to Central Coast Maintenance LLC and Central Coast Supply LLC to Security Investment LLC to the security safekeeping account at the correspondent bank to the bank. Someone had gone to a lot of trouble for evidently no financial benefit.

Matthew then reviewed the account setup information for the LLC checking accounts. The Security Investment LLC account had been opened at the Santa Barbara branch of Bank of America. The Central Coast Maintenance LLC checking account had been opened at the Carpinteria branch. The Central Coast Supply LLC checking account had been opened in the Ventura branch. All three LLC's utilized an address of post office boxes in Santa Barbara. Matthew was again amazed at the effort someone had devoted to whatever was going on.

He next opened the file with the individual identification information from Bank of America. All three LLC checking accounts had been opened by an individual named Don Martin. That was a new name to Matthew. He decided to call Angela to see if she knew this person.

"Angela Falcone speaking."

"It's Matthew."

"I'm sorry, but I'm not done yet with the customer calls about the wires."

"I'm actually calling about something else. And, please don't feel pressured in any way. We appreciate that you're helping us while also completing all of your regular work."

"Thank you. What's the new topic?"

"Do you know if an individual named Don Martin has accounts at the bank?"

"That doesn't sound familiar off the top of my head, but let me run a computer inquiry. Can you hold on for a minute?"

"No problem."

About two minutes later, Angela came back on the line.

"There are four individuals named Don or Donald or Donny Martin who have had accounts with the bank."

"I should have given you a social security number to also use in the inquiry. I apologize."

After Matthew shared the social security number, Angela soon responded.

"Yes, the bank had a couple of accounts for Don Martin, using that social security number."

"Had?"

"Yes. The two accounts are now marked 'closed'".

"When did they close?"

"Let me see... Interesting... Exactly one year ago. On July 31, 2001."

"That's quite a coincidence. Is there any explanation for the closure?"

"I input that inquiry as soon as I gave you the close date. The reason code is 'death of the customer'."

Matthew shook his head. A man who was now dead had opened the three LLC checking accounts associated with the unusual transfers of funds. The individual who had processed the outgoing wire requests to one of the LLCs had collapsed in front of Matthew, dying soon after. This matter only became more complicated with the peeling of each layer of the onion. Matthew then remembered that Angela was still on the phone.

"Thank you again for your help. Please let me know when you complete the customer interviews and we'll meet off-site."

"Will do."

Matthew then opened the final file attached to the most recent email from Elaine. The third Bank of America account that had transferred money into the Security Investment LLC checking account was in fact a loan account. The obligor on the loan was The Fesler Trust, the entity that was the owner and sole member of Security Investment LLC. Well, Matthew thought to himself, it's not unusual at all for a company to transfer funds to a wholly owned subsidiary. On the other hand, in tracing the flow of funds, the money from the loan had eventually ended up in the safekeeping account for the bank.

Frustrated, Matthew walked over to the break room and poured himself another cup of coffee. When he returned to his workstation, he saw that another email from David Morgan had arrived. David confirmed that his valuation of the IO Strip CMO at June 30, 2002 could not possibly be off by $2.0 million, particularly given how little of the original pool of residential mortgages remained outstanding after the refinance wave. David attached a spreadsheet which listed an estimated historical value for the IO Strip CMO at each quarter-end over the past two years. Matthew typed a quick return email thanking David. He then started yet another spreadsheet, this one for reconciling the market value figures from David to the similar information supplied by Melvin. The pattern immediately jumped out at Matthew. A year ago, the difference between the bank's valuation for the security and David's was just over $4.0 million. That difference diminished at each subsequent quarter-end, dropping to about $2.0 million at June 30, 2002.

Matthew looked up at the clock and realized it was time to meet with James Robinson. Once both men were seated in the investigation office, Matthew brough James up to date.

"So, we know a few things for certain, with the rest being conjecture at this point," said James. "Let me recap. In essence, the bank bought a security and incurred a loss of $4.0 million or more. Over the past year, various funds have arrived at the bank from multiple sources, primarily associated with dead individuals. Those funds have been used to write down the bank's basis in the investment, thereby reducing the amount of loss, or, in effect, recapturing the loss."

"Exactly. I wonder if the bank intentionally overpaid for the security as a means of making an implicit loan to some party, with the loan now being repaid through the unusual cash inflows into the safekeeping account?" asked Matthew.

"That could be. There are many individuals and entities blacklisted from the U.S. financial system due to their criminal or anti-American activities. This could be a way of providing financing to such an organization. On the other hand, that would not explain the circle of funds associated with Central Coast Maintenance LLC and Central Coast Supply LLC," opined James.

"I wonder if the perpetrators did not intend some or all of the $4.0 million to be a loan. Rather, perhaps some of the money was an investment or donation of sorts, possibly associated with something that was to be kept from being public," said Matthew. "This approach would keep such off the books of the bank. This valley is highly interconnected. Maybe a portion of the money had to do with some business relationships among one or more of the dominant families."

"That may make sense, at least in part. The wire transfers from the previously dormant deposit accounts could be a way of refunding and thereby permanently hiding the illicit investment or donation by the bank," expressed James.

Matthew thought for a few minutes, and then said, "However, what about all of the cash deposits to the Security Investment LLC checking account? Those were made regularly, with all of the funds eventually being returned to the bank."

"I see your point," shared James. He added, "If there was some type of nefarious loan, investment, or donation, then who or what stood to benefit? We'd have to trace the funds through the seller of the security. That could be challenging, and possibly outside of our jurisdiction. Who was the seller?"

"Huffman Brothers. That was clearly labeled on the orange file from the Controller," advised Matthew.

"They're a well-known investment banking firm. While anything is possible, I don't think an investment banking firm of Huffman's size and reputation would bother with some type of nefarious funding for just $4.0 million, unless it was performed by one or more rogue employees," said James.

After both men thought for a while, James spoke.

"The only ties we have to anyone now alive are, first, that the Security Investment LLC is owned by The Fesler Trust, of which the President of the bank is the trustee; and, second, that the CFO evidently falsified the market value estimates from the brokerage firms for the IO Strip CMO."

"You're the professional investigator, but that doesn't seem like overwhelming evidence of anything to me," replied Matthew. "We haven't proven that the market value estimates from the investment banks over the past year were falsified."

"True. In addition, since we really don't know what Security Investment LLC is or does. You're right in that the Trust could have a legitimate business interest in the LLC, or the trustee was hoodwinked by the dead individual who opened the checking accounts."

"His name was Don Martin."

"We're really not in a position to make any accusations. We also have to be careful about our upcoming interviews with the senior officers. We have to acknowledge their rights and proceed according to our formal procedures. We need to avoid any whiff of abuse of regulatory authority or of improper conduct."

James then looked up at the ceiling for a while, eventually returning his attention to Matthew.

"How about one more email to Elaine and, indirectly, the FDIC staff on site at Bank of America. We inquire about whether there was any collateral for the loan to The Fesler Trust and we also ask if there is any branch video available at the date and time of the most recent cash deposit to the Security Investment LLC checking account."

"Can't hurt," responded Matthew. "Can I mention you suggested such, not to pass the buck, but to share with Elaine that you're actively investigating the matter with me?"

"Certainly."

Later that afternoon, Matthew sent the email to Elaine, copying James. It was now 5:30 PM, and both men were mentally exhausted. Matthew had never seen so many spreadsheets that reconciled almost everything, but proved almost nothing. He grabbed a fast-food chicken salad on the way back to the airport hotel, ate it in his room, and was asleep by 7:30 PM.

Meanwhile, back at the bank, Angela had stayed late to ensure privacy in making the last two of the customer survey calls associated with the wire transfers. The final call was to a Mrs. Franklin, who had signed a $100,000 outgoing wire request form for transferring funds to the Security Investment LLC checking account at Bank of America.

"Hello."

"Hello. Is this Mrs. Franklin?"

"Yes."

"This is Angela Falcone calling from Green Valley Community Bank. Do you have just a few minutes to help us with our customer satisfaction survey?"

"How can I help you?"

"I have just a few questions to ask. The first one is, overall, how satisfied are you with the service provided by Green Valley Community Bank?"

"Is that my bank?"

"Yes. Our records indicate that you have banked there for almost forty years."

"Oh, yes, the bank downtown. Now I remember."

"Getting back to our survey questions, can you comment on your overall level of satisfaction with the bank?"

"I can't remember the last time I was there. My husband used to do all of our financial work. He died."

"I'm sorry to hear that, and please accept my condolences."

"Horace was a very good man. He treated me like a queen. I miss him every day."

Recognizing that she wasn't making progress, Angela tried another approach.

"Do you have someone who helps you with your bills?"

"I think my son set everything up after Horace died. He doesn't live in town. I can't remember the last time he visited."

"I understand. Do you have a helper that visits your home?"

"Oh, yes. A nice woman. She or her friend visit me every day. Let me see, no, I can't remember her name, but she's tall and has blonde hair. She cooks wonderful desserts. Might you know her?"

"I'm afraid I don't."

Now fully appreciating the situation, Angela concluded the call.

"Thank you very much for your time, Mrs. Franklin. It's been a pleasure speaking with you."

"And with you, dear."

"Good-bye."

Angela typed up notes from this evening's conversations, adding to the file she had created for the three interviews she had conducted earlier.

Chapter 77

Wednesday August 1, 2002
Santa Maria, California

Matthew dressed in his best dark suit in preparation for the visitation this afternoon for Linda Morris. He texted James to do the same. By 8:00 AM, both men were together in the Board Room.

"Good morning, James. How are you doing?"

"I've slept better. Our hotel is not exactly a five-star lodging. The mattresses reflect that. How about you?"

"I must admit that I'm stressed. We have two normal regulatory examinations to wrap up, plus the upcoming interviews with the CFO and the President. This case has me frustrated. I still can't fathom why some combination of individuals would have implemented such an elaborate scheme."

"I agree with you, in that we haven't identified any motive that would rationally justify the amount of work invested by some party or parties. Every explanation that I've been able to think of has some gap in the logic."

"Let me see if Elaine has responded to our latest email inquiry," said Matthew.

Looking at his email, he quickly identified the one they sought. Matthew turned his computer screen so that James could also read the communication. Elaine had attached two files. One was the collateral record for the loan extended by Bank of America to The Fesler Trust. The other was a series of still photographs from the Santa Barbara branch. Matthew first opened the collateral file. The loan was secured by a first deed of trust on a residential unit located in Santa Maria. The grantor on the deed of trust was Dale Huffington.

"Why would Mr. Huffington volunteer collateral that he owned as security for a loan extended to The Fesler Trust?" asked Matthew.

"The whole Fesler Trust is more or less a black box to us. We only know that it receives significant disbursements as a result of its partial ownership in Blue Pacific Ventures; and that the current trustee is Mr. Huffington. There could be any number of valid reasons why Mr. Huffington would volunteer some personally owned real estate as collateral for a loan to the Trust. We have no idea what the terms of the Trust are, nor any knowledge of any limitations on the trustee's authority," commented James.

"I'm wondering if this whole matter should be referred to the FBI. They have more resources and more investigative authority than we do," opined Matthew.

"It may come to that. However, we haven't really identified a crime. No one has reported a loss of money as a result of these events. On top of that, most of the funds in question have actually flowed *into* the bank."

"Let's look at the second file."

Matthew opened the second file, which contained three still photographs evidently taken from the security camera footage at the Bank of America Santa Barbara branch. Elaine's email explained that the time-stamp on the video matched the computer record of when a recent cash deposit was made to the Security Investment LLC checking account. The camera angle was taken from behind the teller line. The depositor was wearing a baseball-type cap, but with a Golden State Warriors logo. The depositor was also wearing sunglasses and a high collared jacket.

"Do you recognize the depositor?" asked James.

"That's not much to go on. It looks like a male, no evidence of breasts or long hair, and if I enlarge the photo, I can almost make out an Adam's apple. Other than that, I'm not sure of anything."

"Does it look like the President or the CFO?"

"Definitely not the President. He's older, has very pale skin, with wrinkles, and is likely taller than the person in the photo. It could be the CFO, but there's not enough detail for me to be sure either way."

Matthew and James both stood and paced.

After a few minutes, Matthew suggested, "Let me follow up on the wire transfers to the Security Investment LLC checking account. I can spend the rest of today finishing up the regular examination reports and you can draft the questions for our Friday interviews, unless you have a better idea."

"Can't say that I do."

About twenty minutes later, Matthew received a text from Angela. It read: 'Drive to visitation together?'

Matthew texted back: 'Meet you in the lobby at 1:45 PM'. Matthew selected that time in order to pay his respects during the likely least attended hour of the day.

By 2:00 PM, Angela was driving them over to the Rossetti funeral home.

"Thank you for reaching out and also driving. I'm not yet that familiar with the valley. I might have had a challenge locating the funeral home."

"It's one of the longest-established in the valley, but a few blocks off Main Street on a small cul-de-sac in a quiet district. Remember that Linda's husband is named Carl."

"I remember, but thank you for making sure. I wouldn't want to hurt anyone's feelings at a time like this."

Angela parked her car and led Matthew into the funeral home. The largest visitation room had been reserved for Linda. Upon entering, Matthew saw that it was an open coffin. The chairs immediately in front of the coffin were occupied by a man appearing to be in his mid-sixties, with swollen eyes and a red face. Seated next to him was Dale Huffington, holding onto the man's shoulder and supplying a handkerchief. About ten other individuals were also in attendance, most of them silently praying for the repose of Linda's soul.

"The man with Dale is Carl," whispered Angela.

After waiting at the back of the room for a period, Matthew stood and approached the coffin alone. He was raised Catholic, not so very different from Episcopalian. He paused at the coffin, kneeled in prayer, and then rose and approached Carl.

"I'm so sorry for your loss. I only knew Linda for a brief period, but in that short time I quickly recognized what a caring and loving individual she was."

"Thank you," mumbled Carl, breaking down in tears. Dale kept his arm around Carl, providing physical and emotional support. Dale couldn't help but glare at Matthew, wondering if his behavior that morning had caused Linda's death.

Once Matthew returned to the rear of the room, he again knelt in prayer. Angela took this opportunity to pay her respects.

"Mr. Morris, I worked with Linda. Every single day, she brought a smile into my life and the lives of all of the bank's employees. We were blessed by her presence. You were married to a wonderful woman."

Angela then gently hugged Carl, his eyes still watering. Upon separating, Angela nodded to Dale and mouthed 'thank you'.

Once back in her car, Angela commented to Matthew, "In times like this, I remember a quote I first read in high school:

> *If we really think that home is elsewhere and that this life is a 'wandering to find home,' why should we not look forward to the arrival?*
>
> *C. S. Lewis*

The quote always struck me as an intellectual confirmation of my Roman Catholic faith."

"I understand. C.S. Lewis certainly had a complex relationship with the Catholic Church. Thank you for sharing that with me. A death puts so many things into perspective," said Matthew.

As she was pulling back into the bank parking lot, Angela suggested, "Can I meet you at the Kehoe hotel bar at 5:30 PM to share the results of the wire transfer related interviews? I have some reports that I need to finish this afternoon so we can finish closing the books for the month of July."

"That's a plan."

At 3:30 PM, Dale told Carl that he would be right back and used the restroom at the funeral home. Despite the day's being draining on Dale, he had committed to himself to stay by Carl's side throughout the six-hour visitation period. Linda had been his assistant for years, completely loyal and always eager to please. He missed her, and knew that no one could ever truly replace her. Dale and Anne had shared many dinners with Carl and Linda, particularly at the various community events sponsored by the bank. On the way back from the restroom, he used his personal cell phone to text Joel: 'Condo at 6:30?'. He soon received a reply: 'Y'.

Upon entering the Kehoe hotel bar at 5:30 PM, Matthew saw Angela engaged in an animated conversation with Brendan the bartender. By the body language, it was clear that Brendan thought Angela to be attractive. Matthew noticed that he was a bit jealous, even though he hadn't yet confirmed Angela's interest in himself, much less been on a date.

"Hello. How are you?" asked Matthew.

"To be honest, on the tired side. Between my regular job, the extra work for you, and taking time to honor Linda, it's been a lot."

"I understand. I've greatly appreciated all of your assistance, and will try to minimize any future requests. What shall we drink, perhaps with a bar plate?"

"I'm ready for something stronger. Have you ever had a glass of *nocciola*?"

"Can't say that I have. What is it?"

"It's an Italian *digestivo*, or cordial. The primary ingredient is hazelnuts."

"Sounds interesting. Let's give it a try."

Angela gave the drink order to Brendan, along with requesting a plate of the mixed cured meats.

Turning back to Matthew, she asked, "Are you ready for my report on the five wire transfers?"

"Yes."

"As I mentioned from the computer research, all five of the initiators of the outgoing wire transfers were over 85 years of age. After calling each of them, there was a distinct pattern.

Whether due to dementia, Alzheimer's disease, or simply age, all five individuals appeared to suffer from memory loss and / or cognitive impairment. They were conversant and pleasant. Two of them had a helper nearby with whom I was also able to speak. The helpers confirmed the mental limitations of the customers."

"Wow. That's quite a coincidence."

"My father taught me that coincidences rarely are."

Brendan arrived with the drinks and food.

"We don't get too many requests for this liquor, but I was fortunate enough to have found a new bottle in the back. Must have been left over from some Italian wedding at the hotel."

"We'll toast to our good fortune," replied Angela.

"I poured myself a glass as well. Can't remember the last time I enjoyed this beverage," said Brendan.

Brendan and Angela clinked their glasses and sampled the liquor.

While Angela and Brendan were talking, Matthew's mind was racing. The signatures on the wire request forms were genuine, but the customers would not be able to testify regarding the validity of the outgoing funds transfer. The five deposit accounts had been scheduled for escheatment to the state due to inactivity, which would be consistent with the memory loss symptom exhibited by the clients. The employee who submitted the wire request forms had passed. He'd discuss all of this with James, but this aspect of their investigation looked like a dead end.

"Matthew, did you hear what I asked?"

"Oh, excuse me, I was lost in thought. I apologize."

"I asked if there is any follow-up work that you'd like me to perform."

"No. I can't think of any. You've been immensely helpful."

"You haven't sampled the *nocciola*."

They both sipped the beverage. The taste was unlike anything Matthew had previously experienced. There was a slightly fruity entrance, a rich, velvety middle, and a smooth, aromatic finish that filled his sinuses.

"Outstanding. How have I never tried this before?" asked Matthew.

"You just need to have the right Italian connections," smiled Angela. "Not to be ethnocentric, but food and beverages are almost a religion to Italians."

"Now *that's* a faith where I would never miss a service!"

They both smiled. The remainder of their rendezvous was primarily comprised of small talk, with each of them gradually sharing a bit more about themselves. They also confirmed that they would both be attending Linda's funeral service tomorrow afternoon.

....

Joel arrived at Dale's condo at 6:30 PM as planned. Dale let him in. They took their usual seats at the dining room table.

"Joel, what have you learned thus far?" asked Dale.

"I have a meeting with the FDIC at 9:00 AM this coming Friday. Things were moved back in light of Linda's funeral service. I haven't received any advance questions for the meeting, nor requests for any additional information. The examination exit meeting is scheduled for 4:00 PM next Friday, August 10, in the Board Room. No one has yet asked me anything about the IO Strip CMO. Most of the questions I have received over the past several weeks were from the junior examination staff.

Those were easily answered by providing the applicable reports. How about you?"

"I'd provide a similar answer, with the addition that the Examiner in Charge appears to be quite interested in Angela. Among other observations, I saw them arrive and depart together at the visitation today."

"That could be to our advantage, from a distraction standpoint."

"Could be. On the other hand, Angela is very smart. She could intentionally or inadvertently through questioning highlight some of our activity."

"Should we confront her?" asked Joel.

"That would be risky if done by the two of us. How about if you ask an open-ended question of her tomorrow morning and see if she says anything useful?"

"I'll do that."

"Now, let's practice our questions and answers for the meeting with the examiners. I'll ask you your questions, and you can do the same to me. Practice makes perfect," advised Dale.

"Sounds good."

The men spent the next hour rehearsing their answers to a broad range of potential questions concerning aspects of the coverup plan. They not only wanted to deflect the attention of the examiners, but also ensure that their answers were consistent. By 7:45 PM, their meeting concluded and Joel began the drive south to his mother's house in Goleta.

Chapter 78

Friday August 3, 2002
Santa Maria, California

Matthew and James met in the investigation room at 8:00 AM. Each were holding a cup of fresh coffee, wanting to be as alert as possible for the upcoming interview with the CFO. After they rehearsed their questions and agreed how to coordinate their behavior and comments, they paused to finish their coffees.

"That was quite a funeral service yesterday," shared Matthew.

"Despite being almost the size of a cathedral, the church was packed."

"The longer I'm here, the more I appreciate that this is a well-connected valley, with deep and longstanding relationships."

"I thought the President's eulogy was eloquent. More than that, his voice communicated how he deeply cared for Linda," shared James.

"I agree. The way he linked Linda's life to the essence of one's soul was beyond touching. And his concluding quote was one I'll never forget:

> *The more one loves, the heavier the meaning of death becomes, and the deeper the sense of loss. Love and death are not different things, they are the front and back of the same thing.*
>
> *Otsuichi*

I had never heard of Otsuichi before," added Matthew.

Matthew and James then saw Joel approaching and quickly focused their thoughts on the job at hand.

"Good morning, Joel. I'm James Robinson, on loan to assist Matthew with wrapping up this set of examinations. Please have a seat."

James pointed to the inside chair across from him, again subtly communicating that Joel was surrounded.

"Would you like a glass of water or a cup of coffee?" asked James.

"No thank you."

"I'm a big NBA fan. Can't wait for the new season to start. Do you have a favorite team?" asked James.

"Golden State Warriors."

"We both work out of the San Francisco office, so we agree with you. Not too many Lakers fans in the Financial District," smiled James.

Joel simply smiled back, without a further response. He was cognizant of his practice session with Dale, where it was emphasized to minimize the conversation.

"Let's see, we've completed the review of the bank's regulatory reporting. Just a couple of minor corrections were needed. I must say, your Controller certainly keeps detailed accounting records."

"There's only one Melvin."

"Next, I see that the CPAs issued a clean audit opinion for December 31, 2001, with no accounting adjustments identified," said James.

"Yes, the bank received an unqualified opinion."

"Congratulations. We almost always see at least a couple of passed adjustments."

Matthew leaned in and directed, "Next topic, the investment portfolio."

Joel took a deep breathe, telling himself to remain calm.

"Most of the securities appear typical for a community bank of Green Valley's size. I see that the bank has reduced the duration of the investment portfolio over the past couple of years," commented James.

"Yes, in order for the bank to be able to support more lending to its clients requesting fixed rate commercial real estate loans."

"That's a logical reallocation of interest rate risk. We've seen several other banks behave similarly."

Joel again simply smiled.

"I do have one other question in this area. I see that, about two years ago, Green Valley purchased an Agency IO Strip CMO. That's a bit unusual for a community bank," opined James.

"The anticipated yield was attractive, and the security was a natural hedge to the fixed rate commercial real estate loans I mentioned."

Joel was thankful that Dale had prepared him so well.

"That makes sense. What doesn't make sense to me, and I hope you can help me understand, is why the market values for the IO Strip CMO used by the bank over the past year or so were consistently so much higher than the market values provided by the FDIC's Capital Markets Division," presented James in a deep, monotone voice.

Despite his best effort, Joel flushed and began to perspire. He told himself to calm down and follow the script that Dale had prepared.

"The bank obtains estimated market values for that security from three large Wall Street firms. Those estimates are averaged and then used in the bank's accounting and reporting."

"Yes, we saw that documentation," responded James. "However, we followed up with all three of those investment banks and asked them to verify the market values used by the bank. None of the information in response to our inquiry matched what the bank had on file from the Wall Street firms. In fact, the Wall Street firms' estimates were generally fairly close to those supplied by our Capital Markets Division."

The last statement by James was fiction. They had not in fact contacted the Wall Street firms out of concern for tipping off whoever might be involved. James inserted this line of questioning on a hunch, based upon the lack of internal control over the safekeeping reports as described by Melvin.

Joel's body temperature soared even higher. He took another deep breath and repeated the line practiced with Dale.

"I don't understand that. I'd have to perform some follow-up research."

"Very well. Please do so and advise us of your findings. Now, turning to another topic, we'd like to ask about a company named Security Investment LLC," advised James.

Joel sat quietly.

"Are you familiar with that entity?" asked James.

"Not that I can remember offhand."

"Well, it's the entity that's been wiring additional cashflows into the bank's security safekeeping account each month, with those cashflows processed as principal reductions on the IO Strip CMO. However, of course, an IO Strip CMO does not have principal cash flows, since it is an interest-only security."

"I'd have to look into that."

"I understand. Thank you. Circling back to my earlier topic of questioning, I was wondering why you were recently photographed wearing your Golden State Warriors hat depositing cash into a checking account at the Santa Barbara branch of Bank of America. The checking account is under the name of Security Investment LLC, the entity you mentioned that you cannot remember."

James removed the photos acquired by Elaine and showed them to Joel. While he was not sure that the individual in the photos was Joel, he stated such in an effort to evoke at least a partial confession.

Joel stared at the photos. This was now outside the preparation provided by Dale.

"Might I pause for a glass of water? All this talking has parched my throat."

"I'll get that for you," said Matthew. "Please remain seated."

After Matthew returned with the glass of water, Joel took a long, slow drink. James then re-initiated the questioning.

"Let me provide a bit more background on Security Investment LLC to help jog your memory. That entity owns Central Coast Maintenance LLC and Central Coast Supply LLC, both relatively new vendors to the bank."

"The bank has several hundred vendors. I don't know them all."

"Interestingly, every invoice by both Central Coast Maintenance LLC and Central Coast Supply LLC was approved by you."

James then removed copies of the invoices from his file folder, taken from the bank's Accounts Payable files, and showed them to Joel.

"Are these your initials, approving the invoices?"

"Yes. As CFO, I approve a large number of invoices. It's part of my job."

"I acknowledge that. However, our resident team at Bank of America has provided account statements showing that every dollar the bank paid to Central Coast Maintenance LLC and Central Coast Supply LLC was later transferred to Security Investment LLC and included in the supposed principal payments made to the bank for the IO Strip CMO. It seems that the associated funds went on a long journey, eventually arriving back at the point of origin. Let me show you the color-coded items that document the travel of the funds."

While James removed the documents from the file folder, Joel drank some more of the water.

"Joel, do you have any explanation for what we've observed?" asked Matthew.

"Not offhand."

"Joel, do you know a man named Don Martin?" inquired James.

Joel could answer this question easily and truthfully, as Dale had not shared any of the LLC details with him.

"I don't believe so."

"He opened the various business checking accounts at Bank of America for the LLCs."

"Does not ring a bell at all."

"Hmmm... Let's pause on that and pursue a new line of

questioning. Joel, was the purchase of the IO Strip CMO a vehicle to loan money to an entity in violation of the anti-money laundering laws? That makes sense to us, given the cash flow pattern."

Joel knew that serious violations of the anti-money laundering laws carried huge fines and prison terms. He felt the need to nip that thought in the bud.

"Absolutely not."

"You were the individual who purchased the IO Strip CMO, were you not?" asked James.

"I was. That's clearly recorded."

"If the purchase was not associated with implicit financing, was it conducted because you were paid a rebate or commission? We're trying to understand how a loss of about $4.0 million occurred."

Joel also knew, after more than a decade in banking, that being paid a commission or rebate on bank business was highly unethical and in violation of multiple regulations.

"Absolutely not. I would never do that."

"So, tell us, Joel, why did you purchase an unusual security that led the bank to about a $4.0 million loss that was later apparently covered up by a series of fund inflows from an LLC to which you have been photographed making cash deposits?"

Despite all of the training by Dale, Joel began to panic. In addition, he had already consumed a large glass of water, on top of the coffee he drank at his desk.

"Might we pause for a bathroom break?" asked Joel.

"Of course."

Matthew stood up, allowed Joel to exit the investigation

room, but followed him into the men's room under the pretense of also needing to urinate. Once the three of them were seated back in the investigation room, the two FDIC employees remained silent, staring at Joel. Joel decided to throw in the towel, but avoid implicating Dale. Dale had been supportive of his ascension to the CFO position and had been nothing but sympathetic over the past year. There was no reason to drag Dale down with him.

"I was an idiot."

"In what regard? What are you talking about?" asked James.

Joel took a deep breath.

"I was stupid to buy that damn IO Strip CMO. Looking back, the original investment was probably not great. However, after the Federal Reserve started rapidly cutting interest rates, the investment became horrible. The underlying residential mortgages were paying off like crazy, rapidly reducing the value of the CMO. I tried to sell it, but there was no bid at that point. I was just plain dumb, taken advantage of by the broker and his trading desk and a beautiful, naked woman."

Joel then broke down and started sobbing uncontrollably.

As Matthew left the office to collect a box of tissues from the break room, Joel began moaning, over and over again.

"What will happen to my poor mother?"

James and Matthew were taken aback. They still did not quite understand what had occurred at the bank, much less about how a naked woman had anything to do with the matter. Matthew kept handing Joel wads of tissues. After about ten minutes, Joel calmed down enough for the conversation to continue.

"Joel, let us be clear about something. There is no law against stupidity. If there were, quite a bit of humanity would be jailed from time to time," said Matthew.

"If you made an honest mistake in purchasing the IO Strip CMO, we can understand that. It's a professional concern, but not a criminal concern. Covering up the loss and falsifying the bank's financial and regulatory reporting is, however, a violation of various regulatory statutes," explained James.

"I understand that. I was afraid of losing my job. My mother depends on me, especially after the stroke."

Matthew and James were not without some compassion for Joel. He was obviously not that bright an individual and someone who could be taken advantage of. The man also clearly loved and cared for his mother.

"Do you know anything about the other various funds inflows into or through the Security Investment LLC checking account?"

"No. I didn't have anything to do with those."

"Do you know who did?"

"No."

Despite the ongoing questioning, Joel remained unwilling to implicate Dale. After all, it was Dale who had tried to come to Joel's rescue after being bamboozled by Troy, Duane, and Jessica. Dale did not deserve to be punished for trying to help Joel out of a predicament of his own making.

James and Matthew looked at each other, and shrugged their shoulders. James thought he had already pushed Joel past his breaking point, and did not want another medical incident as occurred with Linda. In addition, Dale was scheduled to be interviewed this afternoon. That could well supply the missing pieces.

"Joel, tell you what. We're going to mandate that you be

placed on paid administrative leave pending the conclusion of our investigation into this matter. Matthew will now escort you down to your office to collect your car keys. You're to drive home and remain there until we contact you. Do not come into the bank unless an FDIC employee requests that of you. Is that clear?" asked James.

"Yes."

The men then stood up and Matthew walked downstairs with Joel. The two men did not say anything to each other. Once Joel drove off, Matthew returned to the 12th floor and again spoke with James in the investigation room.

"I think we pushed him as far as possible," said James.

"I know we're not supposed to make suppositions, but I don't think Joel is smart enough to have concocted the elaborate plan we've discovered, recognizing that there may be tentacles we have yet to unearth," shared Matthew.

"I agree with you. I checked our records on his personnel file while you were with him. He has an undergraduate degree in music theory and an accounting certificate from a community college. No wonder the Wall Street firm was able to peddle that crappy IO Strip CMO to him."

"Did you gain any insight into the involvement of the naked woman?"

"No. We'd better not go there unless we have to. That's the type of topic that can sidetrack an investigation."

"Let's grab a sandwich and rehearse one more time for our meeting with the President at 2:00 PM."

"Agreed."

On the drive south to Goleta, Joel called Dale on his cell phone.

"Dale Huffington speaking."

"I cracked, but did not implicate you. I confessed to my part of the plan only. I'm sorry Dale. They had a lot of evidence and were relentless."

"Gotcha."

Dale then hung up. Damn it! So close to success, and then failure! Dale spent the next two hours quietly evaluating his alternatives in his office.

At 2:00 PM, Dale arrived on the 12th floor. Matthew greeted him by the elevator and showed him into the investigation office.

"Good afternoon Mr. Huffington," said James.

"Please call me Dale."

"Dale, please take a seat."

After the three men were seated, James commenced his line of questioning.

"Dale, we'd like to ask you about an investment security purchased by the bank about two years ago."

"I wish to invoke my right to have legal counsel present."

"Dale, this is not a court of law. The FDIC is allowed to speak with any bank employee."

"And I have the right to decline to answer questions absent legal representation being present."

"Dale, we're not accusing you of anything."

Dale sat silently.

James continued, "Dale, if you refuse to speak with us, we'll have no alternative but to have you placed on administrative leave pending an investigation."

Dale continued to sit silently.

"Do you have anything you'd like to say?"

Dale refused to respond to even that question.

"Very well. Matthew will escort you to your office to collect your car keys. You're to drive home and remain there until we contact you. Do not come into the bank unless an FDIC employee requests that of you. Is that clear?"

Dale stood up, gesturing to Matthew to lead.

After Dale drove off, Matthew again returned to the 12th floor to meet with James.

"Wow! That was unexpected. Where do we go from here?" inquired Matthew.

"I've been thinking about that. Dale could be trying to protect Joel, himself, or some other individual or parties. As you've mentioned, this is a small town that is highly interconnected. Preserving multigenerational relationships would likely be viewed by Dale as more important than whatever trouble we can direct his way," said James.

"Agreed. So, what should we do? This whole scenario is way outside my training and experience."

"Let me bring this matter and all of our documentation to the Criminal Enforcement Division, which will likely contact the FBI," said James.

"Won't that take a while?"

"Unfortunately, yes. Particularly if Dale retains a competent attorney to represent him and argue every step of the process."

"What about the two regulatory examinations, the exit meeting scheduled for next week, and the fact that we just placed two of the bank's senior officers on administrative leave?" asked Matthew.

"You work with our team to complete the two regulatory examinations, but hold them in abeyance. Cancel the exit meeting after contacting Elaine to gain her approval. Explain to her what has occurred. I'll contact the Chairman of the Board and request a face-to-face meeting as soon as possible. The Board must appoint an interim President and interim CFO. The bank needs continued leadership to operate properly. We don't want to inadvertently create even more problems here," concluded James.

Chapter 79

Monday August 6, 2002
Santa Maria, California

All employees of Green Valley Community Bank found the following email in their inboxes upon arriving for work on Monday morning:

> *The bank's Board of Directors has recently taken a number of actions in response to preliminary findings arising from the recent regulatory examinations by the FDIC. Dale Huffington and Joel Johnson have been placed on administrative leave pending further investigation into various matters. The bank's Chief Operating Officer, Gene Phillips, has been appointed Interim President. Gene has been with the bank for over fifteen years. As many of you know, Gene's great-grandfather was one of the founders of the bank one hundred years ago. The Board has retained Sarah Leonard to serve an Interim Chief Financial Officer. Sarah will be working in that position through a consulting contract with her employer, one of the big eight accounting firms. Sarah is a CPA with extensive experience auditing financial institutions. Please join me in welcoming Sarah to the bank and in supporting both Gene and Sarah in their new roles.*
>
> *George Anderson IV, Chairman of the Board*

Upon finishing reading the email, Angela experienced a mixture of emotions. On the one hand, she had worked professionally to aid the bank's regulators. In addition, she was pleased to be of assistance to Matthew. On the other hand, she felt remorse, assuming that her actions had negatively impacted Dale and Joel, two individuals who had demonstrated an unwavering commitment to supporting the bank since her arrival over four years ago.

Angela instinctively thought about calling Matthew to obtain details regarding what had occurred. After taking a deep breath, she realized that such action would not be appropriate, and could put Matthew in an awkward situation. Contemplating the matter further, Angela determined to focus on doing her job and welcoming Sarah Leonard while awaiting more definitive news regarding Dale and Joel.

Chapter 80

Friday August 10, 2002
San Francisco, California

At 2:00 PM in the afternoon, five people assembled in the conference room at the FDIC's office in San Francisco. Elaine opened the meeting.

"Welcome, and thank you for attending this meeting to determine how to proceed from regulatory and criminal investigation standpoints given recent events at Green Valley Community Bank, headquartered in Santa Maria, California. I'm Elaine Harmon, the FDIC Supervision Division Manager. Please take a moment to introduce yourselves."

"I'm Matthew Trentino, an FDIC Examiner. I was the Examiner in Charge of the recent compliance and safety and soundness examinations at the bank."

"I'm James Robinson. I'm an FDIC Investigator. I spent time on site at the bank performing an investigation once evidence of unusual transactions was unearthed by Matthew and his team."

"I'm Lewis Peworchik, the FBI Special Agent assigned to work this matter from a potential criminal prosecution perspective."

"I'm Dennis Murphy, the FBI Regional Director. My role will be to support Lewis and bring in any additional federal resources as are needed, including those from the U.S. Attorney's Office."

Elaine then again assumed the floor.

"We've shared in advance all evidence collected to date regarding the events at Green Valley Community Bank over about the past year. That evidence includes a synopsis of the interview with Joel Johnson, the bank's Chief Financial Officer. In that interview, Joel confessed to participating in at least parts of an elaborate scheme to cover up a loss of about $4.0 million on an investment security. Given the extent of the scheme, which we have yet to fully ascertain, it appears unlikely to us that Joel Johnson operated alone."

"Is the bank President still remaining silent?" asked Dennis.

"Yes," replied James. "More than that, he has retained a high-end San Francisco law firm to represent him."

"Is the FDIC reasonably convinced that the security purchase and subsequent cash flows were not a vehicle to conduct money laundering or lending to a prohibited party?" inquired Lewis.

"We've been unable to identify any evidence of that conduct," responded James.

"And, you've not discovered any evidence of self-dealing, or any monetary gains by the bank employees as a result of these actions?" asked Lewis.

"Correct," replied James.

"So, you're fairly sure that the initial security purchase was simply an act of stupidity?" asked Dennis.

"In reviewing all of the orange security files from the bank's Controller, the selling investment bank did apparently put lipstick on a pig, but not beyond what is legally allowable in marketing to an accredited investor like the bank," advised James.

"And the CFO is no rocket scientist," shared Matthew. "He has an undergraduate degree in music theory and an accounting certificate from a community college. Joel Johnson had no business ever purchasing a security as complex as the IO Strip CMO," opined Matthew.

"Then why did he?" queried Lewis.

Matthew and James looked at each other, both desiring to avoid references to Joel's comments about the naked woman. James eventually spoke.

"We believe the investment bank talked him into the purchase. There was some conceptual justification from an interest rate risk management perspective. We have no evidence of kickbacks from the purchase after auditing Joel's deposit accounts at the bank. In fact, he lives modestly with his mother. The investment bank might have wined and dined Joel, but that's of course not a crime."

"Sounds like the investment bank put Joel through the financial initiation awaiting all individuals with more money than brains," opined Dennis.

"I reviewed the detailed funds flow spreadsheet assembled by Matthew and James," said Lewis. "It appears that you've substantially accounted for the $2.0 million or so used to write down the bank's basis in the IO Strip CMO and therefore hide the loss."

"Correct," responded James.

"So, let me walk through the $2.0 million in inflows to the bank," stated Lewis. He continued, "$535,000 derived from wires legitimately authorized by bank clients based upon signature verification. All of the subject bank clients suffer from dementia or similar conditions and are over 85 years old. The bank employee who initiated the outgoing wires recently died."

"Yes," interjected James, "in addition, all of the $535,000 in funds were from deposit accounts scheduled for escheatment to the state prior to the recent activity."

"That certainly implies someone with a detailed knowledge of the bank," stated Dennis.

Lewis continued his financial recap.

"A total of about $180,000 was sourced through the bank's payment of invoices from the new vendors who were LLCs. This was essentially the bank sending money to itself, if via a long and elaborate journey. The net result was a reclassification of an investment loss to operating expense."

"Exactly," said Matthew.

"$357,500 was sourced from a loan to The Fesler Trust secured by a condominium owned by the President of the bank. The President is also the sole trustee of the Fesler Trust."

Matthew and James both nodded affirmatively.

"$325,000 came from wires from The Fesler Trust into Security Investment LLC, which is a single member LLC owned by the Trust."

"Yes," responded James.

"Have there been any complaints from the beneficiaries of the Trust?" asked Dennis.

"None that we are aware of. However, based upon information from the Chairman of the Board, who is also the General Partner of a partnership that is 22.5% owned by the Trust, the Trust has a large number of beneficiaries, none of whom are directly involved in either the management of the trust nor the operation of the partnership. In addition, $325,000 would be only a minority percentage of the annual inflows from the partnership into the Trust. The Trust may have other investments unknown to the bank Chairman. He thinks the Trust dates back something like seventy years."

"And the only person with a detailed knowledge of the Trust is the bank President?" inquired Lewis.

James again answered, "Unfortunately, yes. The prior trustee was the father of the bank President, who has passed."

Lewis and Dennis paused in their questioning at this point.

Elaine took that opportunity to add, "If you're thinking that this is an incredibly interconnected group of individuals, you are right. I can't remember a bank, or a town or area, where the individuals and the families were so closely connected, often over multiple generations."

Lewis worked to complete his financial recap.

"Then, there's about $150,000 in funds inflows into the bank from the IO Strip CMO itself. In other words, all of the interest generated by the security was used to write down the principal, with no income being recognized," explained Lewis. He continued, "In addition, there were cash deposits totaling about $250,000 made to the Security Investment LLC checking account, with those funds eventually finding their way back to the bank."

"You've summarized the funds flows well," commented James.

"And we're not sure of the source of that final $250,000, other than Joel Johnson's admission that some of those funds were from him personally."

"On follow-up questioning, Joel estimated about $50,000," explained James.

"Why would Joel use his personal funds to repay a loss on a security purchase, if the security purchase was conducted legitimately? There's no law against making bad investments," said Dennis.

"By Joel's own statement, he did not want to be fired for the investment loss. He evidently not only lives with his mother, but is financially responsible for her to at least some extent following her stroke," said James.

Dennis then positioned himself to indicate by body language that he wished to take the floor.

"So, there's no way Joel could have supplied the entire $250,000 in cash deposits?"

"We've seen no evidence of his financial capacity to do so," replied James.

"Therefore, there must have been other individuals involved. Other individuals who would have donated their own personal funds in an effort to obfuscate the investment loss. However, the only photographs we have of an individual making the various cash deposits is of Joel Johnson, and even those photographs are less than perfectly clear."

Matthew and James again nodded affirmatively.

"And the only validated connection to the President at this point is the fact that he is the trustee of The Fesler Trust and that he volunteered real estate owned by him to serve as collateral for a loan to that same Trust?"

"True," responded Matthew.

"Have you discovered any relationship between the man who opened the various LLC checking accounts and either Joel Johnson or Dale Huffington?" asked Lewis.

"Unfortunately, no. However, we have verified that Don Martin supposedly opened the checking accounts about a week after he died. Therefore, someone must have assumed his identity," answered James.

"Were any security or surveillance tapes available?"

"No. The LLC checking accounts were opened so long ago that the tapes were recycled," responded James.

Dennis stood up and paced for a couple of minutes.

After he was again seated, he shared, "Unless you find some additional evidence or Joel Johnson agrees to divulge the other parties involved, I can't see the FBI and the U.S. Attorney's Office attempting to prosecute a criminal case in this regard. I can just imagine the attorneys for the defense telling the jury something like, *ladies and gentlemen of the jury, the prosecution is asking you to find the defendant guilty of a crime for sending extra money INTO a bank.*"

Elaine now gestured that she would like to speak.

"I thought you might arrive at that conclusion. In my decades of working for the FDIC, I've never seen, nor even heard of, a situation like this. What we *can* do, under the FDIC's supervisory powers, is have both senior officers permanently removed from the bank and barred from the financial industry for life. The CFO clearly materially falsified financial and regulatory reporting. The President failed to provide adequate supervision of the CFO, both in regards to the original purchase of the IO Strip CMO and the maintenance of an adequate internal control environment. The President also refused to cooperate with the FDIC."

"That's of course your decision," replied Dennis.

"I'll have Matthew return to Santa Maria to share our decisions with the Chairman of the Board in person. Matthew will also suggest that the Chairman of the Board utilize his connections to have the parties with a legal and / or financial interest in the The Fesler Trust initiate an audit by an unaffiliated CPA."

"That sounds good," said Dennis. "After this chain of events, nothing will ever surprise me in the future."

The meeting participants thanked each other for their time and interest and returned to their offices.

Chapter 81

Thursday August 23, 2002
Santa Maria, California

Dale Huffington was at the gym early in the afternoon when the mail arrived. His wife, Anne, saw the letter carrier drive off, and walked to the mailbox. She noticed several pieces of mail that she had never seen before, including a Green Valley bank statement for an unknown checking account and a loan statement for Bank of America for The Fesler Trust. Both of these envelopes were originally mailed to the bank's address, but had been forwarded by someone at the bank to their home. Curious, Anne read through the two envelopes. Based upon the transactions in the checking account, including a check for a property tax payment, Anne quickly realized that Dale was maintaining a separate residence of some sort. The loan statement listed an address in town as security for the loan. Anne got in her car and drove to the address, observing that it was a condominium in one of the better developments in the valley.

Dale returned home from the gym at 3:30 PM. The energetic exercise sessions only took the edge off the pain from his being fired from the bank – after 100 years of Huffington service. He had told Anne that he was terminated for not maintaining an adequate internal control environment, which was true, as far as that went.

"Dale, honey, how did your workout go?"

"Not bad. A new personal record on the treadmill."

"Can I get you a drink?"

"A glass of iced mineral water with a wedge of lemon would

be great. I'm a bit dehydrated."

After casually serving Dale the beverage, Anne asked, "And how long have you maintained the pied-à-terre?"

She waived the checking account and loan statements in front of him.

Dale almost dropped the glass of water. He quickly analyzed the situation. What a fool! In his disgrace from being suspended and then terminated from the bank, Dale had forgotten to change the mailing addresses for the red checkbook and other items that Linda had taken care of for years. He decided to be direct and honest with his wife.

"About ten years."

"And I assume it was well used on weekends while I was traveling?"

Dale sheepishly replied, "I wouldn't characterize it that way."

"But it was used for trysts. Why else would you maintain a condo in town and not tell me about it."

"True." That was the only response that Dale could muster.

"Well, I guess what is good for the gander is good for the goose."

"What are you saying?"

"Dale, honey, do you think I was alone all of those nights on the road, working various art exhibitions and events?"

Dale was crushed. He simply walked away from his wife and curled up on their bed, a deep depression now setting in. First, the events at the bank. Now, the realization that his wife was regularly enjoying affairs. And, to top things off, he had heard today that the beneficiaries of The Fesler Trust were organizing to have an audit performed. He would soon lose his position as Trustee, betraying the legacy of his father. After ten minutes on the bed, Dale was catatonic. Saliva drooled from his open mouth.

Chapter 82

Friday August 24, 2002
Santa Maria, California

Matthew arrived at Angela's apartment at 7:00 PM, following his drive south from San Francisco. He had made the date during his earlier visit to meet with the bank's Board of Directors. As soon as Angela opened the door, Matthew was overwhelmed with a cornucopia of smells. There was definitely some garlic and other herbs involved, but beyond that Matthew was uncertain.

"*Buona sera. Benvenuto.* Please come in."

"Good to see you. I brought these for you."

Matthew handed Angela a bouquet of flowers and a bottle of red wine.

"*Nero D'Avola* from the Mt. Etna appellation in Sicily. Excellent choice!"

"I must admit that the proprietor at the wine shop guided my selection."

"It will go well with the dinner. The volcanic soil and the altitude of the Mt. Etna combine to produce some outstanding and unique grape varietals."

"Speaking of dinner, the scents in this apartment are overwhelming. Can I ask what you have prepared?"

"Of course. We're starting with fresh *burrata* cheese and *prosciutto di Parma*. Then we'll have some baked *cannelloni*. That's a type of stuffed pasta, with the stuffing being a secret recipe from my family. The main course will be a seasoned roast complemented by *patate arroste*. The dessert is a surprise."

"I wisely anticipated something like that and skipped lunch."

Angela smiled. She was proud of her culinary skills and enjoyed sharing them with others.

"Why don't you pour us some wine while I finish preparing the food?"

As Matthew decanted the *Nero D'Avola*, he couldn't help but stare at Angela. She was dressed in a medium length dark blue skirt that displayed her toned calves. Her blouse was azure and fitted snugly over her breasts. She wore blue topaz earnings. Her long black hair was piled a bit on her head and then French-braided down her back. Matthew was intensely physically attracted to her, finally able to allow those feelings to run free now that his official duties with Angela were concluded.

The dinner conversation proceeded smoothly. Both Angela and Matthew were pleased to be able to share information about themselves and their personal lives. They also discussed art, history, classical music, and opera, with a particular focus on the works of Verdi and Rossini. The bank was barely mentioned. The first two hours flew by.

At 9:00 PM, Angela interrupted the conversation, saying, "We'd better eat the dessert. The fresher, the better."

Angela walked over to the kitchen, pleased that Matthew had eaten heartily and complimented her cooking on several occasions. She had caught herself a couple of times staring a bit too intensely at his face. She had always found his features to be handsome. Now that she knew his personality even better, her interest was intensified.

Angela brought a tray of *tiramisu* to the dining room table along with a bottle of *Amaretto* liquor.

"My family utilizes a special ingredient in the sauce for the ladyfingers. See if you can figure out what it is."

She gave Matthew a healthy serving of the dessert and poured him a glass of the *Amaretto*.

Matthew had eaten *tiramisu* before, but nothing that ever tasted as rich and complex as Angela's.

"This is outstanding."

"Thank you." Angela noticed that Matthew had not tasted the *Amaretto*. "Do you not like *Amaretto*?"

"I don't think I've ever actually had that before, but after sharing the bottle of wine with you, I really shouldn't drink any more before driving to my hotel."

"Who said you had to spend the night in a hotel?"

With that, Angela leaned toward Matthew, initiating a deep and passionate kiss. That *bacio* was quickly followed by several others. After about ten minutes, Matthew paused for some air and took a sip of the *Amaretto*.

"That's it! You included the cordial in the dessert!"

Angela smiled broadly.

"I think you're more Italian than you realize. Now, let's retire to the bedroom for some *preliminari*."

Epilogue

Green Valley Community Bank survived the loss generated by the IO Strip CMO, in part due to the Directors, led by George Anderson IV, each individually purchasing newly issued shares in the bank, thereby replacing the capital lost through the poor investment. Gene Phillips was eventually appointed to the President position on a permanent basis. Gene led the bank to many future years of success, applying a diligent work ethic which echoed that of his forebears.

Troy and Duane both retired on March 31, 2007, after receiving their cash bonuses for 2006. This allowed the unjustly fortunate duo to avoid the financial crisis and Great Recession which began later that year. The two investment bankers were never found guilty of any wrongdoing. They were smart enough to effectively operate within a system already biased in their favor. All of their Dumps were to eligible, accredited investors. Their trades were documented with the usual half-page of fine print about any information being provided as illustrative only, with no guaranty of future performance. Wealthy and still relatively young, they pursued separate hedonistic lives filled with travel, adventure, and entertainment. Neither of them ever developed a meaningful relationship with a woman. Troy died from a cocaine overdose in 2013, alone in a suite at an upscale hotel in London. Duane passed a year later from a skiing accident in Cortina, Italy when he impaled himself on a tree branch.

Jennifer (aka Jessica) admitted to herself by age 29 that she was never going to have an acting career. With her biological clock ticking, she refocused her energies to dating, eventually agreeing to marry a good-looking but somewhat boring executive two years her senior. Mandy served as the maid of honor at the wedding and remained an intimate friend. The executive was from a wealthy family which owned a mansion in Midtown and an estate outside Rome. Jennifer married her husband primarily for lifestyle. She could always call on her acting skills when passion was needed.

Green Valley Community Bank finally convinced Melvin Needham to retire from the Controller position at age seventy. He spent most of his time in his retirement years volunteering as a bookkeeper for a local non-profit entity. While Dewey believed in the organization's mission, what most attracted him was their basement.

Following the events at the bank, Joel Johnson eventually managed to get a job as the manager for a print and copy store in Goleta. He was happy in this position, as it suited his skills set and allowed him to spend more time with his mother as a result of the short commute from their home. Joel dedicated much of his spare time to enhancing his piano skills. After a few years, he began playing at Sunday church services, weddings, and bar mitzvahs. Despite this ongoing exposure to theological and philosophical concepts, Joel never succeeded in integrating higher level thinking with his daily life.

Dale Huffington was emotionally crushed after his termination from the bank. For months, he was unable to show his face around town, forever known as the only Huffington in one hundred years to be a professional and moral failure. He sank into a deep depression, which was exacerbated by his wife's admission. Despite his own behavior, Dale was haunted by the image of his wife having relations with other men. Dale eventually became a regular at the bar in the historic downtown hotel. He often closed down the bar late at night by sharing a glass of Armagnac with Brendan Kehoe.

With her professional skills enhanced by the experience at Green Valley Community Bank, Angela Falcone accepted a bigger and more remunerative job in 2003 at one of the large commercial banks. The position was based in San Francisco, which facilitated her seeing Matthew Trentino much more often. By late 2004, they were married. The wedding was remembered for years afterwards for its extravagant menu of Italian delicacies and a fifty-person dance of the *tarantella*. Angela and Matthew enjoyed a long and blessed life together, including having two children, Enrico and Isabella.

Afterword

I hope you enjoyed *Financial Initiation.* If so, I'd recommend reading my other two books, *Financial Execution* and *Financial Retribution.* Both are historical fiction and financial thrillers. *Financial Execution* commences before World War Two and concludes in the mid-1980s. *Financial Retribution* is set primarily in the 2018 through 2021 timeframe. Each novel addresses various components of the financial and capital markets in presenting an interesting story populated with a diverse cast of characters. As with *Financial Initiation,* the other two books also indirectly incorporate social commentary and some light philosophical discourse. Individuals who enjoy financial and technical thrillers, mysteries, and stories that operate on several levels simultaneously will find *Financial Execution and Financial Retribution* engaging and thought-provoking reads.